JOAB

Also by Jane Bennett Gaddy

HOUSE NOT MADE WITH HANDS

THE MISSISSIPPI BOYS

ISAAC'S HOUSE

JOAB

A NOVEL OF THE OLD SOUTH

*Final Volume
in The Faithful Sons Trilogy*

Jane Bennett Gaddy, Ph.D.

iUniverse, Inc.
Bloomington

[Signed: Jane Bennett Gaddy]
Oxford, MS
May 2013

JOAB
A Novel of the Old South

Copyright © 2013 by Jane Bennett Gaddy, Ph.D.

All rights reserved. No part of this book may be used or reproduced by any means, graphic, electronic, or mechanical, including photocopying, recording, taping or by any information storage retrieval system without the written permission of the publisher except in the case of brief quotations embodied in critical articles and reviews.

Certain characters in this work are historical figures and certain events portrayed did take place. However, this is a work of fiction. All of the other characters, names, and events as well as all places, incidents, organizations, and dialogue in this novel are either the products of the author's imagination or are used fictitiously.

iUniverse books may be ordered through booksellers or by contacting:

iUniverse
1663 Liberty Drive
Bloomington, IN 47403
www.iuniverse.com
1-800-Authors (1-800-288-4677)

Because of the dynamic nature of the Internet, any web addresses or links contained in this book may have changed since publication and may no longer be valid. The views expressed in this work are solely those of the author and do not necessarily reflect the views of the publisher, and the publisher hereby disclaims any responsibility for them.

Any people depicted in stock imagery provided by Thinkstock are models, and such images are being used for illustrative purposes only.
Certain stock imagery © Thinkstock.

ISBN: 978-1-4759-7339-6 (sc)
ISBN: 978-1-4759-7340-2 (hc)
ISBN: 978-1-4759-7341-9 (ebk)

Printed in the United States of America

iUniverse rev. date: 02/05/2013

Credits for photos:
Tracy Gaddy Danner (author photo); Mike Bennett and Dewey Davidson (Mayfield photo)

Contents

Foreword ix
Prologue xi

PART ONE
Chapter 1   Front Porch Swing 3
Chapter 2   By Way of Oxford 8
Chapter 3   Mud Without Mercy 19
Chapter 4   The Last Tattoo 22
Chapter 5   Young Love 30
Chapter 6   Teaching Sam 35
Chapter 7   Sleepless Nights 39
Chapter 8   Fullness of Joy 47
Chapter 9   Plain as Day 52
Chapter 10   Give Them Heart 58
Chapter 11   The Occasion 64
Chapter 12   Beyond the Feelings 70
Chapter 13   Place of Peace 76
Chapter 14   Desire 87
Chapter 15   For Some Reason 94
Chapter 16   The Letter 98
Chapter 17   A Proper Time 113
Chapter 18   Moments Like These 124
Chapter 19   In the Middle of It All 128
Chapter 20   Joy and Grief 133
Chapter 21   Best Place on Earth 139
Chapter 22   Thanksgiving Once Again 145
Chapter 23   Wrapped in Warmth 152
Chapter 24   Sacrifices 160
Chapter 25   One Perfect Day 165

PART TWO
Chapter 26   Journey 177
Chapter 27   His Own Native Land...189
Chapter 28   Some Rich Man's Carriage 195
Chapter 29   The Wind at His Back 200
Chapter 30   Heroism Unequaled...205
Chapter 31   Defining Moment...211

Afterword..223
My Thanks..227

*To the Memory of
Joab Clark
of Sarepta, Mississippi
who, in 1861-1865, was too young to fight,
but who, when he came of age,
dedicated his life to rebuilding his corner
of the Old South
in the aftermath of the Civil War,
a journey and a work that represented his finest hour.*

and

*To Charlie Clark.
Without his endless cache of Clark memories
and his willingness to share his heart and treasures,
I would never have been able to write this trilogy
with any depth of knowledge or poignancy.*

Thou wilt show me the path of life:
in thy presence is fullness of joy;
at thy right hand there are pleasures forevermore.

Psalm 16:11

To every man, there comes in his lifetime,
that special moment, when he is physically tapped
on the shoulder and offered the chance
to do a very special thing,
unique to him and fitted to his talent;
what a tragedy if the moment finds him
unprepared or unqualified for the work
which would be his finest hour.

—Sir Winston Churchill—

Foreword

When Nobel Laureate William Faulkner gave one of the few interviews during his lifetime for the *Paris Review* article *Writers at Work,* he was asked by the interviewer, Jean Stein, why he started his Yoknapatawpha saga. He stated, "With 'Soldiers Pay' and 'Mosquitoes' I wrote for the sake of writing because it was fun. I discovered my own little postage stamp of native soil was worth writing about and I would never live long enough to exhaust it . . . It opened up a gold mine of other people, so I created a cosmos of my own. I can move these people around, like God, not only in space but in time."

Jane Bennett Gaddy has captured in her third installment of the Payne family, JOAB, a piece of the history for Faulkner's "little postage stamp of native soil" with a combination of history and fiction. She places Joab in Oxford, known as Jefferson in the Faulkner novels, at a time when this town was at its lowest.

Joab has made his way to Oxford to help with the rebuilding of "one of the most devastated towns in the South," as one Yankee newspaper journalist wrote. He rallies the local citizenry to start the rebuilding of Oxford after it was completely burned to the ground by General "Whiskey Joe" Smith in August 1864.

The young son of a Confederate Captain, who lost his life at Gettysburg, has come to Oxford in the terrible days of Reconstruction to bring back this small southern town. Who are we to say that someone such as Joab did not make his way to Oxford? History and fiction sometimes come together and Gaddy has given us something, as Oxonians, to think about in our "little postage stamp of native soil."

Jack Lamar Mayfield, Author and Historian
Columnist, *The Oxford Eagle*
Oxford, Mississippi

Prologue

The rural South was cut off, massively immobile. With hearts turned inward and with no alternative, its people looked backward, longing for the way it used to be, but they had no reason to look forward. Not in 1868, not even in 1870, the year they rejoined the Union.

Joab Payne was living in the harsh reality of a cold war that was more demanding and more deliberate than the war with the North had been. At least to him. He had been too young to fight. There were moments when he lamented the fact that, because of his youth, he did not get the opportunity, while his beautiful mother, Rachel, took heart in the reality that the war ended short of calling up her fourth son, but on the other hand the dreadful toll on her was too debilitating to adequately describe. Joab wondered if life would ever get better for her. He hoped she would one day move from the scourge of the past—the past and the memories of a war that took her beloved T.G. and her son, Albert Henry.

Joab had come through with his sanity intact, escaping all but the pain of loss. Perhaps if he could have fought, it would have sufficed for a measure of understanding.

I was born in ill timing, he mused.

The budding spring thickets by the side of the road choked with honeysuckle vines. How could something so beautiful and with such sweet fragrance overtake and stifle everything else? His thoughts tumbled, leaving him dismally dismayed, shadows of a past in which he had but passively participated hovering close. He dismounted Star and began pulling the honeysuckle from the wild plum trees. Feverishly pulling, as if they were wrapped about his neck. The vine would always cling. The scrounger would do its evil, but he would be remiss if he didn't try to take it out. He had a choice to make. He could either continue to battle the choke of the vine, pine away his days in sad remembrance, or give in to the sweet fragrance of the honeysuckle's nectar, rally, and do something judicious instead.

When he recalled the darkness that had threatened Isaac at the close of the war, Joab regretted he was not able to help his brother more. But Isaac had passed through the valley to the other side and was living in marital bliss with his beloved Jennie in the house he had built at Slate Springs. His brother, Jonathan, had married Albert Henry's widow, Cassie, at Henry's written bequeathing. Henry knew his wife and their young son, Robert E. Lee Payne, would need Jonathan. And who better than his own brother to take care of the family he would leave behind?

Joab allowed his thoughts to return to Christmas of 1867, over two years after the war. Such sadness. Everywhere. There was no escaping it. No gales of laughter emanating from the Payne house on that Christmas Day evening. Their beloved Doc Malone, while sitting in T.G.'s chair by the fire, passed from their presence forever. Sometimes Joab sensed a reprisal for his happy-go-lucky life as a boy. How could he have been so naïve; how could he have taken his superlative boyhood for granted?

He had weathered the war and the losses on the fringe, and Joab was now the faithful son, Isaac and Jonathan having draped the mantle upon his shoulders along with the bulk of the burden. He was responsible for his mother and ten-year-old Samuel. But Joab had come of age, his limited knowledge of the war and aftermath, in time, having made a man of him.

He recalled that April afternoon several years ago when Isaac took him to the front porch swing. It was a day much like this, the crocuses blooming in bunches on the hillsides, the massive oak tree on the ridge pushing out tiny green leaves covering the branches that moved mysteriously over the little cemetery where his brother, Ben, was buried. Isaac, reminding Joab that he had once told Rachel he would never leave her, had sat on the swing on that beautiful spring day trying his best to take his father's place, explaining to Joab that he would one day fall in love and then he would know it would be time to leave.

Joab was a man now, and he had taken on the responsibility; however, it was no hard task. In fact, it was a privilege. He had always been there for his mother. The day Ben died, when his father and brothers went off to war, when Isaac ran away from home trying to get to them, when his father and Albert Henry died at Gettysburg, and when Isaac finally came of fighting age and got into the war—Joab had been right there with his mother, loving arms enveloping her. It was not just for her. It was for him, too. He had wanted to be in that safe place. For that matter, up until now, he had not wanted things to change.

But things *were* changing and Joab found himself surrendering to the emotions that were pushing him out of his safe place. He suddenly had a driving desire to know how it had been for those who fought for the South. Only then might he be able to accept life as the war had dealt it and move into a Shiloh of his own—*a place of peace, a healing place.*

Part One

CHAPTER 1

FRONT PORCH SWING

*I regard the death and mangling
of a couple thousand men as a small affair,
a kind of morning dash—and it may be well
that we become so hardened.*

General William Tecumseh Sherman
in a letter to his wife July 1864

―◊―

Winter's End, Early 1870

The March winds blew fiercely out of the North, blackberry winter as predictable as Indian summer, but not as comfortable. It was cold, but Joab needed to go to the swing. The place of conversation with his mother, Rachel. His brothers had done it for as long as he could remember—first Jonathan, then Henry, then Isaac. He pulled a drab gray woolen sweater over his head, ran his fingers through straight brown hair that fell to his broad shoulders. He let the screen door slam behind him, stepped out onto the wood slatted porch, and sat down on the creaky old swing hoping his mother would soon appear. He was sufficiently troubled and Rachel knew it.

The war had ended almost five years ago, and Joab had heard every story imaginable, but now he was beginning to *feel* more. Rachel feared he was becoming embittered, which she wanted to help him avoid at all hazards, albeit that may be hypocritical on her part, for she was experiencing some delayed after-war bitterness that needed to be modified.

"I heard the door slam," she said, chuckling at her son.

"I knew you would, Mama." Joab stood, motioned for his mother to sit, then took his seat beside her. "And I won't say I'm sorry because you know how I've always loved slamming that door since I was two years old, at least that's what you've always told me."

"Yes. And I'm perfectly right about that."

"How come you never made me stop? Isaac always told me I was raised in a barn." Joab laughed at remembrances of Isaac chiding him for slamming the door.

"Son, I love that sound. It tells me you're somewhere close by and as long as it slams . . . you'll be here. Right now, I would give anything—"

"I know, Mama. I know."

Rachel pulled her shawl tight across her shoulders to oppose the cold wind that blew against her back and she and Joab touched the floor to start the swing. There was something about the creak of the old chains that was conducive to conversation. Felicity, she thought. Appropriately auspicious. This front porch that Thomas built with his hands, the swing he added some years later, even the creaky old chains she refused to oil were all a part of her past and present, the swing meant to be a place that either created happiness and contentment or that would lead to it. Some things would not change if she had anything to do with it including the old familiar sound.

Joab spoke, "I might as well say what I've been thinking now that I've read all of those old newspapers you kept in the quilt box during the war years and the ones since, which are almost as telling. And when I think about it, I want to slam the door right off its hinges. It burns me up when I read about what *they* did to the South. And my anger boils down to . . . to Sherman."

Joab was not sure his mother would tolerate anger directed toward a living human being, especially now that the war had been over for five years. Rachel was scarcely flexible when it came to character and conduct. Joab was taken by the way his mother responded to him. She had always known what to say, but this time, and for the first time ever as far as he knew, there was resentment and anger when she spoke, raising her soft southern voice to a pitch he had not heard before. Furthermore, she spoke into the wind as if Gen. William Tecumseh Sherman were standing on the porch in full uniform with his hand tucked inside his jacket like Napoleon Bonaparte, his medallions glowing in the last vestiges of the setting sun, his hideous cigar chewed up and arrogantly stamped out upon the steps of her front porch.

"Gen. Sherman, you wrote the story in blood and branded it with fire. But you would have been court-martialed in a beat of the heart had you disobeyed your Commander-in-Chief. You were a warrior, a magnificent one; you did your job well and as you were told, but in so doing you placed a tombstone upon the South when you took Atlanta and began your infamous March to Coastal Georgia, cutting a swathe forty miles wide, ripping up our land, destroying everything in your path with no regard for human life and existence. You killed our men and boys, symbolic of your 'morning dash', your branding. You said the death and mangling of a couple thousand men was a small affair. That was ruthless and heartless. You took our Nigras, when most of them didn't want to go. You seized our possessions of value and even those with no value. In that forty mile swathe, your people wasted our land, killed or stole our livestock, raided our cellars and smokehouses, burned our fields, leaving the earth scorched beneath our feet; you demolished our bridges and rail cars, and then you pulled our tracks right out of the ground."

Joab leaned forward resting his head in his hands, covering his eyes as if to shut out the rest of the world as his mother continued her one-sided thesis. He was amazed at her endless wealth of knowledge and worldly understanding of the politics of the war.

"You took our cotton to the North, raised tariffs so high we could neither buy nor sell. We're reduced to a diet of milk and bread, even five years past the end of the war. The South is a graveyard, and you tried to bury our people upon the scorched hills of our own country—even before we were dead. The epitaph on our tombstone branded with fire echoes the words that slipped from your lips—*War is Hell.*

"Gen. Sherman, with all due respect to your uniform and office, I have to decry you most for what you did that was unconscionable. Your commander ordered you to 'break them, take them down, destroy them, bury them. Teach them a lesson and while you are teaching them a lesson, take anything that may be left, all they have worked for since 1776, and burn it to the ground'. Your commander wanted this war ended and the South reduced to ashes. You were the man for the job."

Joab listened as the words flowed eloquently from her lips, Rachel delivering her monologue as if it were yesterday that her beloved Thomas and her son, Albert Henry, died at Gettysburg. Those words had been trapped in her consciousness for seven years. Emptying herself of the grief and bitterness was long overdue. Quite frankly, Joab didn't know she was holding to these thoughts. But how could she not be, he wondered?

"Mother, I've never heard you speak so passionately since Pa and Henry were killed, not even at the town meeting in Sarepta last year over the Carpetbagger Simon Graystone."

"Son, I'm sorry. I fear I have added to your anxiety, and what's more, I have somewhat desecrated this old swing, but I have one defense of Gen. Sherman, though it in no way acquits him for his scorched earth strategy."

"Go ahead, Mother. I needed this and so did you. It cannot be good to suppress our thoughts forever. Besides we don't have to tell anybody else."

"Joab, I need to control my emotions better. I was not setting a good example, but the words are out there now. I allow I do feel better, but fear I must beg the Lord's forgiveness. However, when I reflect upon the newspaper writings concerning Gen. Sherman, I do concede that he tried to be more generous with Joe Johnston at his surrender than Grant was with Lee and his men. I said *tried*, for Congress was not going to approve any generosity towards the South. None whatsoever. Whether it was Sherman making the requests or Grant."

"Mother, I couldn't agree with you more, and when I think about the things I've heard that Sherman and Grant did in our part of the country . . . well, I need to see some things for myself. Sarepta was not directly hit by the war, that is, except for all the men and boys who died, which was the greatest loss."

"I know, son. We didn't have anything to offer Grant and Sherman except our blood and finest treasure. They were interested in our waterways and railroads—things they could use to quickly destroy us. And they wanted our cities and towns, the mansions and the wealth of the Delta and the Capitol and River regions mostly."

"Mama, I want to see some of those places. I need to know where our warriors fell, where they're buried. I want to pay my respects and put some things to rest that cause me sleepless nights. As it is, none of it feels real to me. I know it happened, but I was so far removed from it during the war years that I'm having a hard time owning up to it."

"Joab, you're a man now with a man's thoughts. I cannot deny you that. If it will ease the ache in your heart and help with sleepless nights, it will be worth it. What do you want to do?"

"I don't know yet. I'll think it through and piece some things together, and I need to talk to Isaac."

"Then, you should ride to Slate Springs and do just that."

"Thank you, Mama. I knew you'd understand. I'll go when I leave the mill after work tomorrow."

"If I know you and Isaac and Jennie, you'll stay up late talking. They'll be so pleased to see you. Why don't you stay the night and go directly to the mill Thursday morning?"

"That I will do, Mama. So don't worry about me. If for any reason I don't make it to the mill, Jonathan will know something is wrong and he'll come here looking for me."

"Don't say such a thing, Joab."

CHAPTER 2

BY WAY OF OXFORD

Tears from the depth of some divine despair
Rise in the heart, and gather to the eyes,
In looking on the happy Autumn fields,
And thinking of the days that are no more.

Alfred Lord Tennyson
Tears, Idle Tears

Rain fell in sheets, darkness settled in the hills unexpectedly, and the hope of a lovely spring morning reneged as daybreak relinquished its rights and slipped behind clouds that cooled the air and left no light for the muddy path. Joab considered turning Star off the trail and seeking shelter under the trees until the beating rain slacked. He reconsidered, remembering—remembering the long, dark days of the war, though he had not fought. He had been too young. He could not consider this stormy weather to be unpleasant when he thought about what his people had endured for four long years. He had some obscure idea from the letters his mother had tucked away in her keeping place—letters from his father and brothers. He was not oblivious, even in his youthfulness, but he wanted to know more, even if it meant complete invasion of his comfortable place. He rode on, pulling the hills in rain and mud, imagining how it had been.

Isaac, having made the trip several times himself, had drawn the map for Joab when he visited his brother in Slate Springs just a week before. It was all uncharted trail for Joab. He had never been too far outside Calhoun County and he was enlarging the boundaries of the only world he had ever known, the hill country of Mississippi. He refused to take the map out of his pocket until the rain stopped; it would surely melt, or maybe the ink had already run the words together. He hoped not. But he had memorized most of it. The way he figured it, he was nearing Oxford.

He was not wrong.

Oxford took its name from the city in England. The place was most beautiful, situated in the hill country, and its citizens hoped it would become the seat of learning, the home of The University of Mississippi. It had, indeed, and by 1837, it was its own town. Joab didn't know too much more about Oxford.

He rode onto the town's square hoping to find a nice stop, one where he could get a cup of coffee and perhaps a biscuit. It was still dark from the storm when he pulled to the hitching rail in front of the inn on the north corner of the square, wondering deep down if he were about to step outside his cultural boundary. But never mind that. His hunger far exceeded his pride. He looked upward and through the dismal morning fog and rain, read the sign: *The Thompson House*. There was a front entrance and one to the side of the newly constructed three-story brick building. He stepped up on the loosely fitted wood walkway that spanned the length of a small portion of the square, wondering why it came to an abrupt stop. In the darkness, lamplights glowed in the front windows of the few brick buildings on the corner. They looked brand new. In fact, they were. Joab knew a lot about the look and smell of fresh cut wood trim. He worked for his Grandfather Church, having pulled a saw in the mill every day since he was Samuel's age. Despite the rain, and even elevated by the freshness, was an unusual fragrance. He breathed deep the smell of fine fabric, that rare store-bought scent. His mother was a good sewer, but she generally made their clothes from old partially worn clothing. He took a moment to think how splendid it would be to step inside and buy her a bolt of material for a new dress. Beyond the mercantile was the market with its fragrances of oils and perfumes and plums, preserves and spices and onions, and freshly pulled lettuce and early green peas, each of which were heaped in bins outside the storefront. Someone was at work at this early hour. That was as far as he could see in the drizzling rain and fog.

He entered the open wrought iron gate otherwise held shut with brown leather hinges. Prodigious, Rachel would say. He had never seen the likes. The ornate wood swinging door was shut, but he could see by the lamp light in the windows the place was open for business. Savoring the smell of bread baking and syrup warming, he pushed the door open to overwhelming deliciousness. His appetite increased at the aroma of cured ham frying and he hoped, but had his doubts, the biscuits were like Rachel's.

He removed his hat and took a seat in the near empty dining hall. The server smiled and Joab's heart skipped a beat, his masculinity momentarily in full control. He was near twenty years old, still his mother's son, but very much a man. Rachel had taught him well, yet depended on Jonathan and Isaac to take on the man's role in Joab's life after their father died. They had done a splendid job.

"Morning!" she said. "I'm Sarah Agnes."

"Good morning, Miss Sarah Agnes." Her smile, touching the very heart of Joab Payne, was easy to return.

This is not bad a'tall, he thought. His blue eyes glinted. He hoped he was not so obvious. Should he tell her his name? Before he could make a decision, he had already blurted out—

"Joab, my name's Joab."

"Well, Joab, what would you have this morning?"

Words flowed like honey from her southern lips, the accent, a little softer than that to which he was accustomed. Could be the city touch; he wasn't sure. Being in a place like this was new to Joab, and he was a bit perplexed as to how to acquit himself.

He read the chalkboard fare and said, "Hot biscuits, please, and some warm sorghum molasses with lots of butter. Hot coffee, cream and sugar, or honey if sugar's scarce."

That was easy, he thought.

She smiled, nodded, and disappeared. In ten minutes she was back with a large tray, having added to his order a big slice of country ham.

"The ham's compliments of the tea room today," she said, artistically placing each dish in front of him. "Cook just brought up a big one from the smokehouse."

"Much obliged," he said. "I wasn't expecting such extravagance."

I guess she likes me, he thought. Food was scarce in his town, but pork was part of the basics. Hogs they had. In the lot and up on the hill. It was his assumption the same thing was true here in Oxford, so he would not feel too badly about accepting a serving of ham compliments of the cook.

He ate heartily, took the white cloth napkin from his knee and wiped his hands, but not wanting to leave the comfort of this place, he pushed back and sat still for a few minutes. Distracting himself temporarily, he looked about the room at the large wood-framed paintings of what he figured to be local scenes. *The Lyceum*, the caption read. An interesting tall and sturdy red brick building framed by giant live oaks. His thoughts turned to the times. Things didn't seem so bad here in Oxford. But he knew they were. Reconstruction was an intense undertaking that was going absolutely nowhere. The State's economy was in shambles. Grant had just been inaugurated, and former President Andrew Johnson's guideline for re-admission into the Union had been a bitter pill to swallow. Southerners were dogs, outcasts, in their own country. And The Freedmen's Bureau was part of the War Department. The war was supposed to be over. It may *never* be over, because the South may *never* adjust to the new social and political arrangement.

When he took office Johnson was in a precarious position as far as the Radical Republicans were concerned. He was a Jacksonian Democrat with States' Rights views, but during secession he had remained in the Senate, endearing himself to the North, not so much to the South. He was in the stewing pot. The Radicals had not liked Johnson's plan of Reconstruction, so they came up with their own, at the same time placing the southern states under military rule again. They passed laws restricting the President and when he allegedly violated the Tenure of Office Act by dismissing Secretary of War Edwin Stanton, the House voted eleven articles of impeachment against him. The Senate tried him. He was acquitted by one vote. That was in 1867.

Slavery was not something for which Joab's father and brothers had fought. They didn't own slaves and the wealthy farmers who did—those whom the Paynes knew—had no problem setting them free. Sure, there was a slavery issue but not something that couldn't have been settled apart from the war if it had not been for the wickedness and selfishness on both sides, for both North and South had owned slaves. All those thousands of men killed or wounded, crippled for life, blind, all scarred up. What social or political issue could ever have been worth losing thousands of lives?

Joab was still a Confederate, proud to be so, though the North would say the Confederacy was dead. But he was what his country called a "real" son of a Confederate officer. If there were anything more debasing than being required to apply for presidential pardon for having held civil or military office during the war and for owning property worth twenty thousand dollars or more—Joab didn't know about it. His father would never have to face that shame. That was the one and only good thing about his death, for he was guilty on both counts—a Confederate soldier, a captain in Lee's Army of Northern Virginia, and he owned land worth more than twenty thousand dollars.

The law stated once ten percent of a secession state had taken the oath of loyalty to the Union, that state would be permitted to form a legal government to rejoin the Union. The constitutional convention in Mississippi, called the Black and Tan Convention, consisting of a colorful group—twenty-nine white southerners, seventeen southern freedmen, and twenty-four non-southerners—had hammered out a constitution, presented it in 1868, and gained readmission to the Union in February 1870 just a month or so ago. Joab had mixed emotions. Things were not coming up roses in Mississippi. Not by any stretch. The State was full of corruption, but then so was Washington, D.C.

He sipped the hot coffee Sarah Agnes brought.

Enough! I've got a trip ahead of me, he thought. And I don't have any idea what to expect. Besides that, I don't have any answers to the post-war questions. Not yet.

"It's been a pleasure talking to you, Miss Sarah Agnes," said Joab. He put on his jacket and picked up his hat, stood there running his hand around the brim, and spoke again. "I'm on my way to Shiloh by way of Brice's Crossroads." He paused a minute, looking into Sarah's blue eyes that pooled with tears at the mention of Shiloh.

"I need to pay my respects," he said. "And I need to figure why it is I can't rid myself of the clutches of that cruel war. I thought going to the battlegrounds might help get me—well, get me to a place of understanding."

"Did you fight in the war for the South, Joab?"

"No, I was too young. My pa and older brothers did. Pa and my second oldest brother were killed at Gettysburg."

"Oh, I'm sorry to hear that, Joab."

She had touched him again, with her sympathy, and in the moment, Joab had no idea to what extent.

"My papa was wounded at Shiloh. Some soldiers out of General Sidney Johnston's army brought him from the raging battle to the Lyceum here at The University where he died. He's buried out there on the hill, somewhere with a lot of our men. We don't know where. But I do know he's buried there because he died at the Lyceum. So many were dying, one after another. They couldn't keep it all straight, I guess. A lot of the families didn't get to them until they already had the men and boys in the ground. By the time we got word Papa had been brought to Oxford . . . well, it was too late to even say goodbye. The Yankees were not particular how they treated our men and boys. But I'm here every week day, and I can go there to the grassy hill and be close to him, as often as I please, and mind you, that is quite often."

Tears trickled down her face. "I'm sorry," she said, reaching for the handkerchief in her apron pocket. "I can't stop doing that every time I talk about my papa. I dearly loved him."

"Don't be sorry for that," he said. "I can't stop doing the same thing."

"Well, the reason I asked if you fought is because we give a bit of a better price to men who fought."

"That's splendid. They deserve it."

"I hope you will go to the Lyceum before you leave town. It was a hospital in full operation after the Union took over, of course, and mostly for their own soldiers, but they allowed southern soldiers to be taken there for treatment—or to die. It's a beautiful place, built in 1848, thirteen years before the war started. Built for Oxford, not for the Yankees. I've had to learn to love that building all over again. I hated it for the longest time during and after the war, but when I came to understand that bitterness was causing physical and emotional problems for me and if I didn't try to get control of that instead of letting it take over my life, I wouldn't be able to overcome the anguish it was causing. I try to think of it this way . . . that's the place my father breathed his last breath and said his last words. And in a way it belongs to me. Now instead of getting sick to my stomach when I pass the Lyceum, I see it as a shrine to my father and all those who died at Shiloh. But even that doesn't keep me from crying."

"I understand your feelings. And I'm much obliged for the conversation. I live in Calhoun Country, and I've never even been to Oxford until today. I didn't know such beauty existed." Joab was secretly including Sarah Agnes in his thoughts of beauty. "And I see that you have moved farther toward healing than I have. I'm glad to hear it. Every little bit helps me."

Sarah Agnes stood there, gave a little wave when Joab turned around, thinking she had found a kindred spirit, one she may never see again. He tipped his hat, and left a coin on the table. It wasn't much, but he wanted her to have it. He paid at the counter, looked back on eyes that were fixed on him, and walked out the door.

The rain had stopped. He stepped onto the wet hard-packed dirt street; the sweet fragrance of privet was all over him. But there was another not-so-fragrant smell. What should be a fresh and flowery after-the-rain heady scent was the choking, almost overwhelming, smell of mildew. Joab was not opposed to mildewed compost. It was the fragrance of the farm. But here in the big town? He looked around the square, which he had not done earlier. He had come in on the corner where the hotel was situated and had seen nothing else besides the two new stores next door. It had been dark with rain clouds and still early morning when he hitched Star and walked inside. Now he was seeing the entire square. It was ravaged. Every building burned to the ground, mounds of wet ashes and debris untouched, burnt to rubbish, pieces of iron and tin from the roofs protruding from the rubble.

"Oh, dear Jesus," he said out loud. "How did I miss that?" He scanned the entire square, looking at all four sides. "The war," he said. "Sherman!"

He had not wanted to go back in and ask. Surely Sarah Agnes thought he was slightly pitiful when he talked about Oxford's beauty. Maybe one day he would hear the story of how this happened. He mounted Star, tightened his hat, and rode off toward The University, glancing behind him in stark disbelief.

Joab was taken aback. The Lyceum was the biggest and greatest building he had ever seen with rich pompous columns of creamy white against magnificent new red brick and a portico that spanned the entire front of the building, just like the painting in the tea room. He leaned back and craned his neck to view the top windows. He had never seen a building this tall. He imagined how it had been just a few short years ago with wounded soldiers bringing dying men inside on stretchers and mats. He thought of doctors amputating dangling limbs and pushing back viscera that were hanging outside mangled bodies. He thought of his father, T.G., and his brother, Henry, and Jonathan that day at Gettysburg. How must Jonathan have felt—what must he have seen as he lifted their mutilated bleeding bodies into the shallow grave he dug for them both, his father still clutching the flag Rachel had sewn? Surely he had seen their open wounds, the blood, the bullet holes, the slash marks from the bayonet, for Henry was run through. But they were together. They would always be together. In Heaven. Right now, that was sufficient consolation.

Joab rode Star across the road to the cemetery where seven hundred Confederate soldiers were buried, some in unmarked graves, on the grassy knoll of The University of Mississippi. Why, he wondered, if Jesus suffered and bled and died for the sins of men, did it have to be this way? Why do men who live side by side, State touching State, have to fight each other? His mother had taught him Scripture from Deuteronomy that says, "The secret things belong unto the Lord." If not for that assurance, he would be hard pressed to avoid cynicism, because he just couldn't figure it out, nor did he understand the plan when it came to fighting.

Like every student and most of the faculty of The University who abandoned their classes and mustered in, he would have fought for the South, glad to do so, but that didn't explain the minds and hearts of men. Not enough to suit him. He had read a letter from his father once that told his reasoning in a very few words. "I came out to do my duty—" He didn't go to fight because of slavery. Men do what they know to do. If they are honorable they follow the dictates of their hearts. T.G. Payne fought for Southern Independence, for State Sovereignty. Lincoln had aggressively brought his war to the South, not to the northern states. Southern men had to protect what belonged to them. What kind of a man would have sat at home and let his sons go and fight for him? Not much of one, Joab thought. And Joab could never understand the John Brown deal. The North idealized him, but most everybody who had half a mind knew what he did in Kansas. Joab shuddered at the thought of another human being splitting men's heads with axes—for any reason. It was barbaric.

Joab was not the only southerner who didn't understand. When all was said and done, the final battle of war fought, the Confederacy fallen, when the Army of Northern Virginia stacked its arms, the Chaplains of the Confederacy were put into prisons. They had been non-combatants, performing only their spiritual duties, but their disappointments overwhelmed them when the contest for States' Rights and Southern Independence was defeated. These preachers had done their best to encourage the South's fighting men

There was still a lot of resentment that these spiritual giants of the South were shuffled off to Federal prisons at the end of the war. Why? His mother had told him that somewhere miles and miles away in the sister state of South Carolina, a man by the name of John Girardeau was born on James Island near Charleston. He was of godly parents, Presbyterians. After graduating from high school when he was fourteen, and with years of heartache and loss, joy and sadness, John, having been raised up to love the Bible, to respect his parents and elders, and with a burning love and loyalty for his native South Carolina, longed for his own *particular* forgiveness of sin—for his own Lord and Savior.

Rachel had read a portion from Girardeau's life story to the boys. "'It was at the north corner of King Street and Price's Alley in Charleston. Oh, the unutterable rapture of that hour when I found Him, after a month's conflict with sin and hell! The heavens and the earth seemed to be singing psalms of praise and redeeming love.'"

Joab remembered asking his mother just what happened. She told him this, "He had started to college when the gloomy darkness hovered, his conscience pointing out his sinful nature, God's holiness, and the hopelessness of a life without the redeeming love of Christ. He spent an inordinate amount of time lamenting his inadequacies, begging God to forgive him over and over again. And then one day, he rested his case, threw all ritual to the wind, and calmly placed his trust in Christ. He, in essence, raised his hands in surrender. And he immediately knew."

"Knew what?" Joab had whispered, spellbound by the story, in awe of this man Girardeau.

"That he was *accepted in the Beloved*," Rachel answered. "He was struggling, asking over and over to be forgiven when Christ had already forgiven him. It was not until then that he became content, totally reconciled to God.

"And, Joab," Rachel continued, "Girardeau never forgot his loyalty to South Carolina and the fight for Southern Independence and State Sovereignty. And in the midst of all this, he gathered together large numbers of whites and blacks to listen as he preached the gospel of Jesus Christ. He would preach to the white people who filled the building first and then to the Nigras who filled it second. He stopped at the plantations on his rides back home to Charleston and preached to the Nigras there.

"Girardeau dedicated the days of his life to South Carolina. When he was released from prison and journeyed home by wagon, someone announced, 'We are in South Carolina!' Dr. Girardeau shouted, 'Stop!' He jumped out of the wagon, knelt to the ground, rested his head upon the soil and said, 'O South Carolina, my mother dear, God be thanked that I can lay my head upon your bosom once more.'"

When Joab thought about it, he wanted to swear. He was so angry with the Union. It had taken his father and Henry, left Jonathan sorely wounded, and Isaac in his own anguish of heart at the end of the war. And what was worse, it had left his mother a widow and his younger brother, Samuel, without the father he would so desperately need.

Joab wanted to be like Girardeau. He wanted to love his native land with as much passion. He dismounted Star and tied her to an oak tree.

Albert Henry should be riding Star. She belonged to him.

"God, I hate the Union," he swore out loud.

He dropped to his knees by the side of the road and began pouring out his anguish, asking for clean lips, for forgiveness, for a curbing of the anger, knowing that he could not move forward to help his own self, his people, his friends who were left as lonely as he. He could not help his beloved Calhoun County, his Mississippi—until he could be forgiven of the hate and hurt of the war—forgiven by a Holy God who had told him he could be angry, but that in so doing, he must not willfully commit the sin of rage and hate.

He got up, wiped his face and mounted Star. He rode northeast toward Brice's Crossroads with a final destination of Shiloh, wondering just how much anger God would allow him to display without declaring it to be sin.

CHAPTER 3

MUD WITHOUT MERCY

*Listening long for voices
that never will speak again, hearing the hoofbeats
come and go and fade without a stop . . .*

Donald Davidson
Said of Gen. Lee after the War

Brice's Crossroads was no more than four muddy roads in the woods, heavy woods, a natural boundary alongside Tishomingo Creek, over which a flat single wood-plank bridge passed, east to west. Sherman had his mind set on destroying Nathan Bedford Forrest and this was the best place to do it. The North hated Forrest; he was maligned throughout the war for many reasons, not the least of which was for his attack, plunder and pillage, and his 'mobile warfare.' He was a cavalryman of the finer sort, his primary strategy being fast movement. He would sometimes push his horses to the breaking. He pressed his cavalrymen to arrive first and fast, then to fight on foot. He wheeled around the Union army flank cutting telegraph wires and pulling up railroad tracks.

Joab traveled as the crow flies, taking what he hoped were all the right turns on the trail. Isaac had been exactly right. Joab gently nudged Star—not wanting to bog in the mud—turned left across the road from the Presbyterian Church, whitewashed and lovely by the side of the road that was now covered with rain bejeweled purple phlox. He breathed in the fragrance of the familiar spring flower, took the hill up into a golden field of tiny bitter weeds and there it was. The cemetery must have been a cow pasture before it became a killing field. He reluctantly rode a little closer on the less boggy sod then dismounted, an eerie awareness invading him. It was only the second time he had been inside a Civil War cemetery, this morning at Oxford, his first. Brice's Crossroads was a burial place now, but then, in '62—it was a bloody killing place.

After the war, President Johnson appointed William L. Sharkey, a Union Whig, provisional governor to maneuver Reconstruction in Mississippi and to organize an election of delegates for a state constitutional convention. In 1867 Congress placed Mississippi under U.S. Army rule as part of Reconstruction until they could decide what to do with ex-Confederates and Freedmen. A year later, nothing had changed.

That was a scary place to be, thought Joab, as he moved cautiously across the burial ground. The whole State of Mississippi was under arrest for a few years, so to speak. Times are still bad. The Republican Party controls the State and it's full of Scalawags and Carpetbaggers. They're trying to rip our heart out, break our will. If the war could not do that, what made them think Reconstruction could?

He shuddered, remembering the encounter with the Carpetbagger, Simon Graystone, almost two years ago. Isaac handled the situation with the greatest integrity, that is, after his intense anger abated and he abandoned his own selfishness in the matter. His brother was amazing.

But everything that Mississippi had always known, always been, was going away. For the most part, the State was made up of poor dirt farmers and small land owners, those eking out a living off that land except in the rich flat Delta, where the more affluent lived. But everything he had known was in the northeast hills of Mississippi.

How would they make it with money scarce, tariffs high, and the Union stirring up trouble all over the South?

He swore again and pondered how long God would put up with him.

"Help me," he whispered.

Joab tied Star to a tree, removed his hat, and slogged between the graves now covered over with the fresh spring grasses. Oaks and tall pines surrounded the cemetery, but there were few trees on the knoll where the dead lay beneath the wet sod.

Grant's obsession with the South's waterways was the premise upon which he fought many battles. It was an addiction. Grant was addicted to water; Sherman, to fire. Joab knew that much from Isaac. He told him everything he could remember about the war. Joab needed to know. He would one day tell it all to Samuel. Rachel knew most of it. And the newspapers she once hid in the quilt box, after Thomas finished reading, were no longer kept secret. They were history revealed in four long years of fighting. Joab had long since read them all. But he needed to know for other reasons, now. He had followed the war to Gettysburg after the battle, of course. That was as far as he could go. The letters his father and brothers wrote home stopped abruptly, just two weeks before Gettysburg. On June 16, 1863, to be precise. He trusted those letters from his father and brothers. Now all that was available were newspaper stories written by journalists who got their radical information from Washington City, still slanted against the South.

Joab was getting close to the swollen Tishomingo stream. The rain set the stage, William Tecumseh Sherman having sent his troops in on a day much like today. Water rushed over the foot bridge about two inches but the planks were visible in places. Joab walked across cleaning the mud off his boots, thinking about Nathan Bedford Forrest.

He was tough as shoe leather and a strategic cavalryman. Mean as a snake may be a better description of Forrest. But these were not Sunday school teachers. Far from it. Sherman was a cigar-chewing, cursing, hot tempered raving maniac. No doubt about that. He marched from Atlanta to the Sea before the war was over, burning the South and killing its people. I would say he had a bone to pick, thought Joab. That or—just following orders.

Brice's Crossroads was a decisive win for the South. Forrest had accomplished what he set out to do. The Confederates suffered just fewer than five hundred casualties to the Union's over two thousand. Forrest captured huge supplies of arms and artillery and other supplies—as he was wont to do in every battle. General Sturgis, the commander on behalf of Sherman, suffered demotion and banishment to the far West for the balance of the war because of his incompetence in the battle.

Sherman always shifted the blame to someone other than himself.

CHAPTER 4

THE LAST TATTOO

The muffled drum's sad roll has beat
The soldier's last tattoo;
No more on life's parade shall meet
That brave and fallen few.

From *Bivouac of the Dead*
Theodore O'Hara

Joab spent the night on the bank of the Tennessee River, rose with the first light of day, rolled his blanket, and rode up the hill in knee deep grass to Shiloh. The rain had stopped and the early sun cast cheerful rays through hundreds of live oak trees whose fresh green leaves glistened with every drop that clung for moments and then dropped to the acorn-covered ground.

He was seeing a corner of the beautiful state of Tennessee for the first time. If not for the sickening thought of blood and treasure strewn across the hills of Shiloh, it would have been different. He rode slowly through the eerie woods, past the Bloody Pond, its banks slightly overflowing from the rain. It was just that—a pond, not a very big one. In fact, he was surprised. And there was no blood, of course, only a thick layer of fog that would soon burn off with the brilliance of the early sun. He closed his eyes and tried to visualize the South that April morning six years ago. Its men in tattered gray and butternut brown screaming, groping their way to the water's edge and falling into the cool liquid to soothe their burning bodies riddled from cannon fire, rifle shot, and Miníe balls. That day, the water turned brilliant red as men and horses bled to death.

He removed his hat, bowed his head and paid his respects to the brave southern soldiers who had fought fearlessly. It was the closest Joab would ever get to the war. He needed to relive the day, wanted to ride where Gen. Albert Sidney Johnston rode, stand on the spot where he died, wade out into the now infamous Bloody Pond and ride across the Peach Orchard, where the trees drooped from the weight of their blossoms, pink and white.

There was nothing left of Shiloh Church, which had been a crude building resembling a posh corn crib, and until that beautiful spring morning in 1862, it may have lived up to its name, *place of peace*. But it had not withstood the war. Joab thought maybe its people would build it back someday. Or maybe those who once worshipped there would not be able to do so again. Shiloh would never be the same. It would forever be a burial ground. Up the hill and near the front entrance of the battleground stood thousands of grave markers, mostly for Union soldiers. Tennessee was a southern state, a secession state, yet Union soldiers, the men in blue, were given the grave sites on the hillsides. The South's men were buried together in several long narrow trenches with scarcely a marker. Likely as not, there were remains of the dead beneath Joab's feet, for Grant had ordered that the Rebels be buried either in the trenches or where they fell.

Matters not, he thought. God knows where they are, and they will come forth at the Resurrection. Joab was extraordinarily calm at the thought of it. He rode up on the bluff and, perched upon Star for a better view, he braced for what might be ahead of him. He dismounted and standing in the middle of Shiloh ground, he viewed the landing below and began to walk slowly, recalling the full account as it had been passed down to every young Confederate, to every *real* son of a Confederate veteran.

In mid-March, forty-nine thousand of Grant's men disembarked at Pittsburg Landing, which was no more than a hog and steamboat dock on the Tennessee River just twenty miles north of Corinth. The cat was out of the bag. Those who knew anything at all knew about

Grant's obsession with the South's river systems and word got out that steamboats were docking in and leaving out from the Landing and that Yankees were camping all up in the woods and on the hills close by. The rumors spread to Mississippi's brilliant war strategist, Gen. Albert Sidney Johnston, who was at Corinth, at his side the colorful Creole General Pierre Gustave Toutant Beauregard, hero of First Manassas.

Before April 6, a string of blunders and miscalculations took place, soldiers marching in on torrents of rain and mud over the tops of their boots, the rain washing out roads, obscuring paths, causing them to lose their way. A ten thousand man corps under Confederate General Leonidas Polk was on the muddy streets of Corinth, awaiting marching orders, but Polk was not moving his men up one inch until he got those orders in writing. His delay meant wasted time for the Confederates, who were champing at the bits.

Beauregard postponed the attack until April 6.

The North could not know what the South was doing, and that went for both sides. Grant had more men coming down on foot from Nashville under Don Carlos Buell. But Johnston had another army of fourteen thousand men on their way from Alabama under the command of Earl Van Dorn. Beauregard urged an attack before either army of reinforcements could arrive. At the same time, Grant's army at Pittsburg Landing had no knowledge of what Johnston and Beauregard were planning. They camped in the open, supremely oblivious to what was going on around them. They were busy building latrines and doing artillery training of young raw recruits, many of them having never fired a shot.

Sherman, who obviously arose upon the wrong side of his posh encampment bed on the morning of April 6, was in such disbelief of what his men tried to tell him that he threatened to have them arrested for spreading such rumor. After the battle, he had his excuses. If they had fortified at the point of knowledge, they would have looked like cowards.

But too late for Sherman. At sunrise on the morning of April 6, he could no longer ignore the reports. Forty-five thousand Rebels surfaced from the privet hedge that was white with blooms. They were in his face in a surprise attack. When Sherman reached for his field glasses, his orderly was struck in the head, fell from his horse, and died. Sherman, his hand hit by rifle fire, became an instant believer and dashed about yelling, "My God, we are attacked!"

Joab stood there, smiling as he envisioned the tart-mouthed Sherman riding for cover.

That morning had broken cool and delightful with wild flowers in full bloom, peach blossoms pink and fragrant dropping their petals on the green grasses of Shiloh, hedgerows of privet high with the nostalgic fragrance of home, and dogwoods in full white spray, branches hovering low to the ground. Mocking birds sang in the trees that canopied a forest floor spread with the colors of early spring.

The place of peace was about to become the place of pandemonium.

Joab reverently relived foot soldiers in Confederate gray and butternut brown bursting from the woods in waves, their lines two miles wide, flags waving, generals atop their horses yelling orders. As always and as expressed at the end of the war, they were *marching in perfect order*, like a pass-in-review parade. Joab couldn't help but think of Jonathan charging the hill with Pickett and his men as the blistering hot July wind gave way to bullet and cannon and bayonet on that third day of battle at Gettysburg.

The morning sun over Shiloh flashed off rifle barrels and Confederate bands played *Dixie*, a tune that angered the Union soldiers almost as much as the Rebel Yell. On that Shiloh morning, they yelled it, shrill, sharp, penetrating. And they charged at the order, crashing through a line of young untrained Union soldiers shoved to the front by commanders who didn't know what to do with them.

South Carolina born, Rebel Brigadier General Adley H. Gladden from Louisiana, hero of the Union bombardment of the Confederate forts at Pensacola Harbor, had influenced the battle, spectacularly leading his quarter of the field at Shiloh. Gladden was blown from his horse when a cannonball tore off his arm at the shoulder. He fell mortally wounded. Opposite him was Union Colonel Peabody's regiment, hard hit by Gladden's attack. Peabody took five bullets, buying time for the Yankee divisions that were to his rear to come up. The sixth bullet shattered his skull. He fell to the ground, dead.

All morning on that Lord's Day, Confederates pushed back the Union. Bodies from both sides lay in heaps on the once cool ground, now hot with the blood of men and horses. About ten thousand of Grant's men dropped behind the bluff by the river while several regiments of the South were sent to the rear because of their timidity.

Those boys were younger than I, thought Joab. What would I have done? I'm no different.

Then Grant showed up about nine in the morning aboard a steamboat. He was thirty-nine years old with a history of failure, and was friends of another flawed-up questionable character, William Tecumseh Sherman, who was the Union Commander in charge of Shiloh Battle.

The Rebels were importunate that morning, pressing the onslaught until midday when the fighting coalesced around the Union center at a scrubby forest—a place that would soon be called the Hornet's Nest, a place where bullets whirred and hissed and spit and sparked through the air like thousands of angry hornets as the South cracked the web design, aggressively angering the Union Army.

Joab walked through to the old wagon trail called the Sunken Road. The grounds were still wasted, brutally beaten down. It would take years to raise up a forest in this spot where the artillery had riddled the trees. The ones left standing were dead, filled with bullet holes. Joab could see through them with no hindrance. A hive of bees had set up in an old bullet-ridden trunk, honey dripping from the comb. Joab, as much a wilderness boy as his fighting brother, Jonathan, reached into the hole, pulled off a piece of the comb, flicked away the tiny bees, and put it to his lips. It was sweet and luscious and filling. He rode to the Snake River and washed the stickiness from his hands and his youthful sparsely bearded face and continued his thoughts about the battle.

By mid-afternoon, Gen. Johnston looked out over his successes and was pleased. President Jefferson Davis had personally celebrated Johnston as the Confederates' finest officer. Much like Lee, Johnston had turned down an offer of high Union commission to fight with his native South, and Davis had put him in command of the Army of the West.

Gen. Johnston, concerned about the Tennessee brigade that was refusing to fight, took them on. Those timid Tennesseans rallied with the great general at the lead and took the Peach Orchard. Branches perforated with squirrel rifle shot fell to the ground spreading a bed of blossoms—a bed for soldiers, North and South, to die upon. Battered and wounded fighting men from both sides crawled and clawed their way to the pond to cool their mangled bodies, under an unspoken truce. So many dying, so much bloodshed.

And then tragic and costly for the South—Johnston, leading an attack on Union forces near the Peach Orchard, took a shot behind his right knee. He didn't know he was hit, neither did he realize his boot had filled with blood, the leather trapping it inside. One of his staff, Isham Harris was the Governor of Tennessee until he heard Lincoln had appointed Andrew Johnson as military governor. At that, he lost heart and went to fight with Johnston. When he saw his commander slump in the saddle, Harris asked if he were wounded. Johnston confirmed that he was, and Harris and other staff officers lowered their commander to the ground, carried him to safety under a tree and attempted to make a tourniquet, but the general had lost too much blood. He died sitting under the tree in the ravine where his aides had brought him.

Joab shook and wept at the thought of it. If they had only known. A medic could have removed his boot, wrapped a proper tourniquet, and saved the life of that southern hero. Such a loss! Without Johnston there could likely have been no decisive victory at Shiloh. Had he lived, the strategic war lord could have led the South to uncanny victory that would have soon ended the war. The Confederacy would have stayed intact, leaving the two countries, the Confederate States and the Union, both on the continent of North America. What would have been wrong with that? It was the dream of southern people—to be left alone.

But that, thought Joab, is living in the past; it did not happen and I know it's a waste of valuable time to constantly ponder the *what-ifs*.

The Hornet's Nest collapsed long about six o'clock that evening when Union General Wallace was mortally wounded. Soon after, Union General Prentiss was captured along with his entire division. It looked bad for the Union.

Then Buell came in the nick of time for Grant. His adjutant had placed a battery of siege guns in the Union line to drive the Confederates back. While Grant observed, a Rebel cannonball blew the head off one of his aides. Sobering. The battle fell apart for lack of knowledge on Gen. Beauregard's part. Unaware that Buell had arrived, Beauregard called off the attack until the next morning. He was two miles away at Shiloh Church; his plan was to get the remainder of the Union soldiers at the Landing the next morning.

The Union brought out the new forces and at dawn attacked all across the Rebel front. Beauregard put up a good fight. But around two the afternoon of April 7, he ordered his worn-out troops back to the stronghold of Corinth.

Sherman could not leave well enough alone. The next day, April 8, he ran into Colonel Nathan Bedford Forrest at the Battle of Fallen Timbers. That day, Forrest taught Sherman a lesson about the power of the Confederate Cavalry that he would never forget.

Shiloh Battle was ended.

There were many twists to the tales of Shiloh. All things being equal and handled properly, the South had wreaked more havoc upon the North. If the Union had lost badly, it would have been disastrous for them. The South would have likely invaded the North and gained states and they would have rallied with troops pouring in. Instead, Grant, with Lincoln's words ringing in his ears—"Break them. Break their will"—concluded that there must be total annihilation of the South. The Union must take over the Rivers. He had not anticipated such a fight at Shiloh and he was as angry as the proverbial hornet upon the Sunken Road. The South had unleashed horror and inflicted death and carnage unspeakable, like none before, maybe none since. More of the North than of the South lay dead on its rolling hills. Yet, Shiloh had been declared indecisive.

Joab knew the newspapers had played it hard against Grant for the Battle of Shiloh. Congress had censured him for holding up in a mansion several miles from the Landing where his soldiers were encamped and for having no battle plan in case of attack.

At the same time, Jeff Davis wept bitterly over the death of Sidney Johnston. And he was angry with Beauregard for calling off the attack when he did. Hindsight is always clearer, thought Joab.

There were no winners at Shiloh, truth be told.

Shiloh's beauty had somehow softened the blow for Joab. Images that should be remembered lodged in his head and he longed to turn back the clock and declare the Confederacy to be the winner. In every battle, they fought with fewer men than the Union and in most every battle they lost fewer men than the Enemy. He shuddered to think of what the men and boys of the South could have accomplished if the kill ratio had been a proper measuring device.

When the battle was ended, the last soldier had fallen, and the Confederates were pushed back to Corinth, the Union Army was deeply embarrassed over dereliction, something its commanders had to deal with in their own way, including Lincoln. Dead bodies and horses lay strewn from one end of Shiloh Church grounds to the other, through the Peach Orchard, in the Bloody Pond, on the Sunken Road. The war had not wreaked this much havoc since the first shots were fired at Ft. Sumter just a year before. There was nothing to compare, not even First Manassas, which the South had won.

Because there was no decisive victory for either side, only death and carnage, Shiloh was sinister reality that there was more to come. The war that would devastate both sides before it was over had not ended at Shiloh Church grounds.

CHAPTER 5

YOUNG LOVE

The sun slid magically below the hill
on the western side of the house,
sending slithers of gold across the old
wood-slatted porch.

Had they been personal friends, Gen. Robert E. Lee would have been the first to entreat Joab not to lose his southern gentility, his hope for better days for the South, and his love for the country for which his father and brother died. Lee knew—in the moments, the months, the years he had left to live following Appomattox—that the South had begun to lose the charm for which it had been lauded in the years before going to war. Southern hospitality was carelessly being replaced with strong hostility arising out of constant exasperation brought on by the rules of Reconstruction. Somewhere—somewhere far away in the mountains of the Sovereign Commonwealth of Virginia, Lee was likely experiencing the same harsh realities of the aftermath as Joab and his family.

Lee had participated in President Johnson's proclamation for the terms of amnesty and pardon for southern Rebels. At least a path was made for settling old resentments. Heaven knows, they couldn't go on the way they were. Sure, the heart of the Confederacy had stopped beating. Lincoln was dead, and he had by no means preserved the Union. He had simply shut down the South. How could its wounds be bound when northern politicians still desired to have Dixie's leaders strung up on sour apple trees, Joab wondered?

In their purported omniscience, the North was determined that Reconstruction would call the Rebels to America again and that secession would be forgotten. But that would never happen; secession may be over and gone, but it would never be forgotten. The South had bled and died for it, and the memory was indelibly fixed. President Johnson had vetoed the Reconstruction bill. Congress had overridden his veto. The whole country was disjointed, and the Radical Republicans were still in office in the person of Ulysses S. Grant. There had been no southern representation in that contest. The Rebel States had not yet been accepted back into the Union at the time of the election in 1869.

Late in the day, Joab sat alone on the porch of the old farmhouse he had called home for over nineteen years. It was hot as blue blazes, not unusual for early summertime in Sarepta. He dared to take his shirt off to cool his skin, brown from hours in the field and garden and long days pulling the saw alongside his brother, Jonathan, at Grandfather Moses Church's sawmill. He slapped at the mosquitoes with his shirt, wondering which was worse, the heat or the pesky insects.

The sun slid magically below the hill on the western side of the house, splashing slithers of gold across the old wood-slatted porch. He touched the floor with his boot and set the swing in motion, the lonesome squeak of the chains synchronized with his thoughts, something he and his brothers had done one by one through the years. Sitting there dredged up old memories. He missed his brothers, though Sam and his mother Rachel were there. Sam was a regular little man. He had even learned to play the fiddle like his brothers. That was one good thing left. So much was gone, huge chunks out of their lives since before the war in April of '61.

While the sun moved downward and the killdeers scurried to find their ground nests for the evening, the crickets struck chord and refused to quit until Joab tapped his foot on the porch again. Given two minutes, they amazingly resumed on key and in unison. Rachel quietly opened the door, not wanting to disturb Joab's thoughts. He put his shirt on.

"Mama . . . can you . . . can you come sit with me?" he said, standing.

"I was hoping you would ask," she said.

"Where's Sam?"

"In the attic room pouring over *Pilgrim's Progress*. He has a test tomorrow."

"Oh, I remember the wretched thought of 'Pilgrim'—not my favorite."

Rachel laughed. "Some things remain constant. Sam is of the same persuasion."

"A smart little man, I say."

It had always been easy for Joab to have meaningful conversation with his mother. They were close. He seldom kept a thing from her. There was no need. She always knew anyway.

"Remember I told you when I went to Shiloh I stopped in Oxford?"

"Yes, I remember. You had breakfast at the tea room in such finery."

"I kept some things from you," he said apologetically.

"No!" Rachel's eyes popped in interest. She was kidding him.

"Yes!" Joab grinned and began to tell her the story. "I didn't tell you about the girl I met. The girl who served me breakfast. Her name was Sarah Agnes. And she was . . . well, she was pretty. In fact, she was what you might call . . . beautiful."

"Well, did you stop again on your way back home?"

"No ma'am."

"Why not?" The smile on Rachel's face grew wider and her eyes danced.

"Why did you say that?" asked Joab.

"Because . . . because . . . well, you're telling me now."

"Guess I didn't want to get involved with someone so far away from Sarepta. Remember how it was for Albert Henry and Cassie, Houston being in another county? Seemed so far away."

"But you must have been interested. Besides Oxford is only twenty miles from here."

"Yes ma'am," he said. "She fascinated me. The way she spoke. And she was able to do something I've not found to be easy for myself just in the past six months or so."

"I think I know what you're about to say, Joab." Rachel breathed deep, sighed and leaned back on the swing.

"You think so, Mama?"

Rachel knew him, but Joab had to question that she knew *that* much about these particular feelings. Isaac had always said she was omniscient, though it ruffled Rachel. But she had always known *everything* about her boys, ingeniously so. Joab hoped he inherited the gift of knowledge and that he would have an opportunity to learn just how she did it.

"Was she cheerful in spite of the circumstances?"

"Mother, you beat all."

"Well, I'll be quiet so you can tell me about this pretty girl."

"Her name's Sarah Agnes, as I said. In the first place, I like the name. I think if I knew her better I might call her 'Aggie' for short. But it was her smile that took me. She was able to shed big tears and smile at the same time. I wanted to touch her flawless face. But—I daren't. Mother, is it wrong that I wanted to kiss her? I don't even know her."

Joab squared his wide shoulders and ran his hands through a head of brown straight hair that fell to the top of his shoulders. He pulled his fingers through it. When he let it go, it fell right back into place. His blue eyes attractively gave away his present thoughts.

"Sounds seriously like the first signs of love or maybe just the longing to be loved by someone who can relate to your own emotions and passion. Joab, love is magical in the pure sense of the meaning. You don't know where it comes from, you don't know what to do with it, but you don't ever want it to go away."

"You hit the nail on the head, Mama."

"Experience, Joab. I had experience in loving your father for over twenty years before he died. And believe me—that was not long enough."

Joab dropped his head and thought about his father, full of life and love for his family.

"I'm going to leave you with your thoughts and get Sam to help with supper. Come in when you're ready."

Summer winds blew through the trees to cool the evening. Joab watched as the squirrels scampered to a resting place, disappearing until another day. The silhouette of a deer and her fawn faded into the wood line. They would be back. They would be back and so would the thoughts of Sarah Agnes. The evening was heavy with the soft scent of Confederate jasmine, sweetening his remembrance of the beautiful southern girl. Joab leaned back on the swing and, with hands on his head, sought to push back memories of Aggie, her silhouette fading into the corners of his mind. Of course, that meant filling up his brain with other less gratifying thoughts.

He sought to be distracted once more by the scrumptious smell of his mother's biscuits baking. He opened the door and, for old time's sake, he let it slam behind him.

Rachel smiled.

CHAPTER 6

TEACHING SAM

*The South was not just an institution.
It was people.
Living human beings...*

At the fall of Richmond, the epitome of southern beauty and charm, following its capture by the Union forces, Lincoln took his son, Tad, and sailed southward to its shores, just one hundred miles from Washington. Richmond's elite residents had burned their own city, not wishing the Union to pillage and plunder and loot one thing that belonged to them. When his Union General Weitzel, Richmond's conqueror, asked of Lincoln what to do about the captured Confederates that were being held in Libby Prison and Castle Thunder, Lincoln, not wishing to commit himself said, "If I were in your place, I'd let 'em up easy, let 'em up easy."

Joab's ears rang with Lincoln's troubling words about the Confederate prisoners.

"I wonder what he meant by that," Joab whispered. His Uncle Marcellus Church died in a Federal prison at Point Lookout, Maryland. Lincoln had wanted his generals to break the back of the South. 'Break their back—let 'em up easy?' Snuff them out for the sake of the war, but let 'em up easy for the sake of the Union? Is that what he wanted? The South was not *just* an institution. It was people. Living human beings, subject to the same passions as the North.

The three of them gathered close around the table T. G. had built, Joab now seated in his father's place. One by one, the boys had moved up close to their mother, into their father's chair.

Rachel glanced at Joab and he bowed his head.

"Lord, make us thankful for this food and other blessings that are ours only because of your goodness. Forgive us for the sins that beset us and may we rest in the promise that you, and you alone, will never leave nor forsake us. In the name of Christ our Lord, Amen."

Sam. Sweet innocent Samuel stuck his fork into a brown-topped biscuit, picked up the plate and passed it to his brother while Rachel poured tall glasses of milk.

"You know," said Sam, "Kit just keeps on giving, doesn't she?"

They all laughed.

"I think it's time you taught your brother how to milk that faithful old cow, Joab."

"How about first thing in the morning before we head for the mill, Sam?"

"I reckon if that's part of getting to be a man, I'll have to go along with it. What time?"

"Four o'clock."

"In the morning?"

Joab nodded as he filled his plate with butter and pear preserves.

"Then I better skip 'Pilgrim' and get to bed right away!"

Joab stepped out on the back porch and lit the barn lantern. The tree frogs quit singing momentarily, realizing they were not alone, but in another moment, they started up again, willing to share the early hours with Joab and Sam. This was going to be fun. Isaac had taught Joab and Sam was next in line. It was Joab's turn to teach. Milking a cow was no easy feat until the milker could master the art.

Sam rubbed his eyes and splashed water from the wash pan onto his face hoping it would help him walk a straight path to the barn. Would Kit even be awake at such an hour? He followed in his brother's steps wondering just how this milking thing worked anyway. He hoped he would not embarrass himself, though he had never attempted such a disgusting thing. Until now, he had stuck with feeding the chickens and hogs. But he had watched the boys do the milking. Maybe it would be fairly easy. He hoped so.

"Okay, brother, here's what you do. Sit up close, almost under Kit. She won't hurt you. She's real used to this. She'll just be bending her head, getting a mouthful of hay and she'll chew and chew and then she'll start to chew her cud. That means she'll lift her head upright and keep chewing and chewing and chewing, swallowing, bringing it back up, and chewing some more."

"Well, that sounds disgusting."

"You do have to do a little more than that, though," said Joab. "Go ahead, sit down."

"It feels awfully close under here," said Sam. "And I can't half see. It's still dark."

"But you have to do it that way, else you can't reach her. I'll hold the lantern close in a minute. Now, just take this right here and start at the top and let your fingers go straight down. Don't try to squeeze on the whole thing and don't squeeze at the bottom. Nothing will come out. You have to force it down with your fingers in a sort of rhythm, from top to bottom. Understand?"

"All right, I'll try."

Nothing happened. Not one drop hit the bucket.

"Could you just show me first?" said Sam.

"Certainly," said Joab, grinning mischievously, putting the lantern on the ground close up so they could both see.

"Like this. Watch."

He took nature's instrument of milk production, doing exactly what he had described to his brother, but he aimed it toward Sam, filling his eye with fresh warm milk from a nice sated stream.

"Aw, Joab! That's nasty! I may never drink milk again!"

Sam took the washing water and threw it at his brother, and they both laughed until they were bent double.

Finally the bucket was full, but not because of Sam. He just couldn't get the hang of it. It might take more than a dozen mornings of four o'clock instructions for him.

"Joab, did you notice how old Kit just stood there the whole time we were having a good time behind her back?"

"Yes. I feel guilty. Do you?"

"No. It was fun."

They laughed and trekked to the house, poured the milk in the churn, covered it over with a flour sack, and crawled back into their beds until Rachel called them for breakfast.

CHAPTER 7

SLEEPLESS NIGHTS

When the house doth sigh and weep,
And the world is drowned in sleep,
Yet mine eyes the watch do keep,
Sweet Spirit, comfort me!

Robert Herrick

Immensely tired from a day at the mill and from plowing the garden and planting summer vegetables that replaced the early peas and onions and lettuce, Joab led the mule to the barn and helped Sam finish his chores before the sun dropped behind the hills for the night. They took the path home together. And after supper of milk and cornbread, the crusty kind his mother made, Joab took his thoughts and excused himself. He climbed the steps to the attic room his brothers had passed down. Albert Henry to Jonathan to Isaac, and now to Joab. He opened the windows that lined the back wall hoping for a night breeze, then stretched his lanky body across the feather bed. He lay there with thoughts of Aggie that wouldn't go away. What was it about her that had so drawn him? He didn't really know her, yet they had both experienced the war years from the same perspective. They lost their fathers. He allowed that was sufficient. Southern ties were mysteriously binding through the war years and even now that it was over. He hoped memories of Aggie were sufficient justification for his private thoughts to keep him bound to her.

He lay still. It was too hot to move about and he could find no sleep. He got up and stretched out on the wood floor that was much cooler but entirely uncomfortable. Tomorrow was Thursday, and it put him yet another week beyond Aggie. He was afraid of forgetting her. Time could take care of that.

Summer stretched from one endless hot and humid day to the next. But it never happened. Joab could not shake his thoughts of the beautiful southern girl. One thing was certain since the weekend Joab made his trip to the battlegrounds, his life had started to change and he had begun to see from a higher vantage point. The day he rode up on Shiloh Church grounds, he had wanted to curse Sherman and Grant and those responsible for burying Confederate soldiers in shallow trench graves together. To be sure, that desire had not diminished, but he was thinking along different lines now.

Granted, Reconstruction was not working for the powers in Washington. They quickly found they could not order the South around and expect them to roll over and play dead. Nor could they hang them from the nearest sour apple tree, at least not all of them. They were a group with which to contend, and they were not going to succumb to the North's every whim. Joab, in fact, believed that Reconstruction, as it was designed, would soon go by the wayside. He proposed, to himself, that he label it something else—Rebuilding. The South needed to be rebuilt. It didn't need to be radically changed. And they were not about to vanish into thin air over snide remarks and rude slogans. If it meant being hungry, doing without, then so be it. They were used to it.

Joab, weary from sleepless nights with thoughts of the past, present and even the future, began to slowly cut the *binding cords of discord*. Life was taking on a gentler meaning. The war had taught him—taught him that he could ill afford to lose his humanity, his propensity to love and cherish. The hatred was diminishing, but not the restlessness. His country had been at war with itself. Men and boys, North and South, who had survived the killing, would nevermore enjoy life as it had been. They would all have to make some changes. He was sure most of them would rather not have fought each other. Out of necessity, the commanders were taught to study war. Ordinary people were not. And surely that included the North.

Joab's family was scaled down to three. Although it was lonely, there would once again be times when the family would gather and they would celebrate with love and laughter. But right now, Joab was living a restlessness he couldn't explain. Not that he *couldn't* explain it. He didn't want to explain it—not to Rachel. And she was the only one who mattered at this point in his life. Not too bad, he thought, just one person. He was accountable to just one person, humanly speaking.

By summer's end, he had fought the sleepless nights and restless days for as long as he could. It was time to go to the swing. It was not a bad thing.

"Mother, I have to go."

Joab wrung his hands and shifted from one leg to the other. Rachel sat down and so did he. The leaves on the oaks were turning and falling. Indian summer was coming on, the most beautiful time of the year in the South. A cool breeze stirred and gave relief to an otherwise warm evening. The sights and smells of autumn lodged in his senses, adding fire to the flame that burned deep within him.

"I have known for a long time, son," Rachel said with a faraway look on her face as she gazed up the hill to the little cemetery.

"Known what, Mother?"

"Every time I lose a son, I think of Benjamin. I don't mean to make you feel uncomfortable, Joab, but you must know something of a mother's heart when it comes to saying goodbye to each of her children. I had to say forever goodbyes to Ben and Albert Henry and temporary ones to Jonathan and Isaac. I know this is a burden on you, but I thought you would always be here. That was wrong, please forgive me. I have identified the restlessness on your face. I've heard the clamoring for sleep and relief at night. All of that has helped prepare me for the day when you will say you're leaving."

"And I should have known *that*. I don't want to be selfish in this. I'm learning things I never dreamed I would learn. Things that are not in the books. You taught me well from those books. But the trip to Shiloh and a summer's worth of sleepless nights have taught me the balance of what I need to know—to do the things I'm called to do."

Rachel wiped the tears with her apron and cleared her throat.

"Joab, this is your time and it is in God's good timing. He makes no mistakes and He knows best. I will not argue with that. I think I have an idea of the place this will take you."

"Mother, you always know and it is much easier because you do, for in knowing there is understanding."

"It *is* about the *place*, isn't it, Joab? Figuratively speaking?"

"Yes ma'am, it is. Or maybe the places, Shiloh being one of them. The *higher ground* at Shiloh. That's where a gallant representation of our men lie. They were not able to finish what they were called on to do. But I can help finish it for them. Oh, I don't mean fighting another war, dredging up old wounds, running slave trade, hating Negroes. That's never occupied even a single space in my mind. I'm talking about rebuilding the war-torn South. Not Reconstruction in the Union's definition of it, because the majority of us in the South know it cannot work, not like they've put it together. But rebuilding homes and restoring tangible treasure. Building towns and railroads and churches and barns. Touching a life or two along the way. I don't want to stay forever. I just want to go out there for three or four months at a time and see what I can do to help."

"But there's more, isn't there?" Rachel said, glancing up at her son.

"Yes ma'am," he said. "There's more for me, but I don't know if there is more for Sarah Agnes. Of course, I only saw her that one time, but I cannot get her out of my head. Sometimes I think she will never go away from me. That's part of the sleepless nights, the restlessness. Which leads me to the real place . . . the *real place* is Oxford. I have to go back. I have to see her at least once more. I have to know for certain. Does that make sense, Mother?"

"Son, I will be the first to tell you to follow your heart, but in so doing, you know you are leaving yourself wide open for that heart to be broken."

"Yes ma'am, I know."

"Then you're prepared for heartache as well as happiness?"

"I doubt that," he said, "but I will remember what you said, because right now there is no real permanent happiness in this world—North or South!"

"You know Samuel is going to grieve when you're gone?"

"Yes, Mother. Please help me in that regard. I cannot bear to leave him that way. What can I do?"

"Tell him he can go with you when he turns thirteen!"

"I can do that without fail. He will be beside me. It will take a long time to rebuild our country. But what will *you* do then, Mama?"

"I'll cross that stream when I get to it two years from now," said Rachel, forcing a smile.

"My first concern is you, Mother. For a lot of what I will do, there will be no money. But I will make sure I earn enough to send back to you every month."

"I have a small income from the sale of the hogs on the hill. You know, when I think of it, we outsmarted the Yanks by keeping those hogs penned up there until they turned wild. We didn't have any control over that. The pork is good, but they're intolerable. The Yanks didn't want anything to do with them. I'm just glad they didn't shoot them and don't really know why they didn't. Just a thought. Glad those days are past."

Rachel continued her accounting of how she would get along without Joab.

"Samuel can keep working for Grandpa Church. Jonathan will take care of him in that regard. Jonathan and Isaac still send money from time to time as they can and they will plow the garden and the corn field when they come, and as long as Jude Parker keeps the gristmill running, he'll buy corn from us. We will need very little. Also, Papa sends money up from Natchez. I have the sale of my eggs or I can trade them for something I need more. We will be fine, Joab. I've learned to live on meager fare."

"Maybe I *am* being selfish, Mama. Sometimes I think all my thoughts are about me and what I want out of life. Sooner or later, I have to make my way. I have to learn to support a wife and family. And I have to help rebuild this Country. If that is selfish, then I have to plead guilty. But these longings never leave me."

"Far from selfish, Joab. You are a man. That's what men do. Giving of yourself doesn't fall into the category of selfishness. I remember once when Jonathan found it necessary to leave home for several days just to go to the Yalobusha Wilderness. He came back a grown-up man."

"Yes," said Joab. "But he still needed his mama to salve the wounds the old bear made to his face. No. I'll never forget that, and I'll keep my options open."

"Oxford is not that far from us. Samuel and I could consider riding over on the buckboard to see you if we get too lonely."

"That would be splendid, Mama. I'll have to find a place to stay first thing, of course. I hope I can work for room and board."

"An adventure," she said. "A *splendid* adventure."

Joab woke early, not that he had slept much. The night had been long and warm in the attic room, and he had tossed and turned, torn between leaving his mother and Samuel and following his dream, his calling. He kept reminding himself it would not take forever and it would not be permanent.

He hadn't known about Oxford when the beautiful square was lined with trees and handsome buildings. Six years ago in 1864, the Union Army laid it waste, burned those buildings to the ground, and wrecked the town's economy. He had hastily blamed it on Sherman. He knew the South would not—could not make a quick comeback, but he would do his best to encourage its people to rise from the ashes. Every southern man knew how to do the things that mattered—use a squirrel rifle, milk a cow, ride a horse, plow a straight row. They knew how to love passionately—God Almighty and their meeting houses, their women and children, and their country. And they knew how to cut timber and mill lumber. Joab had worked at his Grandpa Church's sawmill since he was Samuel's age. The fragrance of pine and cedar not only filled his senses, but his soul; the pull of the saw was as familiar as the sun that rose over Sarepta of a morning.

He was taking nothing but his bedroll, two changes of clothing, and a two-day supply of food. Rachel put the biscuits and ham in a flour sack, tucked in a fried peach pie and a baked sweet potato. An old iron skillet and a tin coffee pot, a plate, a sharp knife, and a cup lay on the kitchen table. He brought in his saddlebags and packed the items neatly.

Joab is about to learn to fend for himself, thought Rachel. These few pieces will help. "An adventure," she whispered. "We'll see. God, if I can hold to my sanity, my emotions, for yet another good-bye!"

Tears were popping.

Joab swallowed hard, pulled Rachel and Samuel to himself and hugged them both. Then he promptly left in the early morning mist, not wanting to get emotional. He was already there, however. On the verge of tears. There would be many moments like these.

He had obsessed with Sarah Agnes Stephens, with her beauty, her grace and charm. He couldn't get her off his mind. Surely when he saw her, it would help soothe the heartache over leaving his family. And this place called Oxford intrigued him. Its tree-lined trails and hard-packed dirt streets, beautiful old mansions, The University and its peacefulness. In spite of the battle that had raged in 1862 by Grant and Sherman's invasion, it had stayed intact until Union General Whiskey Smith burned the buildings on the square in his 1864 invasion. Joab allowed he had been drunk the morning he burned such a beautiful town. The Yanks couldn't get enough of the Old South.

Lafayette County needs more help with rebuilding than Calhoun, he thought. Grant and Sherman were only interested in key southern towns and Oxford had been one of them. Sarepta was just a one-horse town, so to speak, though it was home to him. Oxford was the seat of learning for Mississippi. But as far as the Union was concerned, the southern dogs were just hillbillies, not university material. They would have no need for such.

He took the familiar trail out of Calhoun County and rode across country through Pontotoc to Lafayette, his stomach in knots for two reasons. He had just left his family for heaven knew how long, and he would soon be seeing someone he had grown extremely fond of if only in his dreams.

The Chickasaw Indians owned the land upon which the town was built. By 1832, they had ceded it to the white men, who hoped it would become a center of learning in the Old South. With a name like Oxford, the founding fathers had a lot to live up to.

At the start of the war, the entire student body and a lot of the faculty enlisted in the Confederate Army, calling themselves *The University Greys*. The sad part was that they suffered almost a hundred percent loss, some of them killed in battles previous to Gettysburg. Joab wondered if those who were left had met up with his father and

Jonathan and Albert Henry on the way to join Lee's Army of Northern Virginia, where so many of those brave men fought and fell together at Pickett's Charge on the hot and hateful hills of Gettysburg.

Oxford suffered slow recovery in the years following the burning because of the frazzled economy and shortage of men to do the work. Many had died in the war, and what had been accomplished so far was but a scratch on the drawing pad.

CHAPTER 8

FULLNESS OF JOY

There was a time when meadow, grove, and stream
The earth, and every common sight,
To me did seem appareled in celestial light,
The glory and the freshness of a dream.

William Wordsworth

Joab rode slowly into Oxford on a cool September morning. A slight breeze caught the first leaves of autumn and strewed them across his path, colors of red, yellow and orange collecting beside the cornerstones of the few buildings of a once-beautiful town that had been ravaged by war. Did the sun shine brighter here than any place he had ever known? Shaking like the leaves that fluttered and scattered, he turned Star and rode toward the Lyceum. He breathed deeply, inhaled the fragrance of jasmine and privet that hedged the row of housing across the grassy hill from the building that once was the healing station for North and South.

Healing—then and now. So many young men who never took a bullet needed the healing place. This—this would be Joab's. God, let it be, he thought.

He dismounted and tied Star to the hitching rail. Campus students mingled and passed, greeting him cordially with a wave of the hand. Southern gentility, he hoped, was returning with each passing day that put space between its people and the war.

He was somewhat out of place, his red plaid shirt and overalls falling short of collegiate attire. But he was there with purpose—not motive. Therefore, it could not matter how he was dressed. It was the very best he had, and with money scarce in the South, he was proud to have clothes of any sort. He gathered his wits about him in hopes of seeing Sarah Agnes once again. He had no way of knowing how she would receive him. No way of knowing if she would even remember him, especially now that the students were back and classes had begun. Likely the faces would blend as one. He took a deep breath and prayed silently for strength to accept rejection just in case.

He scrubbed the night before, having brought up the old tin bathing tub, and Rachel's lavender scented handmade soap lay fragrantly on his skin. She starched and ironed his clothes and Joab polished his boots as best he could. His brown straight hair fell to his shoulders, loose and clean, framing his sun-browned face. Joab was handsome, indeed.

He mounted and rode back to the square, looked around, trying not to focus on the dreadful part, the devastation. Not yet anyway. There was so much to be done.

Joab filled his lungs with air he would need just to lay eyes on her, albeit the shaking had passed. Unable to wait another moment, he pushed the swinging doors open and entered the lobby of The Thompson House. It was eleven o'clock and the tea room was filling up with students. Young men and women with studious faces properly dressed. He stood out like a sore thumb. There were many servers today, a far cry from the near empty dining hall on his first visit.

He searched the floor for Aggie. She was not there. His countenance fell; he looked and felt like a limp dishrag. Maybe she doesn't work here anymore, he thought. Four long months of hot and restless summer had passed. That's it! She's gone, and if someone doesn't know where she lives, I will never see her again. He glanced toward the lobby of the beautiful hotel, his eyes resting on the clerk's desk behind which were letter-sized cubby holes of fine wood—for mail, he supposed. Rachel would call this place exquisite. He allowed some people stayed here on a regular basis. He could inquire there about Aggie if he were so a-mind. Instead, he walked back outside and stood by Star, contemplating his next step. He didn't have a plan. One look at Aggie and that would all come. At least he hoped so. Until then—well, he wasn't sure.

He mounted Star, turned her out onto the square, and rode behind the hotel to the back entrance on the alley. Whoever rebuilt did a good job. Even the alley entrances to the hotel and the two new stores were attractive. However, to the end of the square there was nothing but ashes, piles of scorched brick, and old bent and burnt tin from the roofs.

He wasn't sure what he hoped to accomplish or how he could help, but at least he was getting to know this Oxford town, on and off the square. He felt a surge of energy as he made his way to the end of the alley, turned his horse and started back. A buckboard stopped behind the inn, driven by a young man who, from a distance, looked to be just younger than Aggie. He came around to the passenger's side and lifted out a frail young woman, returned to his rig, struck his mare, and drove away. He tipped his hat to Joab in passing and trotted his rig on down the alley to turn around. The person he dropped at the back door disappeared.

Joab sauntered Star back to the hitching rail in front of the tea room, dismounted, and re-entered the front swinging doors, greeted by the cheerful clatter of dishes, silver and glassware. The students were leaving, returning to classes, he supposed. He was glad. He wished for a cup of coffee, but did not want to take up space belonging to the regulars. He was sure they had more money in their Ivy League pockets than he had in his overalls. Besides, he had food in his saddlebags. He would eat later in the day.

A nice middle-aged lady seated him at a table for one in a front corner of the lavishly furnished dining hall. He sat in the window facing the tables now mostly empty, the kitchen help quietly placing dirty plates and silver into dishpans. He reached in his pocket and pulled out the only reading material he owned. His New Testament fell open to Psalm sixteen, his eyes resting on the last verse. "Thou wilt show me the path of life: in thy presence is fullness of joy; at thy right hand there are pleasures for evermore."

Joab closed the book, lingered in thought momentarily; the verse had spoken volumes to him—"Thou wilt show me the path of life"—the healing place. That healing place is decidedly marked by the Lord's presence—with joy and pleasures, he mused. And are not life and living all about healing, physically and emotionally? Tears fell on the white drape that covered the table. He looked up, and there she stood.

"Joab."

He slowly stood to his feet, towering over her. She was so small. He hadn't remembered just how small. Her eyes were cobalt blue, and they were filling with tears.

"Oh, Joab."

"Aggie."

"I thought we may never meet again," she said softly, "and if I may be presumptuous, I was saddened by that thought."

"Somehow, I knew we would," he said, swallowing hard so that his voice did not crack.

"What may I serve you, Joab?" Her eyes never left his as she spoke. "Hot coffee, cream and sugar?"

"That would be splendid," he said, glad she had remembered. *Joy and pleasures* were the Psalmist's words.

Joab sat down as Sarah Agnes turned and swished her lovely frame to the kitchen and returned with a tray. Not only coffee, but pastries.

"Compliments of the cook," she said, smiling.

Joab prayed for appropriate conversation. He had so much to say to her. He got right to it, not wanting to waste a moment.

"Aggie. I decided to call you Aggie as soon as I left four months ago, and in my thoughts—well, in my private thoughts, you have been Aggie. I hope that's a name that suits you."

"Oh, yes. I quite love that name. My grandmother's name was Sarah Agnes, and we called her Grandmother Aggie. So, yes, that's a fine name, Joab."

"I have so much to say to you, but I think I would like to ask you to join me for coffee tomorrow early evening. Right here is fine with me, unless you prefer someplace else. That way, you will have an opportunity—"

He hesitated, because he was speaking much too quickly. He had left something out.

"Yes, Joab?"

"What I mean to say is, well, I was riding through the alley this morning when a buckboard pulled up. Was that you?"

"Yes, but I didn't see you. Guess I never expected you would be here."

"I was at the end of the square riding back toward the inn on the alley. Quite honestly, I was looking for you. You were not in the tea room when I came in. I took a chance you might come in through the back door."

"My brother, Daniel, brings me to work and then comes for me in the evenings."

"That was going to be my next question. I didn't want to be presumptuous in hoping that was not your husband."

"No, no! I'm not married."

Joab breathed a sigh of relief and cut his conversation short, not wanting to take up her serving time.

"Can you stay after work and have coffee with me? Tomorrow, that is."

"Of course," she said. "I'll make arrangements, but I can only stay for one hour. I have chores to do once I get home."

"Where do you live? That is, if I may ask?"

"Only five miles south of Oxford, toward Water Valley."

"I've been there. Not too many miles from where I live in Sarepta."

"I have to go, now, Joab. I'm . . . I'm awfully glad you're back in Oxford."

"So'm I," he said. And she had no idea just how glad he was.

CHAPTER 9

PLAIN AS DAY

*The air was sweet, high with the
lemony fragrance of magnolia blossoms
that would be gone as winter closed in.*

With Star tied to the nearest tree, Joab slept beneath the stars that night. In the shadow of the Lyceum. Nobody seemed to mind, and the students roamed the grounds on grassy knolls and pine-strewn trails from one end of The University to the other until the late hours. He had picked the most private spot he could find to unroll his blanket, a privet thicket where the oaks canopied and sheltered. Tomorrow would be another day and he would find work and a place to stay, at least he hoped so. In the meantime, he lay on his back, suspended between heaven and earth in his thoughts, thankful for the beauty of this place, thankful for that girl with whom he had fallen in love. He prayed for fine autumn weather with no rain.

He awoke the next morning before daybreak, rolled his blanket, and mounted Star. He was as hungry as he'd ever been, having eaten little the day before. He rode to the edge of town in search of the nearest stream and in the privacy of privet and scrub trees he dug a shallow trench and started a low fire. He took up some stones to wedge his pot, which he filled with water. The aroma of the coffee was almost as satisfying as a cup itself. He set the coffee off the fire onto a stump and heated a ham biscuit in the skillet Rachel had sent along. She was God's greatest gift to a hungry son. He ate only one, drank all the coffee, wishing for cream, then cleaned up his camp. Hoping no one was in sight, he quickly bathed in the spring-fed stream that curled and pushed the water downward over the rocks and tree roots. He changed his clothes, folded the ones he wore as tightly as possible and pressed them into his saddlebag. He leaned against a tree and filled his mind with thoughts of what he would do this day as he waited for the sun to rise. One moment at a time, he thought. That's how I'll take it. God help me.

He rode around the square to the part of the north side that had not been touched. He stirred the ashes and wondered whose store it had been.

"Morning, son!"

The voice startled Joab. He had not seen the gentleman, who looked to be his father's age, approaching.

"Morning, sir!"

"New to Oxford, air y'?"

"Yes, sir, I am. Name's Joab. Joab Payne."

"Pleased to meet you, son," he said, reaching for Joab's extended hand. "I'm Hiram Raines, the constable around here. Work mostly at night while the Sheriff's a-sleepin'."

He chewed on a sweet gum brush, removed it from his lips, and spit.

"Well, Mr. Raines, you may be just the man I need to talk to. Is there someplace we can go for a bit of conversation?"

"Course," he said. "We can go to the Sheriff's Office. I got a key, and I got a corner there, m'self."

"That would be splendid," said Joab.

"What's more, there's a coffee pot, and I just happen to be on my way to make us a cup of coffee. You know, coffee's always better if you got somebody to drink with."

Hiram threw his head back and laughed so loud Joab was afraid he would wake up Oxford's residents who slept till half past five. But he couldn't help himself, he had to join this fine man.

"It's not fer from here," he said, "but I'm gonna get my horse and we'll ride over there together."

Hiram mounted and never stopped talking. "You see, the old Yanks burnt us down in '64. It was an awful time. We should have built it back by now, but the money's short and so many of our young men and boys died in the war, we just don't have the wherewithal to make any progress."

"I've come to help," Joab said, blurting it out with such urgency that it startled Hiram Raines.

"You come to what?" he said.

"I've come to help rebuild. You see, I live in Sarepta and we didn't get much damage. At least they didn't burn us down. There was not much to burn. Grant and Sherman didn't want what we had to offer, I guess. But Oxford . . . well, your city is beautiful, or at least I'm sure it was before the burning—"

"You ain't no carpetbagger, air ye?" Hiram bristled.

"Oh, no, sir. I'm southern out and out. And I'm no scalawag, either. You see, my pa, Thomas Goode Payne, and my brother, Albert Henry, were in Lee's Army of Northern Virginia. They were killed at Gettysburg. My brother, Jonathan lived through it, fought at Pickett's Charge, and made it back home, though he was pretty severely wounded. My brother, Isaac, turned seventeen two years before the war was over, fought with the Mississippi Cavalry. He also made it through and rode away from Appomattox in '65. I left my mother and younger brother at home in Sarepta to come here. I want to work a month or two at a time to help Oxford show signs of recovery."

"Well, son, that's mighty nice. Mighty nice, indeed."

Joab thought he noticed tears in Mr. Raines' eyes.

"Quite frankly," continued Joab, "I don't know where to start, seeing as I don't know a soul in Oxford, that is, except Miss Sarah Agnes over at the tea room."

"You know Sarah?"

"Well, I met her a few months ago when I came through here. I just saw her again this morning." Joab felt his face go red as he told Mr. Raines the story.

"Do I see a fair amount of interest in those eyes?"

"I was hoping it was not that noticeable," said Joab.

"Oh, you can spot *that* look a mile off, son."

"I'll have to find a way to hide my true feelings, I guess."

"Now, do you think that's possible? Besides, why do you want to go and hide something that's as special as true love?"

"I guess you're right about that, Mr. Raines. But I've only just recently met her. How can a man know for sure?"

"Oh, you won't have to be told twice," he said. "It will be right there, plain as day."

Hiram Raines had something. Joab was sure of that.

Strange that it would be so noticeable on my face, thought Joab. I really ought to be careful of that, especially around Aggie. She must not know my real feelings. Not yet. I've only had two short conversations with her.

Hiram unlocked the door to the Sheriff's office and stepped inside. He lit the oil lantern and turned the wick up for sufficient light.

"The sun'll be up soon, and it'll warm the building. I'll not start a fire if you're warm enough."

"Oh, quite warm," said Joab. "In fact, I slept outside last night on The University grounds. Hope that was acceptable with the law." Joab grinned and they both took a seat on cane bottomed chairs, waiting for the coffee to brew on the wood stove.

"Oh my, yes," said the Constable. "We're happy to accommodate law-abidin' men, but we don't cater to the carpetbaggers and scalawags. Don't trust them folks."

"We had a bad experience in Sarapeta, so I understand your feelings about that."

The sun rose over Oxford while the two men swigged down coffee, Joab happy to have cream and honey for sweetening. Hiram opened the front windows. The air was sweet, high with the lemony fragrance of magnolia blossoms that would be gone as winter closed in. But for now, they did their job well, sending trails of perfume with every breeze that stirred the leaves through the red maples.

Hiram blew out the tapers as rays from the morning sun sent slats of silver and gold across the old wood floors. Joab liked it here. And he felt right at home with Hiram. They talked for an hour, draining the old tin coffee pot.

"All right, son, we've got some figurin' to do. You've got to have a job. It's not gonna be hard to get you workin' cause our labor force is still way low on account of the war takin' s' many of our men and boys. The hard part's gonna be gettin' you paid."

"I took that into consideration before I left Sarepta, Mr. Raines. If I can get room and board, that's the main thing. I want to spend the daylight hours rebuilding—matters not what or where. But maybe I can work at the sawmill for some pay. I'm already really good at that. I've worked for my Grandfather Church at his mill in Sarepta for over ten years. I know the business from log to lumber, and it doesn't matter what I do. I can start clean-up and building on the square when the rooster crows, quit before two o'clock, and go to the sawmill for the rest of the day."

"Well," said Hiram, "me 'n Sheriff Macintosh know everybody in these parts, including the owner of the sawmill, Charles Fuller. You and me'll ride over there today and see what we can stir up. How does that sound to y'?"

"Splendid!"

Joab had hit pay dirt with Hiram Raines. What a blessing! Rachel must be praying for me, he thought.

"Thank you, Jesus," whispered Joab.

Hiram heard him, threw his head back, and shouted, "Yes, well, hallelujah!"

He must be satisfied Mr. Fuller is going to hire me, thought Joab. Could this really be happening?

As if he knew Joab's next thoughts, Hiram said, "And as for a place to stay, me 'n Mrs. Raines got plenty of room at our house. You can stay there fer the time bein'."

"Much obliged," said Joab, fighting emotions, thinking this was way too much for one day. "But I don't want to put you and Mrs. Raines out. What about your family?"

"Oh, it's just me and her now, son. Our two boys were killed in battle. Oldest one, Trey, with Jackson at Chancellorsville, and Hiram, Jr. at Gettysburg with Lee—same as your pa. I know it sounds strange we named our second boy after me. That was Mattie's idea."

Joab stood to his feet as did Hiram. He looked straight into the man's faded blue eyes and said, "We, my friend, are Confederate brothers for life."

They wept, hugged like brothers, then stepped outside to the horses.

Joab was awed that Hiram had not mentioned his great loss until now. He was sure he had letters from the boys, as did Rachel, and he would like to read them one day. Just maybe he could. The two men rode to the Yellow Leaf Creek Sawmill.

Mr. Fuller was glad to bring Joab on for four hours a day and on Saturday mornings.

"I don't have that many boys who know the business from start to finish," he said. "Lost most of 'em to Shiloh and Gettysburg."

"Well, sir," said Joab, "I can promise you a good day's work on the saw or sander."

"You're hired," the gentleman about the age of his grandfather said.

"Much obliged, Mr. Fuller, when do I start?"

"How about tomorrow, two o'clock?"

Joab grinned broadly, extended his hand and thought of Rachel, who would rejoice when he posted the first Union dollars to her.

CHAPTER 10

GIVE THEM HEART

Be thou my strong habitation,
wherein I may continually resort . . .

Psalm 71:3

Joab woke early, even before the waking call promised by Mrs. Mattie Raines. He had slept well, at peace with yesterday's decisions and promises to himself. He had a job, a place to pillow his head at night, food to eat. While he needed little more, there was more that he wanted. Aggie had promised to meet him at the tea room tonight. He must stop by at noon and tell her it would be near seven before he could get back from the sawmill.

The mill was just outside of town on the road leading to Pontotoc where the Chickasaw Cession Treaty was signed in 1832. That treaty opened up all the territory in North Mississippi for land speculators and the new white settlers. Pontotoc got its name from a Chickasaw Chief. Joab was learning a lot of things about his new corner of the South. There was also a creek named for the Chief. Pontotoc Road went off the Square on the northeast corner by the University Hotel, that is, before the burning, just like all the other buildings. The route took him across Yellow Leaf Creek that would, in time, become more and more familiar to Joab.

He dressed and slipped out of the house thinking what a lovely southern lady, Mrs. Raines. Their home was quite comfortable, in Oxford town, a cottage under shady oaks and towering magnolias, with ivy growing from the hard packed dirt street to the front porch steps, a porch that wrapped around over half of the house, behind which was a small barn and a corncrib all fenced about. He was blessed to have stepped into such a fine setting. He didn't want to be cynical with thoughts that such extravagance was too good to be true. At the same time, he sought to release his skepticism to Divine Providence, believing the part about *every good and perfect gift.*

It was five o'clock. Joab rode Star to The University campus and turned her toward the stream. He had not wanted to disturb Mrs. Raines at such an early hour; besides, he wanted to remain as independent as he could. He had not come to disrupt anyone's life. Hiram was still on duty, and he would see him before his shift was over. He needed a pick and shovel and he needed to know the location of the town's dumping place.

He dismounted at the stream and let Star drink. He already loved this place. And it was his favorite time of year. The trees were changing color and dropping their leaves en masse on the grounds of The University. Picturesque, he thought. This place is heavenly. He took his bag and scrounged for Rachel's fried peach pie in the flour sack. He would get coffee with Hiram. He scarfed down the pastry, washed his face and hands in the cold stream and rode downtown. He could go in the strength of the peach pie for the biggest part of the day. Tall and sturdy with wide shoulders, he could stand to lose a few pounds, but not many.

"Morning, Hiram!"

"Well, sir, there's not a lazy bone in your body. How did you sleep in an unfamiliar bed?"

"Like a baby," said Joab. "Guess you're ready to head towards home."

"Right after I make us a pot of coffee. Else wise, I might fall asleep in the saddle on my way in."

"I was hoping for a cup. Also, I'd like to borrow a pick and shovel until I can get money enough to purchase my own."

"We've got one of everything they is in the shed out back," Hiram said. "We'll go in a jiffy and fetch what you need. You'll know where everything's at, and you can get what you need as you need it. Don't go buyin' nothin'."

"Much obliged, Mr. Raines. I'll return them each day before I head for the sawmill."

"Now, son, don't you think it would save time and energy if you just call me Hiram? Everybody else does." He spoke in a slow southern drawl, pronouncing every word with an extra syllable or two.

"Well, I don't want to be left behind, sir—Hiram. But, at the same time, you're a giant of a man to me, and I don't want to be disrespectful."

"But you said we was brothers—Confederate brothers."

"That I did, and I meant it—Hiram."

Joab finished a second cup of coffee, with cream and honey right out of the comb served from the quart fruit jar on the square wood table, and they headed out the door to shuffle through the garden tools. Hiram pulled out a pick and shovel, an old rake and a cotton hoe. Hanging on the side of the shed was an old wooden wheel barrow with sturdy iron wheels, in pretty good shape. It would suffice to carry scrap iron and tin and metal pieces to the dumping place.

"This is splendid," said Joab, helping Hiram close the heavy wood door to the shed. "It'll make my work much easier. Does it matter where I start?"

"Not a'tall," said Hiram. "You're the boss man."

"Then I want to begin on the square on the corner opposite the inn, and I will not stop until every piece of rubble is removed."

Hiram's eyes filled with tears at the thought of the beautiful town square once again cleared and ready for rebuilding. He hoped Joab's interest—the fervor of a total stranger—would breathe life back into a bunch of dead men who had no incentive to get out of bed of a morning, much less to revive this war-torn town. The losses had garroted the life out of them.

"Do I need to check with anyone? Don't want to be trespassing without permission."

"If you have any problems, tell them you're working for Hiram!" He threw back his head and laughed. "They'll know—yes, they'll understand what's happening here. And they'll be as much obliged as I am, Joab."

"Yes, sir."

"Why, you'll have s' much help y' won't believe yer eyes. Our people want to rebuild, but they're beset by so much rubble and ruin, still cast down, and they don't know where to start. You'll give them heart, that's what you'll do. They'll rally and get busy, if I know them as well as I think I do. Here, Joab, take these old gloves or you'll have blisters so bad you won't be able to work. Keep these on, now. You've come at a good time. Fall of the year. It's not only beautiful—majestic, but cool besides."

"I allow that's true," Joab said.

"And Joab," said Hiram.

"Yes sir?"

"Out there in the middle of the square—you know the great big heap?"

"Yes sir. I saw that."

"That was our beautiful Courthouse. You know Lafayette is the county seat of government. That should probably be the last lot to clean up. It will be the hardest."

"I'm glad you told me that, Hiram."

Joab left Star tied in front of the Sheriff's Office, pulled on the gloves, laid the garden tools across the wheel barrow and successfully wheeled it to the square then returned to get Star. In two hours he had dug out the scrap metal, tin, and iron and one by one had wheeled nine heavy loads to a vacant space he had chosen, across the alley. He shoveled ashes, piled them high on the barrow, and took those to another spot, dumped, and repeated until he was exhausted. Hiram had said not to be concerned about the ash heap. Someone would take care of that.

It was eight o'clock when the first inquisitive gentleman stopped.

"And just what, may I ask, are you doing here?"

"Oh, I'm working for Hiram Raines and whoever owns this corner," he said.

"Well, that so happens to be me—Isaiah Fleming. And who are you?"

"Joab. Joab Payne, sir. And I hope you like the way I've scraped it to the hard packed dirt. It's amazing to me that your building likely took months to build and just two hours to clean up the ashes. You're ready to rebuild."

"What? What did you say?"

"I said you're ready to rebuild and once I get all of this cleared up," Joab said waving his hand from one side of the square to the other, "I'll come back and help rebuild your store. That is, if you want me to."

"I can't let you do this. I have no way of paying you—that's why it's been sitting here piled up for so long. I'm too old to do the work and there is no money. Grant made sure of that, you know. Are you a carpetbagger? Because if you are, please leave immediately."

"Oh, no sir, Mr. Fleming, I'm the son of a Confederate Army officer who gave his life for you and me in the railroad cut at Gettysburg."

Fleming's countenance lifted, his eyes glistened with tears as he said, "Many pardons for my lack of gentility and thankfulness, son. I'm afraid the war and Reconstruction have caused me to become callused and skeptical about everything. Please accept my thanks for your hard work this morning. As soon as I can scrape together enough money to rebuild, I'll be doing that and I'd be much appreciative of your help. Where can I find you?"

"I'm staying with Hiram for the time being. I'll be going back home to Sarepta before Thanksgiving, but I'll be back. I just got here yesterday. I aim to get as much done as I can before I leave. But I promise you, I will return."

"Well, much obliged, Joab. I'm going home now to tell my wife what's happening. She will be shouting so loud you'll hear her clean over here in town. You see, we have three sons and two daughters. My boys fought—two with Beauregard at Shiloh and one with Lee at Gettysburg. They were all killed. All three of them."

He gasped and choked back tears, then it was no use, the moment had taken him and he wept profusely. "My oldest son was in his second year at The University when the war broke out. He enlisted and joined *The Greys*, fought all the way to Gettysburg where he fell with the rest of his friends that had not already been killed. As I heard it, the carnage was unthinkable. The only thing we could find out was that they buried him on the battlefield. All the *Greys* died. All but one. A hundred and thirty-five of them. That was the entire student body. Such a waste of young life. My other two boys are buried in the trenches at Shiloh."

At that, the man shook and cried so hard it scared Joab though he thoroughly understood his grief.

"I'm truly sorry for your loss," said Joab.

"And I for yours," the man said.

He sauntered off shaking his head, looking back over his shoulder, wiping tears with a worn handkerchief. Joab moved to the next lot where another store of some sort had stood, and he began shoveling ashes. By twelve o'clock he had cleared three storefront lots without another encounter. That would not last long, for Isaiah Fleming would make his rounds from house to house. At least that's what Joab was hoping. It would bring help to get the mess cleaned up, ashes spread on flower beds and gardens, and a scrap metal shack opened up to turn the pieces into Union dollars for building back the stores and businesses on the square. It was a plan, and he hoped it worked. He didn't want to get too excited, because men were scarce, there was no money, and most of them had multiple jobs, just trying to put a little food on the table.

Joab mounted Star and rode to the stream. His overalls were covered with gray ashes and his face was black with the powdery soot. When he attempted to shake the ashes from his clothes, he just made it worse. He was filthy. He washed his face and arms in the stream, slicked his hair back and covered it with his hat. He had no way of knowing he was still black as the darkies who worked at the tea room. He dared not go to the front, but pounded on the alley door until an old Negro woman, whose face and arms and apron were covered with flour, pushed the heavy door open.

"Oh, my lawd!" she shouted. "Is you black or white?"

Joab laughed out loud. "I'm white. Is you white or black?"

She roared with laughter and said, "Come on in here boy. Who you be lookin' faw?"

Joab excused himself for appearing in such a filthy mess and said, "Miss Sarah Agnes, please. I'd like to see Miss Sarah Agnes. Is she close by?"

"Yas suh, sho is. She be in de dinin' room. I'll fetch her for ya. You think she gon' know who you is?"

She brushed the flour from her apron and wiped her hands on a dish towel, took another look at Joab, and threw her head back. "You sho looks black, son. You sho looks black as me!"

She left Joab standing at the alley door and shuffled off to the dining room.

CHAPTER 11

THE OCCASION

*. . . it was not in vain, dear heart,
and we must never let go of our devotion
to them and to The Cause for which
they so bravely fought.*

Joab was hot and tired. Sweat rolled down to his collar, leaving streaks of black on his face and neck. He was ashamed, but seeing Aggie was more important to him than his pride. He had told her six o'clock, but he could not get from the sawmill back to The Thompson House before seven. He had to tell her.

The door from the dining hall to the kitchen swung open. Joab assumed it was Aggie. He could not see past the back side of the stoves and cupboards from where he stood just inside the alley entrance, the aroma of southern food and the sweet smells of honey and cinnamon desserts baking momentarily spinning him off-course. But food would have to wait. His heart raced. Sweat poured down his neck.

"He be back deah by de alley doe, honey."

It was the cook's voice. She and Joab were, by now, friends! She was still laughing, at him he was sure.

"You gon' see. He be black as me."

Joab could hear her loud and clear. He didn't know whether to run or stay put, when Aggie's small frame appeared.

"Joab! What happened? Have you been in a fire?"

"No, Aggie, it's a story I'll tell you later. I wanted you to know I got a job at the sawmill working until six o'clock each evening and I won't get back to town before seven tonight. I didn't want you to think I was not coming."

"Oh, Joab! It was sweet of you to come tell me. But my brother will be here at seven to pick me up. I have no way of telling him not to come that early."

"I see," he said, disappointed. "I was afraid that would be the case."

He thought a minute as he stood facing this beautiful creature, his face as black as the cook's. Aggie's was lily white and glowing, and as usual, her dark hair was combed back and fastened with a cerulean ribbon that enhanced the blue of her eyes.

"What about this," he said, licking his lips, the taste of ash and dirt gritty and disgusting. "When Daniel comes, would it be proper to send him on home with word to your mother that I will bring you on my horse?"

"For all the trouble you're going through for just an hour with me, I think it would be most proper," she said. "But first, Joab, tell me what you're doing right now—how did you get to look like—like Miranda?" She giggled.

"Miranda?"

"Oh, of course, you don't know her name. She bakes the pastries. You know, she's the one covered with flour?"

Joab laughed. "Oh, yes, Miranda and I are now fast friends. I look black, she looks white! And that's part of the story I'll tell you tonight. Just have Daniel let your mother know I'm working for Hiram Raines. Is that a good enough character reference?"

"The best," she said intrigued by the thought of his day's accomplishments, whatever they were. At this point she could not guess. "But, Joab, I've already told Mama about you. It will be fine. We've learned to do extraordinary things since Papa died. Things we would not have ordinarily done if he were still with us. Does that make sense?"

"Yes, yes, it does, Aggie. For that's exactly what we had to learn to do at our house."

Joab rode Star back to his work place on the square and set about to clean the next lot. At one o'clock he rode to the stream and with hopes there were no students about, he chanced to strip and bathe. It was the only way he was going to emerge white again. He pulled yesterday's overalls and red plaid shirt from his saddlebag and dressed, ran his fingers through his hair that was at least free of soot and ashes, which were now in the stream. He took the bone comb from his pack and smoothed his hair. He treasured that comb. Jonathan had purchased four somewhere along the way during the war and sent them to Rachel. They were scarce as hen's teeth, and Joab was proud to own one. Dusting off his hat, he mounted and rode to the sawmill.

At two o'clock he was pulling a saw. It felt good. It felt right, like he was home with Grandpa Church, though he missed his partners, Jonathan and Samuel. He spent the last hour sanding planks and stacking finished lumber. Mr. Fuller watched him out of the corner of his eye, never making conversation. He was taken by Joab's skill with lumber.

Fuller called *quittin' time* at six o'clock and the men scurried to put away the saws and chisels. With the snuffing of the lanterns, Joab mounted and rode toward town with the rest of the men. He couldn't remember when he had been so tired, but he was still sufficiently clean from his bath in the stream, hopefully ready to meet Aggie.

She was waiting with tea and biscuits, homemade strawberry jam, and fresh churned soft butter. He sat across the table from her with a head full of things he wanted to say. Where should he start? He was weary from the day, not wanting to mention it. He didn't have to. She spoke.

"Joab, at one time during the afternoon, this tea room was full of men that looked exactly like you did when you stood inside the alley door at noon. They were sooty black. I heard the story—all of it, and you may be surprised when you go to the other side of the square tomorrow. Or maybe you went there first."

"Why, no, I came directly here from the mill, not wanting to make you wait. Did Daniel mind leaving you with me?"

"He was fine, especially after I told him what happened today. He was going to have a lot to tell Mama."

"What happened, Aggie?"

"The men—about fifteen of them, local men, I know them all—came in for cold tea about four o'clock. They were all hot and tired and thirsty, reluctant to be seated, they were so dirty, but we insisted, knowing something was going on and we wanted to know what it was. They took up three tables and when they talked, they laughed and were so cheerful, something we haven't seen much of since the war. I decided to eavesdrop, so I kept bringing tea, which they didn't mind a'tall, and Miranda kept giving me plates of gingersnaps she had baked and it turned into a party."

"Sorry I missed that. What was the occasion?"

"They were all talking about you, calling your name. You're apparently a hero."

"What?" He was shocked, ignorant of anything that might have been said about him. "Believe me, that's not true."

"Well, yes you are. Hiram Raines and Mr. Fleming are responsible, and I think Sheriff Macintosh got in on it, too."

"In on what?"

"They found out, I suppose from Mr. Hiram, all about what you're doing on the square in the name of southern dignity and hope for a better South, and in memory of all our fallen dead, and so every able-bodied man came out there until sundown, pulled out scrap iron and piled up ashes. They said you wouldn't believe the piles of stuff. Joab, it's—it's just splendid, like a miracle."

Joab sat across from Aggie with tears rolling down a clean face. He didn't know what to say.

"That exceeds all my hopes. I thought maybe one or two men would get the spirit, maybe after a few days, and help. But fifteen? How far around the square did they get?"

"Joab—they finished! Finished the clean-up, down to the hard-packed dirt. That is, except for the Courthouse, which is much too large an undertaking, and the burnt black stumps, you know, the Yankees burned our trees, too. The men will have to blow them out with black powder, dig out the roots and fill the holes with dirt so they can plant some saplings. Then they can start building as each owner gets the money for supplies. They're going to take the scrap iron—there was so much scrap iron and tin and metal, you would never allow—and sell it to get money, although the Union doesn't pay our people much of anything for scrap iron and they get top dollar for their people. They'll divide it evenly among the merchants for a bit of a start on rebuilding. Joab, isn't it just too wonderful?"

Aggie was talking so fast, she hardly stopped for breathing.

"I was going to explain how I got so grimy this morning, and yes, I'm purely amazed that part is done, and so happy for it, but since you already know, begging your pardon, can we talk about some other things instead?"

She blushed and dropped her head, not really knowing what Joab had in mind, then looked up with a smile and said, "I think that would be splendid, Joab."

"All this happened in one day, and I'm now of the opinion I've known you for a long, long time, and getting to know the town people, well, that has made me awfully glad I came. Everything is happening so fast, though I know we have a whole lot more to do, what with all the rebuilding that's needed, it will still take a lot of time, maybe years—"

Aggie interrupted him and said, "I need to say it again, Joab, you're a hero."

"Oh, no! I'm no hero, Aggie. I didn't fight in the war. Our fathers and brothers who gave their lives and limbs are heroes. They're why I'm here. To give back, and I can only give of myself and now all the men are doing the same thing. I couldn't help but think of what my brother, Isaac, told me once. When he was riding home that April morning in 1865, the roadsides were strewn with all the brokenness the war had left behind. Miles and miles of men walked, dragging their tired bodies, pulling their mangled friends as fast as they could put one wounded leg in front of the other, all the old pieces of guns and dilapidated wagons and buckboards, shredded bedrolls and even the carcasses of dead horses, with flies swarming about the carnage—all that was piled up on the roadsides. The men and boys moved with such deliberation trying to get back to their corner of the South only to find their towns and countryside had been ripped to shreds. When I think of those men and boys, I *have* to help. I just have to.

"And Jonathan had seen it all on the hill that day at Pickett's Charge. Longstreet waiting to give the nod to Pickett, Jonathan's head swirling with thoughts of having buried our beloved father and Albert Henry the day before. He saw southern men fall like flies on that hot July morning. He recalled things that, in fact, he could not repeat for there were not words enough, there was not blood red enough to describe as it flowed to the bottom of the hill. Jonathan even thought to teach me the Rebel Yell—the blood-curdling sound of battle that could not be duplicated by a single Union soldier, for they hated it, had no heart for it.

"Lee was a force with which to reckon, and Davis was a faithful one-term president of a country—the Confederacy—that fell, not from the blow of the Union, but from hunger, exhaustion, lack of weapons and artillery. Hunger caused by inflation over which only the Union had control. Exhaustion, because there was no reprieve, no relief, and there were no new forces of men to replace those who fell."

"Joab, we've seen so much with our mind's eye. We've visualized our fathers lying in fields of blood, pouring out the last measure of life for what we have often thought may have been in vain. But it was not in vain, dear heart, and we must never let go of our devotion to them and to *The Cause* for which they so bravely fought. I will be with you in your faithfulness to rebuild, at least our corner of the South. I'll be with you till the end, Joab."

Joab never got around to talking about "the other things," and he was not sure what his visit with Aggie would bring forth. There was a certain gray gloom that hung over the relationship; he supposed it was the heartache of losing the dearest on earth—they both had lost the dearest on earth. He could only hope for a ray of sunshine through the gloom as he came to know this most wonderful southern woman.

Chapter 12

Beyond the Feelings

*... tall transom'd windows on either side of the fireplace
were covered with tapestry curtains that revealed their age,
tattered enough to make him comfortable,
and he quickly felt at home.*

Joab and Aggie rode in silence to the Stephens' farm. He knew little about her mother. Only that her name was Caroline Stephens. Aggie held to Joab as he urged Star into a trot. A woman's touch, he thought. Something I'm not used to. Then he felt her head resting on his back. She was no doubt tired. It was dark and late and he was anxious to get her home. He was not sure what to expect, for he and Aggie had not discussed much of anything personal. Would Mrs. Stephens be angry that he had kept her daughter and that it was now ten o'clock and Aggie would have chores to do and she would have to get up early for work at the dining hall in the morning? He felt guilty.

"Joab, this is my mama," she said.

"I'm Caroline Stephens," the beautiful southern woman said, extending her hand.

"Mrs. Stephens, it's a pleasure to meet you, and may I apologize for keeping Miss Aggie so long. Thank you for letting her stay, you not knowing me at all. I do not take that lightly." Joab held his hat in his hand, nervously running his fingers around the brim.

"Joab, you can call me Miss Caroline if you would like. It's a pleasure to meet you, too. Sarah Agnes told me all about you, and somehow I allowed it would be all right for her to stay with you awhile. And besides that, because of the war, I have learned not to borrow trouble. Here, put your hat on the table and come take a seat in the dining room. I'll bring out some coffee; you'll need to stay awake to get back to your place."

"Thank you, ma'am."

"And, Aggie, don't worry. Daniel took care of your chores."

"Thank you, Mama. I'll make it up to him."

While Caroline was in the kitchen, Joab and Aggie sat by the dining room fire that Daniel laid before he went to bed. It was a low fire; the night, cool enough for one. The room was lovely, tall transom'd windows on either side of the fireplace were covered with tapestry curtains beginning to show their age, tattered enough to make him comfortable, and he quickly felt at home. He looked at Aggie and saw the loveliness of her mother, thinking, Aggie will look like Miss Caroline when she grows older, a fine look, a beautiful one. Then, out of the blue, Aggie began to talk fast as though she had been holding her thoughts for days.

"Joab, I need to confess to you that I have a friend, a very close friend. His name is Will. Will Cavanaugh. I've known him all my life. We attended school together, though he was five years my senior. He graduated after eight years of schooling, which was in 1861 and at the age of seventeen, he mustered in. He's twenty-four years old now."

Aggie was spieling, though Joab knew she didn't intend to be. She wanted to get it all said, possibly before her mother came back into the room, not that it was personal, yet maybe it was.

"He couldn't wait to get into the war. Just like all the other men and boys around here. I was heartbroken when he left. By the time I was fifteen years old, I was already having thoughts of marrying Will, though he had never mentioned marriage. Some men don't understand the subject of marriage I suppose; they think it can go unmentioned and everything will just unfold properly. I figured there would never be another man for me."

Joab clenched his teeth to keep from saying a word. He could feel his face go pale, his world collapsing around him. But wait, he thought, I met her four months ago and we've only talked a couple of times, I have no rights to her as a woman. But she had said, 'I need to confess.' Why would this be a confession if she had no personal interest in him? Joab listened carefully, hanging on every word she said, hoping for the best at the end of her monologue.

"Will took his training up in the mountains of Kentucky," she continued, never considering what Joab was thinking. She was perfectly innocent, though she had already begun to have her own special feelings about Joab. He must never know because what could ever come of it?

"Will was part of the Mississippi Volunteer Army of Ten Thousand. So was Papa. They marched on foot for miles and miles, then took the cars to somewhere up in Grayson County, Kentucky. He wrote letters home. It was cold, bitter cold, and a lot of them took pneumonia and died before they could ever get into the fight."

"Was it Camp Beauregard?" Joab asked. He pushed back from the table and slumped in his chair under the weight of his thoughts.

"Why yes, Joab, it was. How did you know that?"

"Because my pa and my brothers took those same cars to that same camp in January of '62 and they were a company in the Mississippi Volunteer Army of Ten Thousand. I've read the letters Pa wrote to Mama. In fact, my brother, Jonathan, took pneumonia and nearly died before they could get out of Kentucky."

Aggie was crying again. Joab took the handkerchief from his pocket and handed it to her. She wiped her face and choked back the tears. "Papa nearly froze to death up there. It was so cold and he couldn't seem to get warm. Oh, when I think about him being cold, not enough clothing or blankets to warm him . . . Papa was always so cold-natured . . . Their paths crossed, I'm sure, Joab. But for some reason, Will and Pa joined Gen. Johnston's command and fought with Beauregard at Shiloh in April. As I've told you, my papa was mortally wounded and Will—well, he was shot up pretty badly; they brought him to the hospital at the Lyceum and he got well enough to go home, though he has never fully recovered, not emotionally or physically. He was not able to get back in the war, though he tried. He didn't have good use of his legs and he had a bullet wound to the head. He cannot see out of his left eye, but he gets around pretty good with his cane. He's a war hero, Joab. As long as he's out there on his farm, he's as content as he can be under the circumstances, at least most of the time, but sometimes he gets depressed. It comes on him without foreknowledge."

By this time, Joab didn't know what to say. He was sharing pity and sympathy for Will along with Aggie, but he was wondering why he had let himself get emotionally attached to her before finding out more.

"Aggie, I'm sorry about your father," he said.

She shivered and went to the hearth, standing in front of it facing the fire.

"I know you understand and I know you mean that, Joab. You know what it's like to lose the dearest on earth."

"About Will—are you still emotionally attached?"

Aggie turned toward Joab and said, "Yes and no. I know that sounds aloof and maybe harsh, but I don't mean it to be. You see, our relationship has always been one-sided. I know Will loves me in his own way. That's what we southerners do. You know that, being one yourself. We fall in love with love, especially women, and at an early age. But I think Will was in love with that war. And I'm not being unfair. It was not the war itself—just for the sake of war. He was so committed to the Confederacy that everything else took second place. He would have tramped through hell with Gen. Beauregard. He was his hero and for all the love he had for Beauregard, he harbored that much hate for Sherman and he had no respect for Grant whatsoever because of Shiloh."

"I see what you mean, I think," said Joab. "Isaac was the same way. And when he got out, he was a mess. Took him forever to get over it and then Reconstruction came. Came and went almost on the same day. It never amounted to a thing, not the way they laid it out. The Union tried to force-feed their ideology, that of reconstructing the South. Funny, they ripped us to shreds and then wanted to help us put it all back together again with their Carpetbaggers and by employing our people—Scalawags and Freedmen."

"Yes, yes they did. And now, we've been brought back into the Union, but they still hate us, and I don't feel like we belong. Doesn't make much sense, does it? Well, concerning Will, I need more than that, Joab. I need my man to be as bound to me as he was, and is, to the Confederacy, especially if I'm going to consider marriage. And don't get me wrong, I love our Country. I wish we were still intact and that the Confederacy had survived."

They stopped talking about Will and the war when Caroline brought coffee and some pound cake. She served it and went back to the kitchen as if she knew the two young people were in conversation about something in which she did not want to be involved.

"Where is Will now?" asked Joab.

"With his family. They own the land that connects to ours. His father was over fifty when the war broke out and he didn't serve. Pa was a little over forty, like a second father to Will while they were gone, until Pa died, of course."

"Do you see Will often?"

"Yes. At least once a week. We go to church together. We're still close, but he doesn't seem to have the heart for marriage or anything else except farming and keeping his mind off things. He's a smart man, a good farmer, and he has worked hard to bring the place back since the Yankees took everything in 1864 when Gen. Whiskey Smith came through on his burning campaign."

"He certainly left his imprint on Oxford," said Joab.

"Indeed. Will and his pa scarcely had anything left to work with. But at least Will had the presence of mind and heart to rebuild and recover for the most part. It's been nearly six years, now. He even helped Daniel rebuild our place. The Yankees set fire to it, but they were not paying too much attention. They mostly wanted the food in our cellars and smokehouses. It didn't burn to the ground. Thank God. I love this old house."

Joab was listening to everything Aggie was saying, but at the same time, he pondered something he had just decided he wanted to do. He would take a chance of putting Aggie into a difficult position, maybe even setting off a reaction he wasn't ready to cope with, but he should try.

"Aggie—" he paused before continuing, having second thoughts.

"Yes, Joab?"

"Would you—"

"What?"

"I want you and Will to go back to Shiloh with me."

"What!"

"Yes, would you be willing to do that?"

"No! Absolutely not! I've never been to Shiloh. I don't know if I could stand it."

"I think you will be surprised."

"How can you say that? I won't be surprised. I'll be sick, nauseated, and I will likely throw up my insides. My pa was wounded there. He died because of Shiloh." Aggie was crying again. "And Will—he's never been back since the battle. I couldn't ask him to do that."

Joab remained calm, knowing that getting emotional would only make matters worse for Aggie. He put himself in her place.

"I thought the same thing, Aggie. My pa and brother were killed on a battlefield much like Shiloh. I came to the decision that, in order to get some kind of relief from the pain and hurt of the war, I had to go and see some of the places for myself. Put some memories to rest. I don't want to forget, but I want to get beyond some of these feelings of hurt and bitterness; and I know to do that, I must go *through*, I must try to experience what *they* went through. It's working for me. I thought it might help you and Will. You know, sort of like your Lyceum."

Aggie was no longer crying. Joab figured she was just about cried out.

"Well, I don't know, Joab. I have to think this through. I'll talk to Will. And I'll tell him about you. I have never talked to him about you."

"You haven't? Why not?"

"Don't ask me that question, Joab. Please."

What was she saying? Why couldn't people just say what they were thinking? Was it that she was a woman and Will was something like a lifelong love? Joab didn't want to have personal feelings that he was moving in on Will's girl, but he wasn't willing to let four months of sleepless nights go without getting some kind of release in that regard.

"No. I won't ask anything. The decision is yours. Whether or not you talk to Will about going to Shiloh. If Will can't bear to make the visit, then I'll lay that thought to rest."

"It's not just Will and going to Shiloh, Joab," she said. "I mean, there was a reason I didn't talk to Will about you."

"Oh?"

"That's why I said, don't ask me that question."

CHAPTER 13

PLACE OF PEACE

*Shiloh was an extension of heaven
in the spring of '62, that is, before
the fighting started.*

Joab worked at the square until the end of the week, enjoying the company of the men who came out to help. He knew it was the other way around. He had come out to help them. This was their town, their rubble, their scrap iron and steel. He was but one man who had ignited a fire in a few. There was no end to what they could accomplish now that they were all involved.

He dug through the pile of rubble, separating iron and steel, trying to get Sarah Agnes off his mind, thoughts of her with another man consuming him. He had mixed emotions about meeting Will, but he had set the wheels in motion and he would see it through. This was all new to him, life in the big town with lots of people he never knew existed entering his life.

Saturday morning at daybreak, Joab slogged to the barn and did the milking for Mrs. Raines. The fields would soon turn brown on the landscape, the ears of corn once green and tender would be dry at the pulling, and the benefactors would once again be the hogs and chickens. But until then, Joab would pull the fresh yellow ears, drop them in the bushel basket, and lug it to the end of the long row. He took a basket from the wall of the hen house and collected the eggs, brought everything up to the back porch and called for Mrs. Raines. He could see her in the kitchen window and knew she was making breakfast.

"Oh, my, Joab. I'm not used to back door service. I could get terribly accustomed to this. Now, come on in the kitchen and I'll fry you up some of these fresh eggs."

"Do you have some fluffy tall buttermilk biscuits in the stove?"

"Well, you know I do. And Hiram is ready, too. I'll just let those brown while I fry some ham and get these eggs going. Do you prefer sorghum or pear preserves this morning?"

"Whatever you put on the table," he said. "You know I love them both."

He washed at the pan on the porch, threw it out across the backyard and drew fresh cold water from the cistern to refill the pan for Hiram. He dried his hands, took off his shoes and went inside. And he didn't slam the door. It seemed inappropriate except at his home in Sarepta. Besides, Rachel would not be there to hear it. He was experiencing a moment of homesickness for his mother and Sam when Mrs. Raines motioned for the men to sit while she served.

"Mississippi women are the best for accommodatin' hungry men, don't you think, Joab?"

"I allow they're the *very* best," he said. "They know how to treat their men, that's for sure. I hope I find someone so splendid myself—someone like you and Rachel."

He grinned at Mrs. Raines, watching her spoon the scrambled eggs into the bowl and then artfully place ham biscuits on the platter.

"Your mama sounds like an amazing woman, and you're makin' her proud, son."

"Hope so," said Joab.

Mrs. Raines brought the hot biscuits to the table followed by the eggs and ham. Hiram thanked the Lord and without hesitation the men broke open the hot biscuits, steam rising up to melt the fresh butter. They unashamedly ate until the skillet was empty, having overindulged in southern cuisine at its best.

Joab helped with the dishes and swept the kitchen floor, Mrs. Raines marveling at his willingness to do a woman's work. When he was finished, he traipsed to the crib, shelled corn, and fed the chickens. When all the chores were done, he saddled Star and tied her to the hitching post on the street, went back inside, and put on clean clothes. He was going to see his girl.

Aggie's first words were, "Joab, I think he's going."

"You mean it?"

"Yes. We talked for an hour the other night. I told him all about you and he wants to meet you."

"Splendid!"

"There's just one thing, Joab."

"What?"

"He has a tendency to recoil. I don't know how to explain it, but you will see what I'm talking about. When are we going?"

"I can go now if the two of you can."

"Will Star let me ride her? If so, I'll go ask Will now."

"If I put you on her, she'll be fine."

"You stay here with Mama," said Aggie as Joab lifted her into the saddle. "Will may be more agreeable to go at short notice so he doesn't have time to think it over and change his mind. I'll be right back. Talk to Mama. Tell her what we're doing."

She makes me do the hard part, he said to himself. I can do this. Miss Caroline is one splendid lady. I think she trusts me, and obviously she trusts Will.

The Cavanaughs had been their friends and neighbors for years. Life in Sarepta was much like this. The Paynes had many friends, and their home had always been open to all of them. Joab thought about Duncan Jamison and his family. Isaac had picked Jennie from Duncan's girls. He was an amazing man, someone special. He had fought with the Mississippi 42nd with Joab's father. Duncan had mourned and grieved with Jonathan after his father and Henry were killed. He was right there. And Duncan had fought with Jonathan at Pickett's Charge two days later. He was family.

"Depending on how this goes and since we're getting a late start, I think we should plan on staying overnight in Shiloh, Miss Caroline. Will that be acceptable?"

"I think I'll be fine with that, Joab. You'll be in charge, so to speak. But where will you sleep?"

"She'll need a blanket," he said.

"Does that mean—on the ground?"

"Yes'm," said Joab. "I didn't see any place where we could get shelter if it rains, but I'll try to be sensible. At least the weather is getting much cooler and at night under all those trees, it should be nice, no mosquitoes, not hot and humid. I'll take good care of Aggie."

By ten o'clock, the three young people were riding out of Oxford toward Shiloh, Tennessee, Joab in a state of disbelief. He found Will to be quite congenial, not the least bit jealous—he really had no reason to be, but he could have if he were so a-mind. They each had a bedroll and their saddlebags well stuffed with food from both Miss Caroline and Mrs. Cavanaugh. They could expect things made with butter and honey and flour and eggs and milk. Southern women could not cook without such staples.

They laughed and talked as they rode side by side. Will spoke freely about mundane matters, the farm, the crops, and he made a few comments about the war. Joab was impressed with his worldly discussion, but Will never said a word about Shiloh. Joab didn't want to be the first to mention it. But he figured Will knew exactly what they were riding into.

The sun was high in the autumn sky, a slight breeze blowing off the Tennessee River, when the three riders came out of the south toward Pittsburg Landing.

Will reluctantly rode up the hill from the river bank, Joab allowing him to lead the way. After all, this had been his battle, and he knew the field like the back of his sun-browned hand, though he had not seen the battlefield post war. But that was the only side Joab had seen.

Will stopped his horse and began to shake. Joab was apprehensive, afraid of what might happen in the next moments, but he couldn't let on. Above all, he must remain calm for Will's sake. Joab quietly dismounted and walked toward Will, wondering, hoping he was doing the right thing. He reached for Will, pulled him off his horse and handed him his cane. Aggie was crying out loud.

Still holding on to Will, Joab said, "I know this is the first time you've been here since Shiloh Battle. Can you do this, Will? Because, if not, we can leave here this minute and never come back?"

Will jerked himself free of Joab and shouted, "No! I can do this. I *must* do this. I'm supposed to be a man. If I could live through this battle, and I'm not talking about getting all shot up, I'm talking about if I could live through what it did to my head, then I can *relive* it. It's . . . it's just that this was the most God-awful scene you could ever imagine on this earth. For that matter, I thought hell had opened up and was regurgitating right here at Shiloh. There was so much blood on these hills, so many bullets flying, so many cannons rolling and boiling and shooting out balls that were blowing men's heads off their shoulders. You have no idea—nobody knows what . . . nobody who was not here could possibly know what . . . what took place."

"Get on your horses," Will ordered, climbing onto his. He secured his cane and rode back down the hill toward the landing, Joab and Aggie following behind him. "This is where it started, long before we arrived with Pierre Beauregard, and Lord God, that man was a gallant and brave commander. Sidney Johnston must have loved him. I know *I* did."

Will got emotional again, wiping tears, and waving his arms. "Just give me a minute." He was shouting again. "But . . . don't touch me."

Joab and Aggie were quiet, riding behind him to the bottom of the hill. Will rode up on the landing, turned his steed around a couple of times, the shoed hoofs making loud clopping noises on the wood-planked dock, and Will pulled him to a halt. He pointed south and said, "Grant finally made it to the battle, coming from that direction on a boat. Right on the Tennessee River there where we rode up. You might say he was late to work that day, and it didn't set too well with Lincoln the way I understand it. But his man, Sherman, was already here long before Grant came in. We heard Sherman's men knew we were in the woods. In fact, we were all over these woods." Will pointed to the tree line on all four sides of the clearing at the top of the hill from the landing. "You may not know this, because we didn't get too much space in the newspapers after the war, or during the war for that matter, but as ragged as we were, in the pitch of battle, we may as well have been wearing the finest uniforms, carrying the finest weapons—but, of course, we were not—but we were some brave warriors and we knew what to do. Our commanders were West Point trained just like the Blues were and they taught us well. We could assemble for battle with the best of them, and we could pick those Yanks off with our squirrel rifles faster than they could load up their fine black powder Colt Walkers."

Will had gotten his wind and Joab, hoping he was going to make it through this, watched him closely. Will goaded his horse and in a gallop he rode up the dirt road about half a mile.

A breathtaking scene rolled up before them, a panorama of beautiful hills covered with the color of autumn, the trees still clinging to the last of their leaves and sadly on those brightly colored hills, thousands of men lay buried just beneath the sod. Aggie caught her breath and tears began to fall. Joab had seen it in the spring and now he was seeing it in autumn. To the Union soldiers on their tour of duty at Shiloh, it may have looked God-forsaken. But . . . it wasn't. Not to a Mississippian, nor to a Tennessean. Shiloh was an extension of heaven in the spring of '62, that is, before the fight started.

"It's beautiful," Aggie whispered. "So peaceful and beautiful."

Joab, who had been riding close beside her, leaned toward her and whispered back, "Shiloh means *place of peace.*"

"Place of peace." Aggie mouthed the words as if in disbelief, though desperately wanting to believe.

Will turned toward the cotton field that was now thick and white, the stalks high and loaded with fluffy white bolls that would soon be ready to pick. "This field belongs to the Widow Bell," he said, and he kept riding, Joab and Aggie following close behind. Will stopped at the edge of the pond and, perched on his horse, he began to tell the story.

"She came running across the cotton field toward the Peach Orchard. Her hands were full of old rags and torn up sheets. She waited a few minutes until she could see there was a lull in the battle, a cease fire of sorts, and then she commenced to running again. The Widow Bell . . . she was a real hero of Shiloh. She commenced tying tourniquets and pouring coal oil into bleeding wounds and binding them with those old rags. And . . ." Will was sobbing again. "She was helping men and boys from both sides. Mind you, this was her field, she lived right over there." He pointed in the direction of the old farmhouse that had managed to survive the battle.

"She was colorblind that day, at least to Blue and Gray. It didn't matter to her. She could only identify the color red and the hurt and pain on the faces. I know. I was one of those she helped pull from the bloody pond. I'll never forget her. She was small, wearing an apron over her cotton dress and she was as bloody as the rest of us. I don't know of another woman on earth that would . . . that *could* have done such a thing."

Will kept talking, his voice getting hoarse and his face wet with tears.

"I managed to drag myself back to our headquarters right over there where you see the pile of rubble. It *was* Shiloh Church, which on those two days became our hospital. The first night, there was an ambulance wagon pulled as close to the side of the church as they could get it. It may be a tale that's told, but I heard Gen. Johnston's body lay in that guarded wagon overnight after he died and that they took his body to Corinth the next morning. They were trying to keep it from us, that he was shot dead, so we wouldn't lose heart. It was bad enough . . . but with him dead . . . well, it would have been so much worse if we had known."

He took a deep breath and paused to regain his voice. He pressed his horse toward the Sunken Road and the Hornet's Nest and stopped. He looked at Aggie who knew . . . somehow she knew they were close . . . She pulled her horse up near to Joab's as if she were seeking comfort.

"Lt. Stephens was hit at the Hornet's Nest. You cannot imagine the bravery of our men here. I was already in the church building by then, but when they brought him in . . . well, I almost didn't recognize him. I motioned for them to put him next to me."

Joab dismounted and took Aggie down from her horse and held her in his arms. She was shaking so hard, he had to press her close.

"Right here, Sarah Agnes . . . here's where your pa was hit. He was able to talk to me, told me about the Hornet's Nest on what they were calling the Sunken Road, although it really was not sunken, and he was telling me as best he could. It was hard for him to describe. He said to me, 'It beat all I've ever seen . . . I could hear the whistle of the bullets, smell the black powder, hear the groans and cries of the young'uns dying, others thinking that death would be a relief and so they succumbed.' That's what he told me Sarah Agnes. He took a pounding, several shots to the body and one bad one to the head.

They took him to Oxford the next morning and I . . . I never saw him again . . . I . . . I never saw him again . . ."

Will heaved and cried and when he could, he continued.

"It rained and thundered that night. One of those spring rains pelted the church house that was barely standing; the windows were all broken out and the lightning flashed through the open holes and the noise was so loud with men and boys screaming and crying and dying. The rain poured through those holes and we were getting soaking wet. All night long. I wondered what in heaven's name we had done to deserve this."

Reliving those Shiloh moments was the hardest thing Will had done since the war. Joab knew that. He only hoped it would help put some things to rest—just talking about it to people who understood, but seeing Will like this worried Joab.

He was still holding to Sarah Agnes, something that Will surely noticed, but he said nothing. It was not the time or place, besides he could see something clearly in this situation. Joab was in love with her. Will was not presently equipped to deal with it. He could not balance love and war in these moments. Perhaps never.

The three young people spent several hours walking Shiloh ground and when they felt like they had leave to go, they rode back to Shiloh hill near Pittsburg Landing—a place where they couldn't see where the worst of the carnage had taken place.

"Wait here for me. I won't be long."

Joab left the two and rode back the way they had just come, toward the Widow Bell's house. He knocked. The old heavy wood door creaked opened. There she stood in her cotton house dress and an apron, maybe like the one she was wearing the day of Shiloh Battle.

"Ma'am, I'm Joab Payne from Calhoun County. I'm the son of Confederate Captain Thomas Goode Payne of the Mississippi 42nd, Lee's Army of Northern Virginia, who fell at Gettysburg."

"Oh, son, I'm so pleased to meet you," she said in a soft southern voice, such a weary look in her eyes as she shook his hand. "And you must know that I feel your pain at the loss of your father. So many of our good men died. I watched them give up their breath and life that day at Shiloh Battle. I've been hurting ever since."

"Well, Mrs. Bell, I've heard about you, and first of all let me thank you for the way you took care of our men at Shiloh Battle."

"It was my duty, Joab, but it was also my privilege. I could never relate to you or anyone else what I felt at the pond and the peach orchard that day. You know, son, when I think about it now—I have to know it was happening like this—heaven was filling up fast with godly men from both sides. And I fear hell was enlarging with so many more who knew nothing about our Lord. And I must be faithful to ask, what about you, son?"

"Oh, yes ma'am, Mrs. Bell. Not only do I know *about* Him—I *know* Him personally. He is my Lord and Savior."

Tears rolled down the widow's cheeks and she wiped her eyes with her apron.

"What a blessing," she said.

"Yes ma'am, and you are a blessing in this moment. Two of my friends are with me. One, a Confederate private. He was in the fight that day at your peach orchard and the bloody pond. In fact, you helped pull him out of the pond and you bound his wounds like the Good Samaritan. The other is a lady friend whose father was wounded here and who died at the Lyceum in Oxford. I should be bearing gifts of appreciation to you, but I was wondering . . . might we pick a few peaches from your trees? We brought food with us, but somehow I thought Shiloh peaches would be most satisfying."

"Oh, my yes, Joab. Pick to your heart's content. They are so good this season and they will soon be gone. I have both white and yellow flesh out there, so take some of each. You'll see. Wait just a minute." She disappeared into the house and returned with two large flour sacks. "Keep the sacks," she said. "I have a-plenty."

Joab thanked her kindly and shook her tiny hand once more.

"We're going to stay overnight on Shiloh Battleground. Do you think that will be acceptable?"

"By all means," said Mrs. Bell. "Nobody comes up here much anymore. I fear many stay away because what was once beautiful became a hideous place at the battle. But I can't look at it that way. It is sacred to me. It's the burial place of our men and boys who fought, who gave up everything to try and hold our country together. The least I can do is be here and walk from the place where the church once stood to the Landing and know we did our best those two days. My memories are painful, because when I close my eyes and visualize what happened I see those boys, so young, some not yet men, bleeding and crying and running for the cool water that became warm with their blood, as they lay back and died in the pond—that bitter cup never goes away from me."

Joab stood there holding her hands in his. He paused a moment, at a loss for words, not wanting to leave her, but knowing he must, he said, "Good-bye, Mrs. Bell. I will never forget you."

"Nor I, you, son. Good-bye, Joab."

He rode back to Shiloh hill loaded down with peaches from the Widow Bell's orchard. Aggie and Will were waiting where he left them. He wondered, but didn't ask, if they had talked at all while he was gone.

A harvest moon hung low over the Tennessee River, its rays casting ribbons of light through the ancient oaks before night fell on the three Mississippians who made their camp on the Snake River near the landing. They spread their blankets on the ground under the branches. The wind blew cool, scattering golden leaves across the hills. Will, having thought to bring a lantern, lit it, pulled out his knife and began peeling peaches.

Healing, Joab thought. He hoped. Even down to the fruit from the peach orchard on Widow Bell's farm, from the same peach trees that had been stripped bare of their pink blossoms on the sixth and seventh of April of '62. He looked at Aggie who was wrapped in her blanket leaning against a giant oak tree, her face glowing in the light of the oil lantern. She spoke softly.

"Joab, I'm glad I came. It hurt me, but I needed to do this. Thank you for insisting. I'll never be the same after today, but in a far better way than before. I could not imagine what you were telling me about Shiloh being the healing place for you, but I have found it to be so for me, as well. And Will, thank you for sharing my father's exact words the last time you saw him alive here on these sacred grounds. It is now my place of peace. Thank you, Lord," she whispered.

Will handed her the first peach, never saying a word.

Joab tried to watch Will and at the same time he needed to see Aggie's face. When she looked at Will there was no question in Joab's mind that she cared about him, but he couldn't tell if Will had those same kinds of feelings for her. He didn't like trying to look into their hearts and minds, but he couldn't help it. When he thought about it, he and Will were a lot alike. They had been raised up the same, though Will was at least five years older than Joab. And now there was another common bond between them. Quite possibly, they both loved the same woman.

Joab was aware that this bond could turn to a bone of contention. Maybe it had already.

Chapter 14

Desire

*I know that bitterness slows healing
of the old wounds and at all hazards
I intend to dispense with my portion of that.*

On Saturday afternoon, Joab rode to the General Store in Oxford to post a letter to Rachel and Samuel. He slipped ten dollars into the envelope, sealed it and rode back to Hiram Raines' place, feeling good about it. It had been a month since he began working at the sawmill. He had received his first pay from Mr. Fuller, and it was exactly what they had agreed upon. In fact, Mr. Fuller, having never said a word to Joab except to greet him of a morning and bid him good evening at closing time, when he handed him his pay, gave him the highest of compliments, assuring him he would have a job as long as he wanted it.

"I've never seen another man better than you at milling," he had said.

It was Joab's first letter to Rachel since the day he left. He knew she would be on pins and needles until she heard from him, but he had not wanted to post anything until he could send money. He wrote mostly about his adventure, leaving out some of the pitiful details of Shiloh, knowing Rachel would read it to Sam like a story and they would love it. He added something for Rachel's eyes only. Joab knew her well—she would read it later.

. . . I have read, and as you have taught me, living in the past is much like reliving the sins I've committed, and I want you to

know I'm searching for a better way. As we spoke while sitting on the swing before I left, I want to live in the spirit of healing and restoring. I don't like Reconstruction, not in the political meaning of the whole idea of it. It will never work for the Old South. I want to help restore what was taken from us. I think the Lord would be pleased with that. I could not be doing this if you had not said the things you did and allowed me to express my frustrations with what has been going on for years now. We had so much heart. And so much of that is either gone or waning. I know that bitterness slows healing of the old wounds and at all hazards I intend to dispense with my portion of that.

I took Will and Aggie back with me to Shiloh for a purpose. I've learned much from Aggie about facing the trials and heartaches the war caused. We were left with the same lonesome emptiness that comes in the loss of a father. And we have both found our ways to cope. Mind you, I did not say we have gotten over, but that we have come through, and in so doing, we each search for ways to help Will. That is not an easy task. Mother, he was one of the men who waded out into the Bloody Pond of Shiloh, bullet-ridden and battle weary. He was lying beside Aggie's pa that day in the makeshift hospital in Shiloh Church. Her pa was severely wounded. They took him to Oxford to the Lyceum, but he died before any of his family could get to him. Will has a root of bitterness that may be killing him. Pray that I can speak some words of wisdom that will uproot and replace. My hope was to help with the hard work, the physical, which I am doing, but as you know, I expressed a desire to invest in the real treasure loss that came as a result of the war—the very heart of the people. I am getting many opportunities.

I will be home by Thanksgiving and I do not know what a single day holds beyond that particular Thursday. I wish to be led by His hand or not at all, for only as He leads will it be a worthy endeavor.

I want to see you and Sam as bad as I've ever wanted anything. I work hard to turn aside long and lonely nights which I could not otherwise endure. I will post another letter when I receive more pay. Do not worry yourselves, for I am well fed and when in the company of Miss Aggie Stephens, I am supremely happy, though I know not what will become of that.

Hold fast to each other and know that I am ever your faithful son, Joab Payne.

Joab rode to the Stephens' farm, knowing that Aggie had not worked past two in the afternoon and she would likely be there. He would apologize for not letting her know he was coming. It had been two weeks since he had seen her and he was missing her. However, he had made no move toward a serious relationship with her. He didn't dare, not until he knew Will's intentions one way or the other, and he had not heard from Will since they returned from Shiloh.

Joab had purchased a pair of khaki trousers and a blue cotton long-sleeved shirt, trying his best to imitate his brother, Isaac, who had always looked dashing in most anything. Joab liked the khakis best. And blue was a good color for both the brothers. He pulled Star to a stop at the Stephens' hitching post and took the steps two at a time to the front porch of the lovely old country house, thanking God that Union Gen. Whiskey Smith and his men had come short of burning it to the ground.

It was late October, the maples and oaks beginning to drop the last of their leaves. Autumn was coming to a close and he had never experienced a more beautiful one. He tapped on the glass door and waited to hear light footsteps on the old wood floors that were likely polished to a high shine.

"Coming," she said. It was Aggie. Joab swallowed hard and cleared his throat. The sound of her voice sent waves of desire through him.

"Joab! I'm so happy to see you."

"Hello, Aggie." That was all he could say in the moment.

"Come," she said, stepping back so he could enter. "What brings you?"

He wished she had not asked because he still did not have the answer to the question concerning Will. He would, however, be honest and tell her what he did know for sure.

"You, Aggie. I've missed you and I rode hard to get here, so please excuse me if I'm less than presentable."

"Joab, you look splendid. The blue in your eyes is enhanced by the shirt, which I dearly love. You're truly a handsome man if I may be bold and say so."

"Thank you, Aggie. Times are changing and I think we've learned to make every minute count . . . just in case . . ."

"Just in case . . . ?" Aggie was not sure she understood. But she liked what he had said, and she was trying to figure it out to suit herself.

"I guess what I mean is . . . we're blessed to be in the company of someone who means so much, even though we have no . . . Oh, I don't really know what I mean, Aggie."

"Yes you do, Joab. You know. It's just hard to say it."

"Well, I have to be so careful because of . . . because of Will."

"Let me tell Mama you're here and we'll sit on the porch swing. Will that be okay for now? Mama will bring tea."

"Yes, that would be splendid."

The east end of the porch was shaded by the magnolias. The red maples were shedding the last of their leaves, the wind sweeping them away as fast as they fell, the cornerstone catching them in a bed of color. Daniel had rummaged through a pile of burned pieces on the dump heap and salvaged the old wicker swing. He painted it white after the burning in '64 and the paint was beginning to chip.

"This swing reminds me of home," said Joab. "Reminds me of home and my mama, Rachel, and Sam."

"You miss them, don't you?"

"You can't imagine how much, but I'll be going home next month."

"I was afraid of that," she said.

"You were?"

"Yes, of course. I don't want you to go, but I know you are on a journey of sorts."

"I plan to come back here and stay until near Christmas, then I don't know what direction my life will take. I only know in this moment, Aggie, I want to kiss you long and hard before I lose my nerve to . . ."

Aggie moved toward him on the swing and before they could think about what was happening, they were in each other's arms and Joab was kissing her passionately. He could not stop, Aggie clung to him, her lips hard against his, and when those passions had risen to the edge, they stopped kissing but neither of them let go.

"I can't say that was not the most enjoyable moment of my life," he confessed.

"Then possibly you could have imagined the same is true for me," she said.

"I don't know what to say. Do we have to say anything about it?" asked Joab as quickly as he could speak.

"No. Let's not do anything to spoil the moment. It's like eating a piece of chocolate cake and not wanting the taste to go away too soon. Does that make sense, Joab?"

"Perfectly," he whispered. "I guess you don't want to hear that I'm falling in love with you."

"Oh, but I do want to hear that, Joab. More than anything I want to hear that. I think I fell in love with you the day you walked into the tea room for the first time. Could you not possibly tell by the look on my face? That day . . . I wanted to touch your flawless face . . ."

"I spent months of sleepless nights dreaming about you. Dreaming though I was wide awake in the middle of the night and so restless. That's one of the reasons I came back here. I couldn't stop thinking about you. I couldn't stop wanting you, hoping that you wanted me, but having no idea that you felt the same way."

Joab hoped he was not shaking too hard; his emotions were trying his patience.

"Aggie, I must confess, I've never kissed a woman before you. I hope I wasn't out of control."

"Oh, my no, Joab. You were quite in control. I'm sure of that. I must confess, I have kissed Will many times, but . . . but I have known for a while that I am not in love with him, and believe me, I have never been kissed like you just kissed me, not by any man. And until this moment I had no idea the extent of real love. So real that I don't think I could spend one day without you now. I really don't know what will happen, because I am in deeper than I can tell you."

"What do you mean, Aggie?"

"I will leave it at that for the time being, Joab, not really knowing myself. I only know I've never felt this way before."

"Neither have I, but I don't want it to go away."

"Will you kiss me again, Joab?"

Without a word, he touched her lips with his fingers and wrapped his arms around her. He kissed her until they were both breathless. The door creaked open and the two young people moved apart. Aggie's mother was bringing tea.

"Hello, Joab," she said.

"Miss Caroline. It's so nice to see you. I hope you're well."

"Why, yes, Joab. I'm fine. And you?"

"Yes ma'am. I am more than fine." Joab wished he hadn't said that. It sounded a little too fine as he spoke it.

Caroline took the tray and returned to the kitchen.

"Aggie, would you like to walk or do you want to take a ride."

"Let's ride," she said.

They walked to the barn and Joab saddled her horse, put her on it, and holding the reins, he walked back to get Star, mounted, and they rode across the pasture toward the tree line behind the Stephens' house. The sun dropped in the western sky and the October wind blew cold. Joab took the jacket that was strapped behind his saddle and pulled his horse close to Aggie's. He spread the jacket across her shoulders. She touched his hand and held to it for a moment. He pulled closer and reached for her, and holding her face, he kissed her. They rode on, neither saying a word. Joab turned and looked behind him toward Will's house, which was at least a quarter of a mile away. He could see the silhouette of someone standing on the back porch. Was it Will? And had he seen them? Aggie had not spoken to him, for neither she nor Joab had expressed their feelings for each other until this very afternoon on the porch. Joab's heart raced and his chest pained as he thought that if Will had seen them kissing on the horses just now . . . if he thought they were . . . Joab had not wanted to bruise the broken reed. His primary reason for coming was to restore not to tear apart again. He hoped he had not. Chances are Will had not seen them, or maybe he wouldn't have recognized them from that distance, wishful thinking on Joab's part.

"Aggie, is that Will on the porch of his house?"

"Oh, my . . . yes . . . yes, it is."

"Do you think . . . ?"

"Joab, I will talk to him tomorrow. I don't want to assume anything. I just hope he did not see us. He deserves to know . . . not to see . . ."

"Aggie, is there anything about the last hour you want to call back?" he asked. "Because if you do, I'll understand and I'll walk away."

"Please don't talk like that, Joab. It sounds so cold. I love you. I love you past my own understanding. If anything, I want to re-enact the whole scene a hundred times. Do you understand?"

"Yes, Aggie," he said. "Forgive me. I fear I'm not too good at young love."

"Oh, you're better than good, Joab. I cannot resist you. But I'm trying to hold back my words as best I can for the time being. Tomorrow—I'll talk to Will tomorrow."

"What on earth is he going to think? I wanted him to know I'm here to help, not to hurt and now I've moved in on his girl. He will never trust me. I think I should be the one who tells him, Aggie."

"Let me think about that, Joab. Can you come back out here tomorrow after church? Will and I always go to church together."

"I will be hurting the whole time you're with him, I fear."

CHAPTER 15

FOR SOME REASON

*He lugged two buckets of milk to the porch,
took off his boots, and stepped inside
to breakfast of hot biscuits
dripping with butter and honey.*

The night was long and Joab slept little. Tossing and turning, thinking about the task at hand reminded him of the sleepless nights in Sarepta before he returned to Oxford. Was this the true meaning of bittersweet? He was fond of Will and felt a kindred spirit because of the war. Not only that, without motive of any sort, he was hopeful he could help Will. The purpose of the trip to Shiloh was to try and bring an end to the harbored hate and hostility. It was not Joab's intention to stir up a hornet's nest of a different sort, one that could potentially do even more damage. On the other hand, he was so in love with Aggie he couldn't see straight. In moments of reprieve from sinister thoughts of how it would play out with Will Cavanaugh, Joab remembered the scene on the Stephens' porch. The touch of her hand on his face, her soft lips pressed against his own, the warm feeling he had that wouldn't go away. Not that he wanted it to. He hoped it would never go away. To spend a lifetime with a woman like Aggie Stephens . . . well, Joab couldn't find words to describe the thought of such.

It was Sunday morning just before daybreak. Joab, having at long last fallen into a deep sleep, popped awake, hoping he had not overslept. He heard no one stirring as he got up and slipped into his old clothes and boots, stepped quietly out onto the back porch and washed his face in the pan of cold water, threw it out and drew more to replace it.

He took long strides to the barn and in ritual that must be performed twice a day, he sat on the milking stool, filling the first bucket to the brim, pausing in his thoughts to wonder how Samuel was doing. He longed to see him and Rachel. Why did I come here, he thought? Would life always be this complicated? I hoped falling in love would be easy and pain free. But it's not. It has a sharper pain than anything else in life. Joab thought of Rachel and how she had loved his father passionately. And then he was gone—killed in a war that drained every ounce of her being, for she and Thomas had been as one. Joab couldn't fathom the thought of never seeing Aggie again. Being away from her for just hours or a couple of days was near unbearable.

Joab thought, in light of Rachel's loss, my light afflictions are nothing. How could I be so selfish? I should be happy for the few moments with Aggie, and if something happens between us—at least I will not be relinquishing a lifetime of love and devotion like Rachel had to do.

He lugged two buckets of milk to the porch and took off his boots, stepped inside to breakfast of hot biscuits dripping with butter and honey.

"So good," Joab said.

"Thank you for milkin', son," said Hiram. "I'm gettin' spoiled to all the fine help."

"My pleasure, sir. It's the least I can do; you've opened your home to me in splendid ways, and I'm most appreciative."

"Well, Joab, the pleasure is ours," said Mrs. Raines.

"It's coming on fall, I guess, and I'll be going back to Sarepta the middle of November. I want to get back in plenty of time to do some work for Mama before Thanksgiving. Then I'll come back here and stay till near Christmas if that's acceptable with the two of you."

"Would have it no other way," said Hiram. "I don't even want to have thoughts that you will leave us permanently one day. You came to Oxford just when we needed you and you've helped us come through some hard times—but we're not the only ones you've helped. I don't think you realize—"

Hiram choked on his words and paused to take a slurp of coffee from his saucer.

"Excuse me for that," he said wiping his eyes. Mrs. Raines reached for the handkerchief in her apron pocket.

"Sometimes I feel like I haven't done enough," said Joab, "or that maybe I could have done it a better way—"

"Now, don't say that, because we . . . none of us in this town . . . none of us would trade what you've done, not for all the cows in Texas, and we'll not ever forget you. Why, you gave us reason, hope, just by your fine example. You show some good raisin', son."

The two men excused themselves and went to the porch. Hiram spoke.

"Joab, you ain't just right this morning, air ye?"

"You know me well by now, Hiram."

Joab reluctantly began to tell Hiram some things that were going on concerning Will and Aggie, and then he let it all spill out, leaving nothing to Hiram's imagination.

"Well, son, let me enlighten you just a little on Will Cavanaugh. He's a fine man; at least he was before the war. But the war changed him, like it did a lot of young men and boys, and he ain't been able to make a comeback like what would be ordinary. But who 'm I to judge that. I wasn't in the fight, but I lost my boys to it. I could have gone either way, and at first I was fightin' mad m'self. Then I went through every emotional battle of the heart until I came to realize I was gonna have to put some things behind me just to carry on. It was a journey for me. Didn't happen overnight, and I ain't there yet. I still get waves of feelings I don't understand. But I don't get angry any more. I just get overwhelmed with homesickness for Trey and Hiram, Jr. Sometimes I think I can't wait for the Resurrection to see them. It's hard to explain, son, that feelin' of just wantin' to get out of this old world."

Joab couldn't speak for the tightness in his chest. For some uncanny reason, he felt more of a kinship to Hiram than ever before. He could almost see him in heaven with his boys. He shook himself when Hiram continued.

"Back to Cavanaugh. He's several years older than Sarah Agnes, I believe, and I think he missed his opportunity to have her as a wife. Women don't like to be dangled on a string a-waitin' for a man to make up his mind. But, between you 'n me, I don't think Will Cavanaugh will ever get married. I think he's too smart for that because he knows he would mess it up if he did. You can't go through life in turmoil and expect a good woman to stay with you. It gets wearisome. A woman can get depressed herself, but she don't want her man living in that condition.

"I hope you won't let Cavanaugh stand in the way of your feelings for Sarah Agnes. Remember, I've known from day one how you feel about her, and you didn't know a thing about Cavanaugh. I think I'm a good judge of that for some reason."

"Yes sir. I think you are—for some reason."

"Air you a-goin' to church with us this mornin'?" asked Hiram.

"Yes sir. I'll just help Mrs. Raines with the dishes and then I'll get on in there and get ready. Then . . . then I'm going out to Aggie's house. Hopefully she will have made a decision on which of us will be talking to Will. One of us must do it today. We can't take a chance that he saw us yesterday without taking care of it. They will be going to church together as usual."

"How do you feel about that?"

"It's making me sick," said Joab.

"Well, if you want my opinion, and you don't have to take my advice, not for a minute, I would let Sarah Agnes do the talkin' to Will. He won't like it comin' from her, but he would *hate* it comin' from you. As a matter of fact, he might break down on you. Course, now, he might break down on Sarah Agnes, too. He's unpredictable, possibly explosive. You need to be out there close by to protect yourself and Sarah Agnes."

Joab wondered what he had gotten himself into, but it was too late. He was in over his head in love with Aggie and his emotions were coming down strong. He didn't understand some of his own feelings.

CHAPTER 16

THE LETTER

*Thou shalt guide me with thy counsel,
and afterward receive me to glory.*

Psalm 73:24

Hiram opened the cedar chest at the foot of the bed in the spare bedroom, the one temporarily occupied by Joab. In a corner and on top of some clothing that had belonged to his sons, tied about with strands of material from his wife's quilting room lay two small stacks of letters. He took the envelopes marked *Trey* and gently pulled the tie. Confederate soldiers paid no postage during the war, hence there were no posting dates, but Trey had been careful to date each letter as he wrote. His writings were like stories, a soldier's journal of sorts, each mentioning his Commander, General Stonewall Jackson, with endearing words and for whatever reason at hand. Hiram opened the letter on top, Trey's last writing before he fell at Chancellorsville.

April 15, 1863
Near Chancellorsville, Virginia

I believe in my heart that Gen. Jackson knows we are nearing the end, whether it be the end of the war or our last days on this side of the River. He is a man of valor and great faith in Almighty God with an uncanny discernment of the wicked system that we fight. I am most influenced by his Christian walk, and if I must go to my death in battle, I would much rather be following Stonewall than any other commander on earth. It is a privilege, at certain moments along the way, to drop to my knees in reverence to a Holy God, when my commander gives pause to pray. I can hear him as he cries out to our Creator God, invoking His guidance and protection—protection not for himself, but for his men. And Papa, you should hear him pray. It would set your heart on fire.

I know not what the next day will bring, nor even the next hour, but I want you to know that you, my dear Papa, have been my stronghold through the years. I believe God in His infinite love and grace placed me with Gen. Jackson as a confirmation that what you and Mama taught me was not only right but perfect, because God makes no mistakes. From my testament, I read Psalm 73: 24 where the Psalmist says, 'Thou shalt guide me with thy counsel, and afterward receive me to glory.' What man could ask for better than that. Hence, if I should die upon the battlefield, it will be all right. I, too, will rest on the other side, as I have heard Gen. Jackson say many times. So do not worry about my safety. I am in His care and keeping. I remain ever your eldest son, Trey Alexander Raines.

Hiram folded the letter, touched it tenderly, carefully returned it to the envelope, and wiped his eyes. It was the last one he received from Trey before he died at Chancellorsville. He put the letter back on top and reached for another one deeper into the stack. He continued until he found the one for which he was searching.

. . . Papa, this is not meant to place a burden upon you, for you have no idea the depth of feelings I have about this subject, because I've never told anyone, but for some strange reason that may never issue in understanding, I want you to know something about your son that no one else knows and may never know. As you can see from the way I write, I am going the long way around to approach it. Please don't read ahead because I am preparing you and myself for what I am about to say.

This is it . . . for a long, long time, I have been in love with Sarah Agnes Stephens. There, now that I have said it, I feel much better, though I hope you will keep this private until such time as you need to mention it, if ever. I do not want Sarah Agnes to know of my feelings, for if something happens to me on the battlefield . . . well, I don't want her to suffer any more anguish than she already has over the death of her father. I know that she and Will have been sort of promised to each other for years, but nothing seems to be happening with that.

I wanted you to know my feelings, perhaps only to receive relief from being the only one who knows. It's like carrying around a burden, for to suffer unrequited love is as debilitating as fighting a war with these old Yanks. I know this is placing an added burden upon you, but please promise me you will not let Sarah Agnes be hurt by anyone. I have received letters from Daniel Stephens that cause me to worry about her future safety, letters confirming Will's instability. The war took its emotional toll on Will. I think that is enough said and I will trust that you will somehow see this to completion. In the end, I do not want her to know that I have designated you as the Hound of Heaven to watch over her, but that, in essence, is what I have just done. I post this letter understanding that these thoughts may perhaps cause you great foreboding and I sincerely apologize, not intending to add one wrinkle to your beloved brow. I just need to know that you will grant me this petition.

At the present time, I remain not only a foot soldier in the Army of Commander Thomas J. 'Stonewall' Jackson and proud to be serving the Confederate States of America, but also even more proud to be your loving son, Trey Alexander Raines.

Hiram wiped more tears, tucked the letter in his pocket and closed the trunk, slipped to his room and dressed for church while Mrs. Raines and Joab finished the dishes.

Anxious to get to Aggie's house, Joab would not be taking dinner with Hiram and Mrs. Raines after church. He and Hiram stepped out on the porch as Joab was preparing to leave.

"Son, I know you're on edge about the situation with Will and Sarah Agnes, but I might have something here that will help you make your decisions. I have waited until now for reasons you will understand when you read it. Take it with you, but please bring it back to me. I want you to go somewhere by yourself and read it. You, of all people, will understand, for my son has been where you are. I trust that you will show the letter to no one, not even Sarah Agnes—especially Sarah Agnes. That is, Joab, unless sometime far in the future and when I am gone you allow it might be useful for Sarah Agnes to know."

"No, of course not," Joab said, not wanting to think about *sometime in the future.*

He took the letter, having no idea what Hiram was talking about. It had crossed his mind that someday he might like to read some of the war letters written by his sons. But why had Hiram said, ' . . . my son has been where you are'?

After meeting, Joab took leave of Mr. and Mrs. Raines and rode toward Water Valley, October wind blowing hard against his face still intense with expression from his conversation with Hiram concerning Will Cavanaugh. Before he reached the Stephens' farm, he pulled Star to the side of the road, took the letter from his pocket and opened it. It was addressed to Hiram Raines. He sat in the saddle resting his foot on a fence rail and read the words of a man at war. *It's like carrying around a burden, for to suffer unrequited love is as debilitating as fighting a war with these old Yanks.*

My God in Heaven, thought Joab, Trey Raines was in love with Aggie. Things are going from bad to worse. Or were they? He was trying to figure out why Hiram had trusted him with the letter. He read on.

"Oh," he whispered, as he read Trey's words aloud, ". . . *please promise me you will not let Sarah Agnes be hurt by anyone . . .*"

Now he understood. This was Hiram's moment in life to fulfill the promise made to his son and he would do it through Joab. Somehow both Hiram and his son, Trey, knew that Will was not the man for Aggie, and it had everything in the world to do with a war that had left Will less than reliable, though due to no fault of his own. Since the war he was hot-blooded, easily incensed, and quite frankly, Joab was beginning to feel terribly responsible for making sure Aggie did not get hurt, not just for Trey and Hiram, but for himself.

Joab didn't know how he would enter into discussion with Aggie. She must not know about Trey Raines' letter unless and until Hiram was ready to tell her, and he would have to do that himself. Joab knew Hiram to be an exceptional gentleman, and the more he pondered the letter, the more he realized he was releasing his son's personal hopes for claims to Aggie into the hands and heart of Joab Payne. It was complicated but in the South there was a protocol for relationships and Joab was in the cross hairs of a triangle that could likely have no pleasant ending. To know that Hiram had taken private sides with Joab gave him a measure of comfort and satisfaction, but from Hiram's point of view only.

Joab took the stone steps to the porch he had come to love. He dared to glance at the wicker swing on the far end, hoping, wishing for one more hour like that first experience. It seemed far in the past, though it was yesterday, Saturday, when they sat there, Joab enfolding Aggie in his arms. The kiss was still damp on his lips and the thought of it etched in his memory, hopefully forever.

Before he could tap on the glass door, Aggie opened it quietly.

"I've been waiting for you, Joab. I've missed you and it has only been hours since you left—just yesterday." She slipped onto the porch, still wearing her meeting clothes, as was Joab.

"We look good together, Joab."

"Please come to me," he said, sweeping her into his arms.

The porch was surrounded by trees and shrubs that shadowed and sheltered. It crossed his mind that, unlike yesterday, no one could see them. He kissed her long and passionately. She never resisted, but clung to him as if it were for the last time.

It wasn't that Joab was testing the waters, but after sleeping on the thought that Will may know, he needed positive assurance that Aggie felt the same as yesterday. He could not be more certain than in this moment.

"We can sit on the porch and talk, Joab. Are you hungry? Did you take Sunday dinner with the Raines?"

"No to both questions. Perhaps I will be hungry later, but not now."

Aggie did just as Joab had hoped. He was not going to be the first to mention the situation with Will Cavanaugh. There was a two-fold problem. Joab was in love with Will's girl and someone on Will's back porch had likely seen them together on the horses yesterday.

"Joab . . ." Aggie paused wanting to align her thoughts properly. Joab's heart raced, his emotions privately out of control, but he was silent, allowing Aggie the privilege of parsing her words. She obviously had something to tell him.

"Will came here last night after you left, which was kind of him; that is, waiting until you were gone. Either kind or cowardly and I could have given him the benefit of the doubt until he spoke.

"He did see us on the horses. I had no thought of denying it. Joab—this is hard because I'm so in love with you, I can scarcely breathe. I've never felt this way before. It is my sure confirmation that what we're doing is right and proper."

Joab listened intently without saying a word.

"I have been taught the Scriptures all my life. I memorized the Songs of Solomon privately, hoping through the years, that I would have a love as meaningful and safe and splendid as the bride of that book. I never had thoughts of Will as the bridegroom in the story of my life, and I must confess that I did wrong by letting our relationship go on and on—though there was really no reason for it to go on and on. Please believe me. The only thing that has happened between us is mostly time—dead time and assumption that we belonged to each other and then a sort of kindred tie because he was the last to see my father alive and to talk to him before they carried him away.

"I know I'm going on and on, Joab. Forgive me. I'm getting to what happened last night. Will pounded on the door. I answered, but I wouldn't let him come in, not wanting to upset Mama and Daniel. I closed the door behind me and we stood here on the porch. He was sobbing and said, 'Sarah Agnes, I knew—I knew Payne was in love with you when we went to Shiloh. I could tell by the way he looked at you and held you when you cried. I know I don't have anything to offer you but a broken down body and a mind that's half gone, and I know I have held onto you for years falsely presuming that we would always be together but never doing a thing to make you want to be with me. But when I saw you and Payne on the horses this afternoon, I wanted to—I wanted to kill him.'"

Joab's expression never changed. He was not in the least surprised. He spoke. "Quite frankly, Aggie, I think that is exactly what I expected him to say. I'm not so sure I wouldn't have said the same thing given the same circumstances."

"But Joab, I don't think he's going to kill you, do you?"

"No, of course not. He's not that kind of man. But the war did and is still doing strange things to our men. I have added misery to Will's helplessness and I'm less of a man for doing that. I will have to make up for it somehow, because what I have innocently done makes a mockery of my purpose for coming here."

"Joab, no! It's my fault. I should have either broken off my relationship with Will, what little existed, the moment I laid eyes on you or I should have at least told him about you. But—if I had, we may never have known real and passionate love the way we know it in this moment. That has to be a redeeming truth, doesn't it?"

Joab moved close to Aggie. "I do love you immensely. I cannot bear the thought of being without you. But I am going to put some space between us. Not because I don't desire to be with you every waking moment of my life. Being apart will be another one of the hardest things I've ever done. I have to allow you and Will time to either bring what used to be to a close or to rekindle it. I will leave that all up to you, knowing it could well mean that I will never be with you again. In the meantime, while I wait, I need to concentrate on the other reason I came to Oxford."

Her eyes filled with tears. "I hate what the war continues to do. I never had any intentions of hurting Will. He has been hurt enough. Ever since Shiloh, he has talked about wishing he had died. He thinks it was wrong that my papa died and he lived. He has trouble understanding God's reasoning behind things."

Joab put his arms around her. "I will work on the square as usual this week and at the mill in the afternoons. And I will stay away for at least a week, giving you time and space to think about all of this."

"You know best, Joab, but this will mean sleepless nights and long days at the tea room. Not seeing you is punishment for my carelessness and thoughtlessness in all of this."

"Aggie, I'm not trying to punish you anymore than I'm punishing myself. You did nothing wrong, and how can I possibly say it was wrong for me to fall in love with you? Yesterday when we kissed on this porch, surely I could have refrained . . ."

"No, don't say that, Joab. I was making a move toward you before you said you wanted to kiss me before you lost your nerve. I wanted you to kiss me. I wanted you to be in love with me as I am with you."

"We've lived a lifetime in these past few weeks, Aggie."

"But a lifetime is not enough, Joab."

"You're right," he said, standing to leave. "Until next Saturday, I will think of little but you. Good-bye, Aggie. I do love you."

He mounted Star and never looked back. Aggie was crying and he didn't want to see it. He rode hard toward Oxford, wondering what on earth had possessed him to make such a decision.

It was mid-afternoon when the sky turned dark and rain began to fall in torrents. A storm out of nowhere cast an eerie gloom over a situation that was turning more dismal by the moment. Thunder clapped and rumbled and lightning skittered across the sky spooking Star.

"Steady, girl. Everything's fine. Just an unpleasant continuation of a mysterious day."

The pouring rain reminded him of his first trip to this country—the country belonging to Sarah Agnes Stephens and so many of his new friends. He was not yet halfway home, but he was cold and he could scarcely see. He sought shelter in an old abandoned barn that had been partially burned by Union soldiers in '64. He dismounted and patted Star. She was dripping wet and so was he. Tying her to the post of the only stall left standing, he searched around for some dry hay. He climbed the rotted steps to the loft on the side that was not burned and kicked out as much as he could find then climbed back down. He dropped some of the hay for Star and pushed the rest to the corner of the stall, unsaddled his horse, and spread his blanket. He sat down to sort through the unfolding drama. The little pile of hay brought the slightest bit of comfort. He was missing Aggie already. Selfish maybe, but she was his girl now, and he didn't want the path to a perfect future with her to play out on any other stage. He was paying the price. But was he handling the situation in the best way?

What would Rachel do? What would be her advice to me, he questioned? Truth be known, Joab, while he had ignited a fire in the hopeless and helpless men in Oxford town, had dashed cold water on a man that had fought for the South and lost everything. What was he thinking?

The war was still taking—not only from Will, but Joab and Aggie. And from Hiram, too. Joab remembered the look of hurt on Hiram's face when he handed him the letter from Trey. It was safe and dry inside his saddlebag.

To believe the war ended at Appomattox was but a trick of the times. Joab was beginning to feel the crunch of his youth. Shiloh was to have been a coming of age experience for him, a reckoning with the madness of seeing the war from a perspective different from letters and newspapers and Confederate graveyards. Nothing as personal as having fought with a squirrel rifle or of suffering the degradation of fighting barefoot and without sufficient food or clothing.

But there were also battlefields of his personal choosing. A sort of rebellion that any southern father killed in the fight would perhaps have been proud to see in a son. It meant one thing—they had not died in vain. But Joab had a difficult time absorbing that. He was on a mission and that task had been carelessly interrupted. He had to sort through whether he had caused it or whether he had rescued Sarah Agnes Stephens from a life of misery with one of those Confederate Veterans who suffered from traumatizing anguish left over from one of the cruelest battles of the war.

A cold gray fog hung on the atmosphere figuratively and literally. Joab, too weary to think, leaned against the rough-hewn wall of the mossy-smelling stall while the rain beat fiercely against the old dilapidated barn. Thunder rumbled noisily and when the lightning cracked it temporarily rolled up the darkness, sending streaks of light and revealing torrents of rain. A bolt of lightning hit the side of the barn, starting a small fire. Just enough to warm Joab, to shed a small flicker of light, and to make him wonder if this old building had nine lives.

Hiram would be worried about him; he had been gone since meeting ended early in the day, and he had not said he would stay overnight. Daybreak would come soon, and Joab needed to be up and on his way when the rain slowed. He was committed to helping with the Courthouse rubble before he left to have Thanksgiving with Rachel and Samuel. He had sent his mother an additional ten dollars with a letter, this time giving her little information, not wanting her to worry about him. Quite frankly, he didn't want her to know the drama that was unfolding—not until he had a better idea of the direction it would take.

While Joab was stranded in the old half-burned barn in a fierce storm, Will Cavanaugh was half walking, half running as best he could with his cane, the quarter mile to the Stephens' house in the same thunderstorm.

Dripping wet but sheltered from the rain on the porch, he tapped on the glass pane in the front door. Daniel answered the knock, turned around and called to Sarah Agnes without inviting Will into the house, afraid the drama was getting the best of his mother.

"Will, you're soaking wet. What are you doing out in this storm? Do you want to come in? Daniel made a low fire in the dining room."

"No, Sarah Agnes. I don't want to come in."

"Then why are you here?" she said. "And why didn't you wait until the rain stopped?"

"I've come to tell you that I'm finished with all of this. The commotion is getting the best of me. I'm on the losing end of this and I can't take it any longer. Not that I had any binding hold on you anyway, but you're free. Free, as far as I'm concerned, to go to your lover."

"Will!" Aggie was indignant. Will had misunderstood everything. There had been no long, drawn-out love affair. In fact, nothing of the kind. She had simply fallen in love with Joab Payne. She was not engaged to Will and he knew it. Sure, they had somewhat of a silent understanding, but that was going nowhere and he knew that, too.

"You know better than that, Will Cavanaugh! What's come over you? We've known each other all our lives. Do you really believe that is the truth?"

"I don't know what I believe any more. Most of the time I can't think straight, and all of this has piled in on me. And when I saw you with Payne yesterday . . . well, I don't want to deal with it any more. For that matter, Sarah Agnes, I don't want to deal with *life* anymore."

"Don't say that, Will," she said, quietly, not wanting to cause him further anxiety. "We can work this out between us, don't you think?"

"It's already worked out, so I'll be going now. I won't bother you anymore."

Will turned and hobbled away, leaving her crying on the porch.

"No, Will! Please don't leave like this. Not in the rain."

He walked faster, as fast as he could. Aggie saw him toss his cane as he slogged through the mud, dragging his leg. He fell to the ground and struggling to pull himself to his feet, tromped and limped onward through the muddy cornfield toward his house. Corn stalks, long since pulled together in shocks awaiting removal to the crib, now lay soaked on the ground. Aggie could still see him stumbling over the shocks, falling, staggering from one stalk to the next. She stood on the porch ringing her hands, then ran back into the house and called for her brother.

"Please go after him, Daniel."

"Get back inside, Sarah Agnes, and don't come out."

He grabbed his coat and pulled on his boots, slicked his hair back and tightened his hat down, cleared the front porch steps, then commenced running across the same muddy cornfield. The creek between the two farms, lined with trees and privet thickets curled and took another direction. Will had to have taken the road to get to the Stephens farm, but now Daniel could see him, and he was headed toward the creek. Daniel's heart was in his throat. He kept running hard trying to overtake Will. The creek was ordinarily just a few feet deep, even dry bed for part of the summer, but its banks were swollen now since the fall rains. Why on earth was Will heading for the water? There would be no crossing it. Not in his condition.

Daniel knew something of the problem between Aggie and Will. He was not totally oblivious, but he didn't understand too much about that sort of thing and had not tried to interfere. He had, however, been watching his sister. He was not going to let her get hurt. Not for any reason. Besides, his friend, Trey Raines, had made it a point to implore Daniel to help take care of Sarah Agnes while he was away at war and especially if something happened to him during the fight. Daniel had never mentioned that to Sarah Agnes. He momentarily lost sight of Will, reached in his pocket and pulled out his handkerchief and wiped the rain from his face and eyes so he could see, then stuffed it back into his pocket. Will appeared in his view once more and Daniel kept running, wishing Will would stumble and fall so he could overtake him. If he got into the creek, there may be no way Daniel could get him out before he . . .

In that moment, Will leapt headlong into the swollen stream. Daniel was still a few yards behind him, and when he got to the bank, he could not see Will. He was gone. The water was moving fast, the rain beating down in sheets and the sky growing darker, making it impossible for Daniel to see. He took his jacket and boots off and swam the stream, fighting to avoid the debris himself. If he could get to the other side, he could make a run for the Cavanaugh farmhouse and alert Will's pa. He couldn't do this alone. On the other side, he pulled himself to the bank, and ran, following the stream down the hill for a few more yards when he saw Will, caught in a mass of limbs and debris, face down in the water. Daniel gasped, jumped into the stream and held onto a limb from the thicket to steady himself while he attempted to set Will free so he could get him out of the water. Daniel pulled him to the bank and tried to revive him, but to no avail. Will was dead. His head was pouring blood. He had obviously struck it on a limb when he jumped into the stream. Daniel slogged to the back door of the Cavanaugh house and banged on it as loud as he could.

"No, God no!" shouted Mr. Cavanaugh as he ran behind Daniel toward the creek bank, his tears mixed with the pouring rain.

Long before daybreak, Joab fell into a deep sleep from exhaustion. He shot straight up when a loud clap of thunder rattled the old half-burned barn. Something was wrong. He sat for a moment to get his bearings. A tiny brown barn mouse scurried across the hard packed damp ground and disappeared beneath the hay. Feeling disconcerted and fearful that something had happened to Aggie, he jumped to his feet, saddled Star and rode fast back to the Stephens' farm.

A lamp burned with a high wick in the front windows. Now he was sure something had happened. He jumped the stone steps to the porch and removed his boots.

Mrs. Stephens came to the door.

"Miss Caroline?"

"Oh, my, Joab! Thank God, you're here. Something dreadful has happened."

Joab panicked. "Is it Aggie?"

"No, son," she said. "Come on in the house. Sarah Agnes is by the fire in the dining room. I'll bring coffee."

"Thank you, Miss Caroline."

Not wanting to ask, Joab held his questions until he was with his girl. If something dreadful had happened, who did it concern? If not Aggie, who, or what? She sat in the rocking chair holding her face in her hands. Had she been sitting there all night? She was still dressed in her meeting clothes, just like he left her in the late afternoon. She didn't move, but he could hear her sobbing. He reached down and lifted her into his arms. She buried her face in his chest and cried aloud then looked up at him. He kissed her face and wiped the tears, then gently sat her back in the rocking chair and knelt on the floor beside her. For the first time, Joab was seeing her imperfect. Her beautiful face was swollen and her long wavy hair was frazzled and falling in her eyes. He pushed it back, held it, and spoke.

"Can you tell me what happened, Aggie?"

She was losing control. "It's Will, Joab."

She threw her head back and sobbed aloud.

"He . . . he drowned in the creek. Daniel ran after him and near drowned himself, trying to get to him. The water was too deep and it kept moving Will downstream just out of Daniel's reach. He tried so hard—but it was like Will didn't try at all. He didn't want to be saved. Daniel said it looked like he jumped in knowing the water was going to take him under and besides that he hit his head on a limb or something and knocked a hole in it. Why, Joab, why?"

By now she was hysterical, her tiny frame shaking at the thought and she said it again.

"He wanted to die . . ."

Joab left her briefly, stepped out into the kitchen where Caroline Stephens was getting coffee ready.

"I would like to take Aggie to her bed, Miss Caroline. She's hysterical."

"She's been that way ever since Daniel came back in with the bad news, Joab."

Caroline told him the story of how Will had come to the porch last evening and then left running, stumbling across the field toward the creek, and how Aggie had sent Daniel to try and stop him.

"He was finally able to grasp Will and pull him to the bank but it was too late. He was dead. Daniel had no way of knowing if it was the lick on his head that caused him to black out and then he obviously drowned. The fact is, Daniel saw Will deliberately dive into the stream."

Caroline Stephens wiped her eyes with her handkerchief. "Take her up, please, Joab. I'll show you."

He climbed the stairs following Miss Caroline with Aggie in his arms, laid her on the bed, took the hand-sewn quilt from the foot, and covered her shaking body.

"Please sit with her, Joab. I'll bring your coffee up here, but none for her. She needs to sleep. She's been awake all night. She's exhausted."

She motioned for Joab to step out into the hall and said, "She's blaming herself for this. Someone needs to help her. She won't listen to me."

"Yes ma'am. She probably won't listen to me either, but we'll face that problem after we help Mr. and Mrs. Cavanaugh take care of Will at the first light. That is, if they will let us. Daniel and I can take care of the arrangements. Where is Daniel?"

"I made him go to bed about an hour ago. He was in bad shape, having to go fetch Mr. Cavanaugh, tell him what happened and take him to where Will's body lay. Daniel saddled Mr. Cavanaugh's horse and they took it down to bring the body back up to the house. It's all so dreadful. So very sad."

"What about the Cavanaughs?"

"They talked to Daniel, said Will had been in despair ever since he came home from the war and it never got better."

"I should never have taken him back to Shiloh." Joab buried his face in his hands.

"Joab, don't. And please don't think the Cavanaughs are going to blame you or Aggie or the trip back to Shiloh. I've talked to them many times because I didn't want my daughter to marry him, not in his condition. I don't mean his physical infirmities as a result of the war, but how it left him with half a mind. I think they knew he would take his own life sooner or later. That Shiloh Battle must have been terrible."

Joab lifted his head and Caroline Stephens was not sure she had made herself clear to him. Now she was scolding him. "Joab, you must square your shoulders and be a man. You are not to blame and the sooner you get that in your head, the sooner you will be able to help me with Sarah Agnes."

"Yes ma'am. I understand."

Caroline touched Joab's hand, patted it, and walked downstairs. He went back into the room where Aggie lay with her eyes closed. He leaned down and kissed her cheek. She opened her eyes and pulled his face to hers, kissed his lips, and lay back on her pillow. He knelt beside her for a moment, tightening his arms around her until she was no longer shaking. Finally she dropped off, and when she was sleeping soundly, Joab took the stairs down to the kitchen and spoke with Caroline Stephens before leaving.

"Miss Caroline, what do you think I should do now?"

"First, go home and get some rest. And please let Hiram and the Sheriff know what has happened, as I'm sure you will. Ask the two of them to ride out as soon as possible tomorrow to help get Will's body to the undertaker. I'm sure Hiram and Sheriff Macintosh will take care of the burial arrangements. They usually do when it concerns a veteran."

"Yes ma'am. I'll take care of that."

CHAPTER 17

A PROPER TIME

*When he thought about it,
a double portion of darkness had unraveled
every bright ray of hope that had eked through
since he arrived in this part of the country.*

Joab scarcely remembered the ride home, the horror of the past hours consuming him. He couldn't think past the day as to what he would do, how he would handle things, much less what shape his life would take after all this. He knew one thing—he must put into practice what his mother had taught him about life. 'Hard days will come for you, Joab. Life will be what you make it, so make it good.' How was he going to make good on all of this?

He was weary when he arrived in Oxford shortly before noon. Mrs. Raines, fearful that something dreadful had happened, met him at the back door.

"Joab, dear, I can see from your face that something is wrong. Hiram's still sleeping. Do you want me to get him?"

"No ma'am, not just yet," said Joab, trying to decide how to handle the bad news.

"Well, then, come on and take a seat when you're done washing up, and I'll fetch you a cup of coffee. I've a fresh pot made, and I'm just getting ready to put dinner on the table and then we'll call Hiram."

"I should be serving you, Miss Mattie."

"Oh, no, son. You've obviously worked hard today and with little sleep last night, I take it. You need rest. Things will look better when you've eaten and prayed and slept. I always said that to my sons."

"You sound like Mama. That's something she would say, Miss Mattie. Thank you for the sound advice. Ah . . . do I have time to run over to Sheriff Macintosh's office and fetch him before we eat."

"Of course, and tell him he can take dinner with us if he would like. I'll set another plate."

Joab dashed out the back door and ran toward the Sheriff's Office, leaving Mrs. Raines with a perplexed look on her face. Hiram shuffled down the hall and out to the kitchen and joined his wife. In minutes, Joab was back and Sheriff Macintosh was following him. The sheriff greeted Hiram and Mrs. Raines and they all sat down.

Another dismal day had cast long gray shadows over Oxford, symbolic of the mood. Without saying a word, Joab went to the shelf in the dining room and took Hiram's violin from the case. He walked back into the kitchen and sat down.

"Do you mind, sir?" he asked his friend.

"Not a' tall," said Hiram, wondering what Joab had in mind, not knowing he was an accomplished violinist; Rachel had taught all of her boys to play.

Joab pulled the bow down on the strings and as he played an old Confederate tune, sad and lonesome, the three other southerners sat quietly, though with emotion. He played through the verse and gaining his own composure, Joab sang the chorus. He apologized to Hiram, Mrs. Raines, and Sheriff Macintosh, feeling he had done nothing to bring a moment of joy. But there was no joy to bring. Only sadness. His place of peace and healing had been interrupted by a tragedy, the worst since the war had ended, at least to him. Had he expected too much? Was it not true that it would one day completely pass? He would not give up until it began to make sense. He was too far into it to turn back. The events of the last forty-eight hours started on the front porch swing of the Stephens' farm with Aggie. When he thought about it, in the last few hours, a double portion of darkness had unraveled every bright ray of hope that had eked through since he arrived in this part of the country.

Joab placed the fiddle in the case and Sheriff Macintosh broke the silence. "That was splendid, Joab. I would never have known you could do that. It touched me to the heart."

"Joab, is they airy a thing you can't do?" asked Hiram.

"Oh, yes sir. Many things. I can't right the wrong and I can't soothe the hurt. I wish I could."

"Son, your job is to make music and do what you can. Life and breath and even death belong to Almighty God and that's not your job, nor mine, nor the Sheriff's. We're only responsible for what He allows us to do."

"Thanks for reminding me. Sometimes I act like my brother, Isaac. When he returned from the war, he wanted to fix everything. Just like Isaac, I'm learning the hard way. I love my brother with a passion, but I don't want to be like he was before he surrendered to the will of Almighty God."

"Well, I think you can continue right down the same path you're on. Just don't try to carry the load when it's impossible."

"Right now, I need to give you some very bad news. I don't know how to break it gently. I don't know why I played the Rebel tune. The stage is already set, and it is dismal and sad. So I'll just tell you. Will Cavanaugh is dead."

"What! God, no! What on earth happened?" Hiram was stunned.

"It's a disturbing situation, to tell you the truth. It seems Will found out that Aggie and I . . . well, that we . . . It happened like this . . . . I . . . Aggie and I, more or less at the same time, announced our feelings for one another. Mind you, Aggie had given up on ever having a life with Will because of what the war did to him mentally and emotionally. To make the story short, and to be perfectly honest with you, Aggie and I took a ride on the horses on Sunday afternoon late. Of course, that was yesterday, though it seems like a week now. We stopped for a few minutes and as young love would lead me, I moved close to her horse and kissed Aggie on the lips. Shortly after that moment, I turned around toward the Cavanaugh place, and although we were at least a quarter of a mile away, I could see the silhouette of someone on the back porch. I motioned to Aggie and she said it was Will. It disturbed her because she had not had a moment to tell Will about us. I told Aggie that I would talk to Will, but she said let her think about it. I started back to Oxford late yesterday and got caught in the thunderstorm, stayed a few hours in an old burned out barn. I was exhausted, but found it impossible to sleep. Lightning struck the end of the barn and I thought it best to stay put until the storm passed. I threw out some hay and piled it up against the stall and finally fell into a deep sleep, only to be awakened for some strange reason I can't explain. I jumped up, saddled my horse and rode fast back to the Stephens' farm. When I got there well before daylight, the lamps were burning and I could see something was wrong. That's when I found out from Miss Caroline what had happened. Aggie was in a state, I mean she was delirious. Before I left she had settled down and was asleep."

Joab told them how Daniel ran after Will but was not able to overtake him in time.

"Did you talk to the Cavanaughs?"

"No. Miss Caroline did and she assured me they knew that Will was not right and hadn't been since the war. From all indications they were not surprised he took his own life. But that doesn't relieve me of the responsibility I feel. I was longing to right some of the wrong that has been inflicted on the South, but in so doing, we've lost another Confederate veteran. You don't know how much I hate that. What can I do to make up for my part in causing Will's death?"

"In the first place, you had nothing to do with that," said Hiram. "In the second place, I think you should play the violin on the hill during his burial. And if I know Will Cavanaugh, he would love to hear *Dixie* played in fine fashion, nice and slow and solemn. Do you think you could do that?"

"I would be pleased to if you could first ask Mr. and Mrs. Cavanaugh if that is what they would like."

"Consider it done. Now, Sheriff, are you ready to head out to the Cavanaugh place?"

"Yes, we better be on our way. I'm going to suggest we have the funeral on Thursday at high noon and that we bury him on the hill at The University with his friends and Lt. Stephens."

Joab shuddered and nodded his head. "Do you want me to stand your watch tonight, Hiram?"

"No, son. You've been up way too long. I'll get Fuller to do it. He's always handy to help me out when I can't make it of a night."

"I know it's too late for me to mention this," said Hiram, "but don't you go worryin' y'self sick over this, fer they's nothin' you can do to change airy a thing. And don't go blamin' y'self. Most all the Oxford folks will likely feel the same as me. Will has been in a bad way ever since he came home from the war. I think you understand that by now."

"Yes sir. I allow you're right, Hiram."

On Thursday morning, Joab rose before daybreak and did the chores as usual. His private thoughts were of Aggie. He had not seen her since Monday morning. In all of the heartache over Will, Joab was touched by other emotions. He missed his girl, needed her arms around him. Sometimes a man just needed to be consoled. He saddled his horse and rode to the campus, sauntered her down to the stream and tied her to a tree. The creek was cold and clear. He shuddered when he thought about it and wondered if he would always be reminded of that dark Sunday when Will took his own life in the moving waters of a stream not far away. Joab scrubbed and washed his hair with the soap Mrs. Raines had given him, dried off, and dressed. He rode back to the Raines' home feeling the least bit invigorated. He prayed as he rode, asking for a strong measure of peace and a release from the burden of guilt. If Rachel had taught her sons one thing it was the utter uselessness of carrying a burden once it was released to the Lord. She always wondered why people continued to get detained on life's journey when it would never change a thing.

At half past eleven, Joab dressed in his best trousers and clean white shirt and rode Star to The University. He tied her to a tree in the edge of the woods and waited for Hiram and Miss Mattie to arrive with the violin. He knew Aggie and Daniel and Miss Caroline would be coming soon, but he would wait until after the service to see them. In fact, Joab thought it best to wait for them to approach him and if they didn't, he would understand. Hiram had arrived and was walking toward him with the violin case.

"I take it you spoke with Mr. and Mrs. Cavanaugh?"

"Yes, I did. And they have just arrived. Would you like to go and meet them?"

Joab swallowed hard and said, "Yes. Yes, I would." He squared his shoulders and walked beside Hiram across the grassy knoll toward the crowd that was gathering.

⸺※⸺

Thursday afternoon following the service, Joab rode to the sawmill, and deliberately avoiding conversation, he went right to work. He had not talked to anyone after the funeral. It was best that way. Friday came to a close without Joab making an appearance at the rubble heap, something he had no control over. He would explain to the men on Monday. He stayed close to the Raines' home and did all the chores. He had, however, made it to the sawmill by two on Friday afternoon, once again pulling the saw, mindlessly doing his job, feeling much like a marionette, allowing his thoughts to be pulled first one way, then another. His state of mind had caused confusion and when he thought about it, he compared himself to Isaac. Had he done the exact same thing as his brother? No. This was entirely different. There was no triangle with Isaac. He was a rogue, acting alone and in self-disapproval. Joab had not allowed himself to take on the roguish characteristic. And Rachel would never agree that he was a self-inflicted rogue of a man. Neither was he so self-absorbed as to hold himself hostage to depression and despair. For moments, yes. For long periods of time, no.

But in these moments, Joab could only think of one thing. Will Cavanaugh was alive Sunday when he left Aggie's. Today he was dead, his body lying in a grave on the hill and Joab felt very much to blame. He admired Hiram's son, Trey, though they never had the opportunity to meet in this life. From all indications, he was absorbed in the goodness of God. At the same time he stood in firm opposition to deliberate selfishness, which he considered characteristic of Will. Trey had been in love with Aggie, but he never told her as much. He didn't want to give her added reason to worry. It was bad enough her father was killed in battle and Will was badly wounded. He never wanted her to endure the war worrying about him and possibly losing him along with her father and Will. That would be too much for a young girl to bear.

When Joab thought about it, he had a better understanding of the kind of man Trey was. He had experienced the same unanswered love as Joab had those first few months after he met Aggie. The only difference was Trey had died for the Confederacy, never having pledged that love. Joab had been able to express his feelings for Aggie and have those same feelings returned. A very powerful experience, he thought.

He rode from the mill to Hiram's house, wondering if Aggie had returned to work, or if she was not yet able to face people. The Thompson House had only been open since February, and she had worked there from the beginning, endearing herself to all its patrons. Joab thought about the funeral on Thursday. Half the town had gathered around, consoling her and the Cavanaugh family. Joab had watched from the hill, not wanting to assert himself. He had wished with all his heart to be beside her, holding her hand. It was not the proper time, and he wondered if ever again there would be—a proper time.

Joab allowed two weeks to pass without seeing Aggie. He did not step into The Thompson House even for casual conversation. He wanted to give her a proper portion of time to mourn and to think about everything after the funeral. He loved her endlessly, but she needed time to absorb all that had happened with Will. Joab would be leaving soon. He would spend time with her, if she would allow it, the weekend before Thanksgiving, and on the Tuesday after, he would be going home. Home to Rachel and Samuel.

Caroline Stephens pumped water into her kitchen bowl and washed the few dishes at her sink. No one was hungry these days. Maybe that was best since food was scarce, except for jars of vegetables and fruit she had canned and preserved from her summer garden and a few pieces of pork her kind neighbors had brought. Daniel had helped her salt and hang those pieces in the smokehouse to cure.

Daniel was still distraught, fighting his own battle, because he was not able to save Will Cavanaugh from drowning. Perhaps more distressing than *how* it happened was *that* it happened. Daniel was eighteen years old, mature and responsible, having taken on his father's role from the day Lt. Stephens died in the Shiloh Battle, but Will's drowning lay heavily on his youthful heart.

Caroline pushed back the time-yellowed lace curtains and gazed out the window over her sink, thankful for the trees that rose up tall to block the view of the Cavanaugh house. She needed no reminders.

She thought about her husband and Will, both dead now, and Daniel and her daughter, Aggie, so touched by the war's aftermath. It may never end for us until we are all in our graves, she thought, brushing tears. She hoped Daniel would soon recover from the shock that Will Cavanaugh had deliberately taken his own life.

"But Mama," he had said, "I was just a few minutes behind him. Did I not run fast enough? Dear God, Cavanaugh was crippled. Was I not quick enough to get to him and pull him out? Truthfully, Mama, I would rather he died a hero at Shiloh than this way. It's just not right."

Caroline had dealt with her son as best she could, believing that to have endured the war years and now the aftermath required either a theological degree or that of a physician. The South had not provided mental help after the war. She would have to take care of her children herself, with the help of the prayers of Reverend Phillips. He had been her mainstay after Lt. Stephens died.

"Mama." Sarah Agnes spoke softly, knowing her mother was thinking, pondering. Her eyes were fixed on the window.

"Oh, Aggie—I'm calling you Aggie now, since that's what Joab Payne calls you. It's comforting to me. Guess I'm being reminded of my own dear mother, wishing she were still alive and here with me. Somehow I need help to get through these days."

"Mama, I'm so sorry. I never meant to add to your sorrow and pain."

"Why should you be sorry, Aggie?"

"Because if I hadn't fallen in love with Joab, it may never have happened."

"You must not talk like that, child. Do you not know that God made us women to love with all our hearts, and nobody has the right to tell us who we can and cannot fall in love with? It's something that can't be helped. And it's not wrong."

"Mama, I dearly love you and I agree with what you are saying. But how can I get past this, and how can I take some of this burden from you?"

"I have no university education, Aggie, but—"

"You are wise beyond mention, Mama, even more so than a university degree could offer."

"Then let me explain it to you this way. Your papa died in the war. Nobody made him go. In fact, he was to the age where he could have stayed home and nobody would have called him a coward for doing so. But now he's gone, cruelly shot up and mangled at the hands of the enemy. Am I supposed to chastise myself because I didn't do anything to stop him?"

"Why, no, Mama. Of course not. You couldn't have anyway. Papa was determined to fight for Mississippi, for States' Rights. You know that. It was his duty, and he was duty bound. Remember he always said that?"

"Then was it your fault that Will joined the Army, that he fought for our country and was severely wounded at Shiloh?"

"No ma'am, he made his own decision."

"So am I to understand that Will had a choice? Why, he could have chosen to fight for the North. It would still have been his choice."

"Yes ma'am, because he joined up. He didn't wait to be conscripted. And no, he would have never fought for the North."

"What kind of young man would have stayed home when the rest were going to war?"

"A coward."

"Will was no coward, but when he came home, he was a bitter man. That, too, was a choice he made. He was just one among thousands who joined up for *The Cause*. It was a privilege to fight for the Confederacy. But Will made the decision to let the war and what it did to him and thousands of our men take over and conquer his mind."

"But Mama, the war was so cruel. That day we went to Shiloh, you should have seen Will describing it. Why, he was beside himself, flailing his arms and crying. I could almost see our men bleeding and screaming and dying. He was reliving it and instead of letting the return speak peace to him, it riled him. But, you know, Mama, I thought after a while when he settled down and maybe thought about it he seemed to get a better attitude. He even peeled me a peach from Widow Bell's orchard. Joab went up to see her and talked and then he pulled peaches for us."

"If only—but it's too late for that," said Caroline. "Will had a choice. He chose bitterness over peace, and it literally drove him to take his life. It boils down to one guilty person. Not you, not Daniel, and not Joab. It was a matter of choosing."

"Yes ma'am."

"When you went to Shiloh, what happened to you?"

"I felt peace, indescribable peace and tranquility. It was amazing, Mama."

"And what about Joab?"

"Why, that's why we went. He had the same inner peace, which he had already gotten. That's why he so wanted us to go."

"Joab tried. You tried. Daniel tried to rescue Will. He refused it all."

"Aggie, if you require further vindication or absolution, or even wisdom, you must simply pray and ask for it. The burden is not yours to carry. You bore Will's burden for several years. Now, you need to let go. You cannot outthink God. But neither can you outlove Him. Make it easy on yourself, child."

"Yes, Mama. Yes."

Caroline dried her hands and hugged her daughter. Aggie laid her head on her mother's shoulder and cried.

"Mama, I miss Joab so much. I allow my love for him is making me lonesome and sick. I have so many emotions vying for my attention I hardly know which way to turn. If I could just have his arms around me I would be better. I just know it. I won't be seeing him for another week. He wanted to give me time to mourn over Will. And believe me, Mama, I have mourned his death. A big part of my life is over, and while I have not been in love with him for a long time—in fact, maybe never, for I never knew real love before Joab—I still cannot just drop my thoughts of Will. I keep seeing images of him at Shiloh, hoping, praying that he was somehow able to get that inner peace.

"Mama, can a man experience inner peace without showing it outwardly?"

"I don't know the answer to that, Aggie. I think we can try and leave it with this—war wreaks havoc with the mind. The Bible says 'as a man thinketh in his heart, so is he'. That leads me to believe that the heart and mind are connected. We think with our minds and our hearts reflect who we really are. I'm going with the heart, which is what

God looks upon. The Will we knew was a godly man, and God saw his heart."

"Yes ma'am. I think we must leave it right there, too. 'Man looks on the outward appearance. God looks on the heart'. That comforts me, Mama."

CHAPTER 18

MOMENTS LIKE THESE

*When the dearest on earth are gone from you,
nothing else matters in moments like these.
Nothing else but the touch of the hand of a good friend.*

Joab would turn his energy entirely toward Oxford for the weeks before leaving for Sarepta. While he longed for home and Thanksgiving with Rachel and Sam, his heart ached for Aggie, and he couldn't help wondering what she was feeling since the days following Will's death. Joab feared he had been hasty in his decision to let time pass before he once again stepped inside The Thompson House. He wondered why life was turning out so complicated for both of them.

A lot was taking place in the South and Joab was only getting bits of local information. L.Q.C. Lamar, a man of integrity, citizen hero, beloved by the state of Mississippi and the city of Oxford, had hammered out the official Ordinance of Secession for Mississippi in 1861 and then fought as a lieutenant colonel in the Mississippi 19th. When Mississippi seceded from the Union and joined the Confederacy on January 9, 1861, Lamar said, "Thank God, we have a country at last: to live for, to pray for, and if need be, to die for." In 1862, President Davis commissioned Lamar to go to the Court of the Czar in Russia but he never made it there. He only made it to London and Paris, and despite his southern charm and skillfully chosen words, he failed in his commission of getting the European powers to acknowledge the Confederate States of America as a sovereign country because of slavery. Like every other southerner, he suffered loss during the war. Both of his brothers were killed in battle. He believed, along with General Lee, that

Confederates who had served in top positions during the war should remain on the sidelines, at least temporarily, during Reconstruction. It grieved Lamar, however, to watch as Mississippi endured carpetbag rule and military occupation. But since February 23, 1870, Mississippi had been accepted back into the Union with a newly ratified Constitution and at least ten percent of its people had re-pledged allegiance to the Union.

Joab, certain L.Q.C. Lamar had frequented the tea room at the hotel, wished he had been privileged to sit next to him during those weeks, months and years. What an honor that would have been! Just to watch as southern patriots poured over the laws regulating secession. And now some of those same patriots had drafted a new Constitution, and Lamar had spent endless hours crafting proper words that would deal with the healing of the South in a far better way than the Carpetbaggers and Scalawags had done. It would not take a Union politician to accomplish that. Lamar was a southerner who took his charge seriously. He had always done a splendid job. Joab was glad to be temporarily living in Oxford, the seat of teaching and learning and the home of L.Q.C. Lamar, who himself was a professor at The University of Mississippi.

Ivy clung tight to the trunks of the hardwoods as late fall rustled and scattered the last of the leaves, the limbs naked now as winter was coming on. If not for the green of the ivy and the evergreens and the red berries on the Ilex that glistened in the dew and fog that hovered early of a morning then burned off by midday, the landscape would be drab and distressing.

Joab was up early, taking on his responsibilities with Hiram and Mattie Raines. He trekked to the barn and milked the cow out of habit, scarcely remembering he had done so. His thoughts were someplace else. Quite frankly, he was afraid—afraid of what he would learn when it came time to see Aggie. Afraid that she had already dismissed him, perhaps believing that Joab had come into her life to stir the most unpleasant of memories and that she would have to say goodbye as a way of least resistance to unbearable heartache. He loathed those feelings, longed for the sensations of loving her, the emotions that were stirred when he thought of life with her by his side. He dared not let his dreams take him to that place, not yet. Not again.

Joab reached in the old hen's nest. She pecked him hard on his hand drawing a steady stream of red blood from the vein she had targeted. He mindlessly filled the basket with eggs, using his other hand, stepped outside the henhouse and reached for the pump handle. Water gushed and he held his hand under the icy cold flow until the bleeding stopped long enough for him to wrap his bandana around the wound the hen had left.

He shelled corn and threw out kernels to the chickens that gathered at his feet. Funny, he thought, they bite the hand that feeds them. These pesky chickens are like the North. The South was the country's breadbasket before the war. The North apparently loathed the fact the South had anything to offer. They certainly bit hard.

"Good morning, Miss Mattie."

"Good morning to you, Joab. Oh, did that dratted old hen get you again?"

Joab laughed. "Yes'm. I don't think she likes me. It's okay. I washed it good at the pump."

"Well, here, let's get a clean rag on that until it stops bleeding." She wrapped Joab's hand and said, "You sit down at the table. I've got hot biscuits. That should help."

"Yes ma'am, better than anything." Joab poured a stream of sorghum onto his plate and dipped his biscuit. "Where's Hiram?" he asked.

"He was not feeling well when he came in this morning. In fact, I'm a little worried about him, Joab."

"What seems to be wrong, Miss Mattie?"

"He won't complain and he won't say, but I can tell."

"Would it be all right if I check in on him after breakfast, or is he already asleep?"

"You go right ahead. He might be asleep by now, but maybe not."

Joab washed his hands at the pump on the sink, dried with a clean flour sack and headed down the hall to see Hiram. He was lying still with his eyes open, looking at the pictures on the wall. Trey and Hiram, Jr. They each had ambrotype photographs taken during the war. Hiram treasured them far more than silver or gold.

"They were handsome men, Hiram."

"Joab! I'm glad you're here. Sit beside me."

"Yes sir."

"I was just thinking about them."

"The most pleasant of thoughts, I'm sure."

"Indeed."

"Two great men who fought for our *Cause*. I will always be grateful you allowed me to read their letters. I've never been more richly blessed. The thought of Trey fighting side by side with Stonewall Jackson fills me up. But, Hiram, I am even more blessed to be personal friends with your sons' father. And I must say, you have been a wonderful father image since my own pa is no longer here. I don't take that for granted. It's high time I told you."

Tears rolled down Hiram's cheeks. "I can't even say what I'm a-thinkin' right now, Joab. I miss them both every minute of every day, and you have been the redeemin' grace in all of this. Thank you for bein' here with us at such a time as this."

"Yes sir, Hiram. The pleasure has been mine. Now, I'm going to let you be so you can get some sleep."

When Hiram had closed his tired eyes and drifted off, Joab slipped out and back down the dimly lit hall.

"I think he's okay, Miss Mattie. He's just missing those boys."

Mattie burst into tears and Joab put both arms around her, consoling her as best he could.

This is why, he thought—I know this is why I'm here. Not just scraping rotted debris off the square in the beautiful old city of Oxford, Mississippi, where the Yankees set fire and tried to burn their way across our country. I'm here for Hiram and Miss Mattie. When the dearest on earth are gone from you and the times are so trying one can scarcely sleep an entire night through, nothing else matters in moments like these. Nothing else but the touch of the hand of a good friend.

CHAPTER 19

IN THE MIDDLE OF IT ALL

*Just when Joab thought that Shiloh
held the Balm in Gilead,
he found the bitter gall of the tomb,
the burial grounds of those who gave a full measure.*

Joab glanced up the street toward The Thompson House. Soon. He would be seeing Aggie soon. He was dirty from work on the square. Some of the men had already begun to dig the footers and lay their cornerstones. Time would pass slowly for them before they could get the funds to rebuild and open their places of business, but they would do it. They were regaining momentum and better than that—courage. It would likely be another two years coming. His secret goal concerning the square was to get Mr. Isaiah Fleming's store rebuilt.

Joab mounted Star and headed for home. He took the shortcut, crossing the creek bottom in less than a foot of water and rode hard for the Raines' home. He was tired; it had been a long day, as usual. He got an early start loading scrap iron onto wagons for the men on the square before heading off to the mill where he pulled the saw and sanded wood planks for five hours. He stopped off at Yellow Leaf Gristmill and purchased a bag of flour and one of meal for Miss Mattie. He would surprise her.

It was nearing seven o'clock, already dark, and the wind blew cold out of the north. He would remember to layer on some more clothing and wear a scarf for the rest of the week, and the same would be required on his journey home not too many days from now. Home. He could hardly wait.

He rode Star to the barn, unsaddled her and slogged to the house.

"Sorry I'm so late, Miss Mattie." Joab handed her the two bags.

She hugged him, expressing thanks for the lovely staples.

"I guess Hiram has already left for work."

"Why, no, Joab. Fuller is going to pull his shift tonight. Hiram is not feeling well."

"Oh, no, not again!"

"I'm getting worried about him. I think I should fetch Doc Nelson soon. What do you think, Joab?"

"By all means, Miss Mattie. Do you want me to go now?"

"Do you mind, son?"

"No ma'am."

"Well, wait until you've eaten supper. I have it ready for you."

"No ma'am. I'm going now."

Joab grabbed his jacket and hat and rode past the ivy-clad South Street Presbyterian Church to Doc Nelson's office and home.

"Yes sir, Doc, Miss Mattie thinks you should come. I know it's late, but she wouldn't ask if she didn't think it was necessary. Do you want me to saddle your horse?"

"Yes, son, that would be splendid. I'll just get my coat and bag, let my wife know, and I'll meet you at the back door."

They rode together to Hiram's house. Mattie ushered Doc Nelson to Hiram's room while Joab led both horses to the barn and tethered them to the fence post, leaving them saddled for the time being.

"What seems to be the problem, Mattie?"

"He's so lethargic, Doc," she said softly. "It's not like Hiram."

"That's the truth," he said.

Mattie opened the door and lit the lantern for the old doctor. She held it on Hiram's face.

"Well, well," Doc Nelson said. "What's your big problem, old friend?"

"What in the world are you a-doin' here, Doc? I didn't send for you."

Doc laughed. "I know that. If it were left up to you, why I might never see you, my friend. So I have my spies a-workin' for me. Now, tell me where it is you're a-hurtin'."

"No where. Oh, I have the normal cain't-hep-its. But other than that, nothin'. Absolutely nothin'."

"Then why are you at home a-makin' Fuller do your job?"

"You got me there, Doc." Tears rolled down Hiram's cheeks.

"Well, you just take it easy and don't do anything you don't want to do. You've earned some good down time, Hiram."

Doc Nelson patted Hiram's hands and left the room, made his way to the kitchen where Joab was sitting at the table and Miss Mattie was serving him hot ham biscuits and beans.

"Sit down, Doc, and I'll bring you a plate."

"I've already had my supper, Mattie, but I'll never turn down one of your ham biscuits for dessert. You got any honey?"

"You know I do, Doc. Now, please tell me what's wrong with my Hiram."

"Nothing physical, Mattie. But emotionally he is drained. I know he's still grieving over Trey and Hiram, Jr. And I allow Will Cavanaugh's death likely brought on this added bout of depression."

Mattie wiped tears with her handkerchief.

"Now, Mattie, I know you're trying to be strong for Hiram. I don't want to know that you have come down with the same depression. You don't have to hold back tears. Sometimes that's the best cure for these hard times since the war. God help us!"

"What can we do about Hiram, Doc?"

"There ain't a thing except try to keep his mind off the boys as much as you can, and I know that's nearly impossible to do, and you don't ever want to forget or let go, but let's make it a little easier on him if we can." Doc Nelson spoke softly and deliberately. "Can you think of any other reason he might be down in the dumps, Mattie?"

"Well, yes. Maybe that Joab will be leaving soon. But Hiram knows he'll be back. Joab has filled the vacant space in our hearts for several months now, and maybe Hiram is having thoughts that there will soon be another permanent good-bye. I don't know."

Joab sat quietly taking it all in. What was he to do? Could he be all things to all people? He knew that was not possible, but he was feeling the tightening of the vice. He couldn't stand to see Hiram in this frame of mind. If he weren't so homesick for Rachel and Sam, he wouldn't even consider leaving right now. Oxford needed him. He had two jobs. There was his beloved Aggie, who he kept thinking was getting pushed to the back, though not at his choosing. In fact, in the midst of all this turmoil, he could scarcely wait to stand in her presence, to look into her beautiful blue eyes and to hold the woman he loved. And now Hiram needed him more than ever.

Joab took Doc to his horse and rode with him back to his house on South Street.

"Goodnight, Doc. I'll take your horse on down to the barn and unsaddle her. You go on in to Mrs. Doc. Don't worry. I'll let you know about Hiram if anything changes. I worry about leaving in a few days, but I must go home to my family. They need me, too."

"I understand that, son. Truth be known about Hiram, I think his biggest problem is that you're leaving. He's come to lean on you, especially for comfort in the loss of his boys."

"Yes sir, and I've grown to look to him in place of my pa. Every father needs a son, every son, a father. He's been that to me."

"Goodnight, son."

Joab ambled Star down the dark street, pulling his jacket close for warmth. It was quiet in Oxford except for the wind that whistled and blew hard through the limbs of the oak trees. He turned his horse toward The University and slumped in the saddle as Star clopped along on the hard packed dirt street. The lamps were turned up to a high flame, standing vigil over the few students that were still out and making their way to the dormitories. He rode up on the hill, the little cemetery for Confederate soldiers killed at Shiloh and Corinth, where Will Cavanaugh was buried. Just when Joab thought that Shiloh held the Balm in Gilead, he found the bitter gall of the tomb, the burial grounds of those who gave a full measure—then and now.

He remembered the day he walked the wood planked bridge over the Tishomingo Stream at Brice's Crossroads, the ride up the ridge to Shiloh hill. And now he was in Oxford where "Whiskey Joe" Smith under the Union flag had tried to melt the city down. Joab thought Shiloh was his place of peace until he realized there would be no peace until yet a stronger measure of inner healing could take place.

And Joab scarcely had time to mourn the death of Robert E. Lee, his father's commanding officer. T.G., Jonathan, and Albert Henry loved Lee with a passion. Joab read in the Oxford paper that *The General* suffered a stroke on September 28, and died of pneumonia just a couple of weeks later in Lexington, Virginia. On October 12, to be precise. That was just a few days ago. Someone said his last words were "Strike the tent!" speaking to A.P. Hill, another hero who died at Petersburg in '65. Come up and take the tent down, move on—Lee was moving on to better things. And what could be better for a man of faith than Heaven. "Strike the tent, indeed!" thought Joab. Rachel would be grieving along with Jonathan and Isaac. Even young Samuel would be touched by the loss of this great Confederate general.

In the middle of it all, Joab wondered how on earth a southern boy could forget. How could one forgive when it just kept coming?

CHAPTER 20

JOY AND GRIEF

*The truest end of life
is to know the life that never ends.*

William Penn

Joab lamented the final loss of the Confederacy. For Mississippi it was February 23, 1870 of this very year, the day the State returned to the Union, a lack-luster occasion, certainly no reason to celebrate. It did mean the end of a significant era for the South. It had happened and Joab was trying to make the best of it. He and Rachel had hashed it out that day on the front porch. They had ranted about Sherman and his total disregard for human life in the South; those words—Sherman's words—would always sting.

Mississippi's patriots had presented the new State Constitution and it was accepted. However, loyalty to the South—to its heritage, its fallen men and boys—would never, never diminish, and as a matter of fact, Joab was still not completely satisfied with his knowledge of what took place for his own father and brother.

On a better thought, Joab had grown to love The Thompson House. It was the present cornerstone of Courthouse Square at Oxford, the symbol of good things to come. The once vibrant Square laid waste during the war was now thriving and active again with men removing the remains of stagnate, mildew-infested, burned-out buildings that had long since crumbled to dust. Soon, the new buildings would blend with The University and, once again, the city would be proud.

Those who worked tirelessly took the first part of every morning at The Thompson House. The owners had pledged to prepare breakfast free on Wednesday of each week, a sort of incentive for the workers to keep up the pace.

On Wednesday morning just a week before Joab would travel home to Sarepta, he took a seat beside the workers, the first time he had been inside The Thompson House in two weeks. He gripped his legs under the table to keep from shaking. He was about to see his beloved Aggie. He glanced about noticing all the men were staring at him. He wondered what they knew that he did not, but he was in no condition to ask.

He nervously cleared his throat and waited for Miranda, who would soon be serving coffee. Her laughter was now her trademark, and she appeared on the dining hall floor dressed in "chef's white" moving from table to table spreading love and cheer. She was getting closer to where Joab was sitting, but there was no sign of Aggie. God Almighty! He missed her. Longed for her. What was happening between them?

"Mawnin', Mas Joab."

"Good morning, Miranda. How's my favorite lady?"

"Oh, Mas Joab, you knows I ain't yo' fav'rite lady. Yo' fav'rite lady be Miss Sarah Agnes."

"What makes you say that, Miranda?"

"You knows. You knows. Sho as de sun shinin' over Mississippi, you knows."

"Hope so, Miranda."

"Well, jes look a-there, Mas Joab. See fo yo'self." She pointed toward the kitchen.

Joab looked up and swishing through the double swinging doors to the dining hall from the kitchen was such beauty as he had not seen in what felt like months.

"Aggie!" he whispered. Joab couldn't help himself. He pushed back his chair and stepped out into the space between the tables and where she stood. When she saw him, Aggie set her tray, loaded with pastries and preserves, on the nearest empty table. Joab stopped, not knowing her thoughts or intentions about him.

She commenced to run across the dining hall floor, her arms outstretched. Nothing had changed; the look on her face and the tears streaming down her red cheeks, gave Joab to know that her heart was exactly where it was when he had last seen her and that every ounce of her pride was gone.

He stood there and as she got closer, he stretched out his arms and she rushed into them. He began kissing her lips. The longer they clung to each other, the louder the men yelled and clapped and whistled. And then Joab understood.

"Aggie, darling Aggie!" He could hardly speak, but there was no need. He put her down and looked around. The men were still standing, still applauding. Joab's obvious love for Aggie was common knowledge. But he had no way of knowing the whole town's passion for the two of them. It was obviously something they had discussed behind his back and they all seemed to be in one accord.

Joab's great southern grin spread across his sun-browned face. He had never been more proud. Finally, he knew that this very moment was worth all the events of a long hot summer and an exceedingly stressful autumn.

"Joab, I have missed you," Aggie whispered. "Time has made my love for you grow immeasurably. I don't ever intend to lose you, dear heart."

"Aggie, you are mine forever. Please don't doubt a word of that."

"Never, Joab. Never."

Aggie picked up her tray and began to serve the men. Joab returned to his seat and found it impossible not to watch every move she made.

"Mas Joab, I better get you some hot coffee. Yo's be done turned plumb cold by now."

"Thanks, Miranda! My best *colored* girl!"

Miranda threw her head back and laughed until every part of her large body moved in rhythm. She shuffled off to get Joab a fresh cup.

After breakfast, he stepped into the kitchen to speak with Aggie.

"You know I'll be leaving a week from today."

"Yes. How could I forget that?"

"I may be gone a couple of weeks. I need to help Mama and Sam. Mama has never been without one or two of us big boys to help keep things up. I don't know what to expect."

"I'll pray for you, Joab, every day, *upon every remembrance of you,* which will be every waking moment."

"I need to see you as often as possible before I go. How about if I ride out to your place on Saturday?"

"Oh, yes. Mama will be so happy to see you. She has been a little quiet for these weeks. Maybe you can bring her out of it, Joab."

"I'll do my best, Aggie. I have given a lot of thought to her especially these last few days. Hiram is not well. I fetched the doctor for him a few days ago. Doc Nelson says he's suffering from depression. Hiram and Mattie both are depressed. I thought maybe we could get your mama and the Raines together for a bit of comforting company."

"I think that's a splendid idea. And, Joab, plan to stay the night with us Saturday. You can go to meeting with us Sunday. I know Mama and Daniel will love your company, and . . . and Joab . . . I am breathless thinking that we could have more than a few minutes together."

"So'm I. I will stay over. You make sure it's okay with Miss Caroline. In the meantime I need to see you. I want you to do something with me."

"Of course, Joab. Just come and get me."

Joab looked around. There was no one. He pulled her close and kissed her, lingering, not wanting to leave her. When he knew she was breathless, he let go and slipped out. He heard her sigh as he left, but he never turned around.

"He is mysteriously wonderful," Aggie said aloud then returned to her work.

At the snuffing of the lanterns, Joab left the sawmill and once again crossed the shallow end of Yellow Leaf Creek and headed for town. He was light as a feather in the saddle, remembering every event of the morning, having relived it as he pulled the saw and sanded planks for the balance of the day.

The lamps were high all over the house, but it was early yet. He rode Star to the barn and spent a little time with her, something he had not done lately. When he had brushed her dry, he fed her and trekked to the house. As he took the first step, Mattie flung the door open and wailed in such a fashion that it startled Joab.

"Miss Mattie! Miss Mattie! What's wrong?"

"It's Hiram! Come quickly! Please hurry, Joab."

Joab ran, jumping the steps to the porch and grabbed the screen door, this time letting it slam behind him. He took huge strides down the wide hallway to the last room on the right. Hiram lay clutching his heart.

"Hiram! Hiram!" he shouted.

"Joab. Is . . . is that . . . you, son?"

"Yes sir, Hiram. What's wrong, sir?"

"Nothing is wrong, son. Everything is right, just right. I'm going home."

Mattie was sobbing. Joab pulled her in beside him and they both hovered over Hiram. There was no reason for this conversation. Not to her way of thinking. There was no reason for Hiram to be *going home*. This was a strong man, one who had endured, a man who had excelled in living life to its fullest. He was a friend to the whole town of Oxford. He had given two sons to the Confederacy . . . given two sons to the . . . Yes, he had given two sons to the Confederacy and now he lay dying and there was nothing Joab or Mattie could do. The cruel war was taking again.

"Hiram, don't talk like that. You're going to be fine," said Joab clinging to them both, tears streaming down his face.

"Yes, fine. I'm . . . I'm going to be fine," he gasped, his breathing getting more shallow with each spoken word. "Mattie, I think I've left a-plenty for you to make it . . . they's money here in my mattress . . . money you don't know 'bout." Hiram patted the side of his bed. He struggled to breathe but wanted to finish speaking.

"The house and barn are paid off," he whispered. "Don't be a-stewin' over anything. You know where I'll be after I close my eyes . . . for the last time. So don't worry. Sorry I'll get to see Trey and Hiram, Jr. before you . . . but I'll talk to them about you. They'll know . . . they'll know how much . . . Mattie . . . goodbye Mattie . . . and Joab . . ."

Joab squeezed his dear old hand and pulled Mattie near. She sat on the side of the bed and draped herself across her husband's body for the last time *on this side of the River*, as Stonewall would have said. She cried out, "Oh, Hiram! How I will miss you! I didn't want you to leave. Ever!"

And she cried tears of agony and hurt. "Joab, what am I going to do?"

"Miss Mattie, I don't know, but the answer will come. It always does. Trust . . . trust in the Lord. He will see us through this. My Pa used to read to us from Isaiah 61, and I've never forgotten the depth of comfort in those words. It goes something like this, and I can't remember all the words . . . 'The Spirit of the Lord God is upon me . . . to comfort all that mourn . . . to give unto them beauty for ashes, the oil of joy for mourning, the garment of praise for the spirit of heaviness, that they might be called trees of righteousness, the planting of the Lord, that he might be glorified.' Miss Mattie, does that give you any comfort in this moment? Any at all?"

"Oh, yes, Joab. Yes, indeed. I needed to be reminded of that. Life has just dealt me the harshest blow. My husband is gone from me. I will see him no more until the Resurrection. But when I think about that, I have to rejoice and know that I have not two but three waiting for me. My three men."

Miss Mattie commenced to crying and shouting. Shouting for joy and crying out of grief. *The greatest paradox of all time. Joy and Grief. Beauty and Ashes. Praise and Heaviness.* All coming from the same lips, orchestrated by the Spirit of the Lord God.

Chapter 21

Best Place on Earth

*He struck his mare for a gallop
to the house in the valley.
The old place looked lonesome and rundown,
almost as if no one lived there.*

Joab topped the ridge and pulled Star to a stop on the crest of the familiar hill, thinking about the last few days in Oxford, some of the toughest of his entire life. So much loss, so much heartache. He took a moment to thank the Lord for the time he had with Hiram Raines. What a gentleman, husband, father. A patriot, a great southerner. And the bond had far exceeded friendship. Hiram had become father-like, filling the shoes of Joab's own war-hero father. He relived Hiram's funeral service at the church, his heart pounding with thoughts of this man who had come to mean so much to him.

Joab could see the lamplight in the kitchen. He was home, home where life, he hoped, would take on a semblance of sanity. Back to the real place of peace, memories of his childhood rushing him by surprise. He had not told Rachel exactly when he would return. But she knew it would be before Thanksgiving. He was certain Jonathan had taken care of the turkey and that Isaac and Jennie would help with the vegetables and Rachel . . . well Rachel would have everything under control.

He had left Aggie behind, a hard thing . . . possibly the hardest thing he had done, that is, since the war and all the death in his own family. Life, fragile at its best, had dealt Joab a few losses. He hoped Aggie would not be included. He could not bear to lose her, to death or for any other reason. He had experienced a fair measure of the brittle thread over the past few months. He thought—life is as fragile as Aggie. But she is beautiful, delicate, like a piece of lace or a crystal prism through which I see life as carefree and lighthearted. I want her in my arms in this moment.

He struck his mare for a gallop to the house in the valley. The old place looked lonesome and rundown, almost as if no one lived there. It was late fall, though, and all the leaves were on the ground. The trees were stark and bare. The flowers were gone. Maybe that was the reason it looked . . . desolate. He choked back his emotions, hoping to greet his mother and Samuel with smiles instead of tears when Samuel cleared the porch steps and ran up the dirt road toward his brother. Joab dismounted and held his arms open. Samuel leaped into them.

"Whoa, little brother, you have grown a foot since I left."

Sam grinned but couldn't say a word. His blue eyes glistened as he swallowed hard and fought tears. He cleared his throat and said, "We didn't know when you were coming back, but Mama has been planning every day, knowing she would soon get it right."

"I've been counting the days, myself, Sam. I've missed you and Mama, wishing every day you could have been with me. It will take a while, but I'll tell you all about it."

Joab would tell only the lovely parts, leaving out the darkness and death. Samuel and his mother had experienced enough of that, as had he. Rachel could take it; however, Sam was too young. He would not lay that upon him.

Joab looked up toward the house and there stood Rachel on the porch, smiling. She was beautiful as ever, her long dark curly hair with very few strands of gray touching her shoulders, pulled back by her ribbon of red. She looked thinner, so much thinner. He mounted, gave Samuel a hand, pulled him up onto Star, and rode to the porch. He jumped off and gathered Rachel into his arms and swung her around as he had done for as long as he could remember then put her down. She held his face and then buried her own into his chest.

"Thank God, you're home. It hasn't been the same without you, has it Sam?"

"No ma'am."

"Come inside. I must have known it would be today. I have a cake warm from the stove."

"Confirming your omniscience, Mama!"

Rachel had to laugh. "And don't forget Thanksgiving! We have so much to talk about."

"But first, I have presents," said Joab, "then we'll eat cake. And how about some coffee, too?"

"I'll put it on and be right out."

"Sam and I will be in your room, Mama."

Joab crossed the threshold of his mother's bedroom with the keeping room to the side. It was just the same, the same room where each of her five boys and her grandson, Lee, were born.

Joab ran to his horse and took the package that was tied down with his blanket. Rachel put the coffee on and hurried into her room with the boys.

"Joab, you shouldn't have spent your hard-earned dollars. Besides you were not even getting paid except from the mill, and you sent money home to us. We received thirty dollars in three separate letters. Is that correct? We're still not able to count on the mail. And that was a lot of money, much more than I ever dreamed you would be able to send."

"I'm glad to know you got it. And don't worry about that job at the mill. As long as I'm in Lafayette County, I can count on it," said Joab. "Now for the package. I had to roll it. I hope it's not too crumpled."

He untied the string, unrolled the package perfectly wrapped in brown paper, and first handed Samuel a pair of khaki riding pants and a long-sleeved blue cotton shirt just like the ones he had purchased for himself.

Samuel drew in a deep breath. "I've never had store-bought clothes except for overalls. These are splendid. Thank you, Joab. I'd like to try them on. Would that be all right?"

"Of course, little brother."

Samuel scurried to the bunk room. Joab handed Rachel her package. She unrolled the brown paper, unfolding a beautiful piece of indigo blue fabric unlike any she had ever seen.

"Like your eyes, Mama. I don't know too much about things like this, so I asked Aggie to help me. Just yesterday we went to the only merchandise store on the square. They have splendid things to choose from. Actually, Aggie picked it. She was glad to do so. Don't you think she made a good choice? Mama, I've told her all about you."

"Son, it's the most beautiful piece of cloth I've ever seen and so smooth. City material is a far cry from what we have here." Rachel pressed the fabric to her face and breathed deep. "I love the *new* smell Joab. I'll have to get a dress pattern. And, yes, Aggie made a perfect choice."

"Keep looking."

Rachel carefully laid the fabric out on her bed, unfolding until she found the pattern. "Oh, I love this," she gasped. "It's . . . it's so fashionable."

"Aggie knew just what to pick. And there's thread besides, in my saddlebags."

Rachel was good at holding her emotions at bay, but she couldn't help herself. She burst into tears. Joab took her into his arms and hugged her, smoothing her beautiful silky hair.

"All you need is a bonnet, Mama. Hope there's enough material for that."

"I'll make sure of it, Joab. Thank you, son. This is a really beautiful gift, but of course the greatest gift is that you're home. But for how long? We might as well get that out in the open."

"I'll be home for a week after Thanksgiving, Mama. That will give me over a week before I go back to Oxford. And I'll return to Sarepta for good before the end of December. I'll be home for Christmas, without fail. I remember how Pa always wanted us to 'make merry' at Christmastime, and I don't think you could do that without me."

"In no way could we do that without you, Joab."

"There's just one thing, Mama."

"Oh, break it gently, if you will."

"I'll try. I will be going to one more battlefield before I settle down. At least one more."

"Let me guess," she said.

"You wouldn't be able to—not in a million years. But go ahead and try."

"Gettysburg!" Rachel burst into more tears at the mention of the town.

"Mother, Isaac has always been right about you. Omniscient!"

They both laughed, Rachel with tears still streaming.

"There's yet another announcement, Mama."

"Oh, there's more?"

"I'm going to marry Sarah Agnes Stephens. I can't help myself. I'm so in love with her—I cannot tell you just how much I love that girl. She's more than I ever dreamed . . . well . . . I never even thought about having someone like her."

"Son, your first trip to Oxford was a continuation of the war's nightmare, but out of heartache and hurt came something wonderful. Real love. It's kind of like childbirth in a manner of speaking. The pain is unbearable and then you lay eyes upon the beautiful rendering and you know—"

"More magic?" said Joab.

"More magic," she said.

"Mama, I want to marry her at Christmas, although she knows nothing of this. She doesn't even know I want to marry her—at all. I haven't asked her. You must know, I'm scared."

"You needn't be, son, for she is likely waiting anxiously over there in Lafayette County."

"I guess you sheltered me well, even after Pa and the boys went off to Grenada to muster in. You hovered over Isaac and Sam and me. I will need your help to understand what on earth I'm supposed to do."

Rachel laughed and hugged her son again. "Oh, Joab, the directions come with the proposal. It's a packaged deal, but you know I will be right there and so will your older brothers who have their own experiences now. They may have a few tips for you. I'm better with the woman-type things."

"Now, Mother, I have to tell you something sad and I don't want Sam to hear this. He's awfully young to take on so much sorrow."

Rachel's countenance fell. Would it always be this way? Something good and wonderful; something sad and disheartening?

"Tell me, son."

"Hiram Raines . . . Hiram died just a few days ago. Mother, he died of a broken heart. There's no two ways about it. I've been around a lot of heartache and pain in the last few years since Pa and Henry died, but I've never seen anything like this. He took sick about three weeks ago, just gave in to the hurt of losing his sons in the war and then like I told you, Will Cavanaugh's death, and he just succumbed to grief."

"Oh, Joab! I'm so sorry to hear that. Were you with him when he died?"

"Yes ma'am. With him and Miss Mattie, of course. It was awful. I didn't know what to do, really. I just quoted some Scripture Pa used to read to us from Isaiah, and assured Miss Mattie that God would ease the pain for her and that she needn't worry over Hiram, because he would already be happy seeing the boys again and being with the Lord. I didn't know what else to do."

"You did it exactly right, son. And I'm so proud of you for taking on just like you were one of his boys. Miss Mattie must have appreciated that."

"Mother, she was amazing. She cried one minute and shouted the next. It reminded me of when you got word about Pa and Henry. So you know how she felt in that moment."

"Yes, son. I know exactly how she felt."

Darkness gathered about the cabin in the valley as the day came to an end. Joab took a stick of kindling and lit it in the slow burning fire in the fireplace. He rolled the wicks up on the lamps and said, "Samuel, looks like you've been doing your job well, as I knew you would. All the wicks are trimmed."

Sam grinned and said, "Yeah, that's my job now, Joab. Mama says I do right well with it."

Rachel had hung the coffee pot low over the flame and it was bubbling. She brought out fresh cake slices and the butter dish.

"Here, boys, spread a little while the cake is still warm. This should be good, a buttermilk cake with figs and peaches and apples and nuts and some vanilla."

"I have been longing for this cake," said Joab.

The three of them relaxed by the warmth of the fire with cups of coffee with heavy cream and honey and the wonderful fruit cake made with ingredients from the cellar.

"Home!" said Joab. "The best place on earth, Mama."

"The best place on earth," said Rachel.

CHAPTER 22

THANKSGIVING ONCE AGAIN

*. . . as the last signs of a beautiful day faded
into a glorious sunset of pinks and blues,
Joab slipped outside and walked up on the hill,
wishing for Aggie.*

He and Samuel slept in the bunk room and talked half the night; Joab was amazed at how much Sam had matured in just a few months. With the crowing of the first rooster, they both jumped out of their bunks and dressed. They had work to do. Rachel, already up and stoking a fire in the oven, greeted her boys with fresh hot coffee.

"Mama, I'm so glad to be home where the coffee tastes better than anyplace else. And do I smell some bacon frying?"

"You do, indeed."

"Sam, let's get that fire going in the other room, and after we eat, I'll help you milk old Kit."

"Aw, Joab, I can milk her now—by myself."

"What?"

"You don't believe me, do you?"

"Well . . ."

"It took a while, but Mama had patience to wait it out. Now, I'm good as you."

Joab laughed. "All right, then. I'll start the fire and you do the milking after breakfast and I'll help Mama. We can get twice as much done."

They sat down to bacon, eggs and biscuits. Joab bowed and thanked the Lord for blessings he was enjoying in these moments.

"We've got to move quickly after breakfast, boys. Our house will be full of people in no time, and we want to be ready."

"What do we need to do first, Mama?"

"Well, Sam and I cut the decorations late yesterday before you got here. They're on the back porch in a tub of water. I wanted them to be fresh and green. And you know what to do—just like always. The mantle, the dinner table and sideboard and any place else you want to decorate. There are also some pumpkins and gourds on the porch. I've got plenty of candles, and I think some of those holly berries might be nice for some added color."

By ten o'clock all the chores were done, the house was decorated and Rachel's pan of cinnamon and cloves bubbled on the stove. The smell of Thanksgiving permeated the Payne home and, once again, they were ready to receive the guests—both family and friends.

Joab was beside himself with joy. It had been months since they had all been together.

At eleven o'clock, Sam saw Jonathan's rig on the hill. He shouted for Joab and the two of them ran out to meet Jonathan and Cassie and eight year old Lee.

"He looks exactly like Henry."

"I think so, too, Joab. Exactly, and he acts a lot like him, too. As best I can remember my brother." Tears welled up in his eyes at the thoughts.

"That's good. Keeping brother alive in our hearts, Sam."

Before the buckboard had stopped, Joab grabbed Lee as he jumped from the back.

"Hello, sweet boy!"

"Hello, Uncle Joab. Where you been so long?"

Joab choked back tears, memories of his brother, Albert Henry, overwhelming him.

"Uncle Joab, don't cry. It's just me. Robert E. Lee Payne!"

"I know it's you, Lee . . . it's . . . it's just that you grew up a foot while I was gone. I missed you little man."

"I missed you, too."

Jonathan reached for his younger brother and the two hugged.

"Mother's been keeping me up on you, Joab. I'm right proud of you. Very proud of you, in fact, for all the hard work in Oxford. And I want to hear all about your trip to Brice's Crossroads and Shiloh.

Maybe you and me and Isaac can all go back to Shiloh one of these days. We might even stir up the ghost of an old Yank or two. Oh, and by the way, what's this about a woman? Not sure if I'm supposed to say anything about that."

"There's one thing about it, Jonathan. I've tried to follow your instructions on how to love a woman and I allow I've been successful with that."

"I don't remember sharing my secrets with anybody," said Jonathan, grinning broadly.

"You didn't have to. Your feelings and love for Cassie were written all over your face. If a man was so a-mind to, he could have gathered that much. And I reckon I did."

"From what Mother's told me, you must have, Joab. May I be the first, then, to congratulate you, even if prematurely?"

"I'll gladly accept that."

By one o'clock that afternoon, the house was so full of people Joab could scarcely turn around. It reminded him of a smaller Thompson House when school was in session. He felt at home in more ways than one, but sad when he looked around and Aggie was not there. He began to move about the room greeting old friends and family and found himself looking forward to the end of the day when only his family would linger.

Isaac and Jennie arrived after Jonathan and his family. They had stopped by the mill and picked up Grandpa Church.

"Son, when air ye a-comin' back home? I need y' at the sawmill, even though Samuel is a-doin' a good job for me. He can handle a saw as good as any of y' and Jonathan, he brings him out every day."

"Grandpa, don't give up on me. I'll be home for good after Christmas, that is . . . well . . ."

"Well, what, son?"

"I wasn't going to tell you this because I don't want you worrying about it. But I might as well. You're going to find out about it anyway."

"Well, course I am. Now, what is it?"

"I have decided to go to Gettysburg soon after Christmas. I'll be gone just long enough to travel there and back and to do some searching while I'm there."

"Searchin' for what?"

"I want to try and find out what happened to Pa and Henry and to Uncle Marcellus. I guess what I'm saying is, I want to see that battleground for myself."

"Well, son, you know Marcellus was captured by the Union and taken to prison in Maryland. He died in that prison."

"I know, but if I can see something tangible that will help me understand more about what they went through, I would be satisfied, at least I think I would be."

Jennie arranged the homemade goods she had made on the sideboard and, clinging to Isaac, she took the little bell Rachel had left on the table especially for this occasion, for Rachel knew—

Jennie cleared her throat and spoke with all the fervor and diction of Sarepta's former school teacher, "I want all of you to know at the same time . . . Isaac and I have chosen this glorious Thanksgiving Day to announce that we are going to . . . we're going to have a baby. Yes—a baby! Isaac's House in Slate Springs will finally ring with the laughter of one of many. We hope!"

Applauding and shouts of good wishes broke out all over the house. For the first time since the war, actually since Pickett's Charge in 1863, Jonathan did the Rebel Yell, followed by Isaac and Duncan and Joab and Samuel and Robert E. Lee Payne. Isaac had made certain the younger boys all knew just how to do it. A brilliant show of love and happiness for Jennie and Isaac ended in pandemonium as family and friends celebrated the hopes and joys of a little one in the house once again.

Dr. Whitaker had been killed in the war and his son, Jeb, had taken on his practice. He dropped by for a cup of cider and some sweet potato pie. Then Dandy and Tibby, old Doc Malone's people came.

"Mas Joab, I ain't seen you in way too long," said Dandy. "Wheah you be stayin' now?"

Joab squeezed the old Negro's hand, remembering the last time he saw Dandy and Tibby. It was when Doc Malone died and he rode out to the old place with his brothers in Winfield Cooper's carriage to take Doc's body. It was Christmas Day evening. He would never forget how those two people moaned and cried, Tibby running up the hill screaming and Dandy running and crying behind her. Their beloved master was dead.

"Dandy, my friend! I still live here with my mother, but I've been over in Oxford helping clean up the mess from the war."

"Yas suh, Mas Joab. It sho be a mess aw'right."

"Are you and Tibby loving Doc Malone's old house, Dandy?"

"Yas suh. It sho be nice. Tibby 'n me, we never 'magined we could have anything that fancy. But we ain't changed ourselves, Mas Joab. We still be the same old black folk we wuz."

"Well, you two have always been a special part of our family, Dandy. You know that."

"Yas suh, Mas Joab. I knows dat. The wa' didn't change nothin' for us. We always had it jus' right. Most folks don' understand dat."

"No, they don't, Dandy. But we do, and that's what counts."

"Sho nuf, Mas Joab. We sho knows what count."

This is good, thought Joab. A lot of splendid memories, a lot of wonderful people. Preacher Banks, Jude and Fran Parker, Duncan Jamison and his family. And even Jonathan's old Army friend, Andrew McAllister was there.

Cal Worthington and Anna Jamison sat as close together as was permissible. They had pledged their love and would be marrying in the spring at the end of the school year. Their life was all planned, simple, unchallenged, straightforward. Together they were teachers at the Sarepta School. Jennie had groomed them both.

Joab thought, I admire them, but I don't think God has designed my life in that fashion. Thank you, Jesus! My life is complicated and intense. I like it that way, at the risk of bringing yet more of life's fury down upon me. Anything worth having is worth fighting for, worth travailing over. Maybe the war and the aftermath gave me those kinds of feelings.

Visions of Shiloh flashed before him, of Aggie, and Will the day the three of them sat on their saddle blankets talking about the evils of the battle. The blood, the screams, the death.

Joab deliberately willed himself back to the moment and shook hands with Winfield Cooper, once Scalawag, now devoted friend of the family. His presence in their home was as natural as any Payne's. Joab was smitten with Winfield's knowledge of the livery business and the purchase of fine rigs. He had a splendid life-story of redemption and restoration, had made good on all his promises to the Lord and his Calhoun friends and neighbors, though he had no family of his own. Everything he touched turned to success and he, of all men, knew where to extend thanks. God Almighty had blessed him abundantly. Not only that, his laughter filled a room and was like icing on the cake.

The women had this Thanksgiving party under control. Everything had calmed and friends were beginning to leave. Finally as the last signs of a beautiful day faded into a glorious sunset of pinks and blues, Joab slipped outside and walked up on the hill, wishing for Aggie, vowing that he would never spend another holiday without her, God helping him.

He tramped through mounds of acorns to the huge oak on the grandest spot on the ridge. Ben's grave. Joab thought about the day he and Isaac and Ben went to the woods to cut a Christmas tree. Samuel and Rachel stayed behind making cookies and cider. His father, Jonathan, and Albert Henry were at work at the mill. Joab would remember that day as long as he lived. It was all very innocent, their younger brother, Benjamin, wandering off toward the stream. Isaac was cutting down the chosen tree while Joab held it when they realized Benjamin was gone. The stream . . . he was in the stream. He had tired of waiting for the boys to find the perfect tree and decided to make his own entertainment. Isaac had rescued Ben, but he died of pneumonia just a few weeks later, the year the war broke out. The saddest day of their lives to that point.

And there had been so much loss since then, Joab having experienced the latest with Will Cavanaugh and Hiram Raines. He shivered, wishing to push back the thoughts for now.

He sat down under the tree and recalled cheerful moments with his little brother. He could see his face, hear the laughter as he threw his little head back riding the sled Isaac pulled to the woods for the tree hunt. Ben's laughter would ring in Joab's ears forever. He wanted it that way. He wanted the pleasant memories of that Christmas. He would leave it there, if possible.

> *Lord, protect and preserve the remnant of my family. Give Mama strength and courage to press on as her family dwindles at home and increases in Slate Springs. I long to give her even more family. Lord, please let it happen. Take care of Aggie. Give her inner peace as she waits. Save her only for me, I selfishly and unashamedly beg, through Christ my Lord, Amen.*

Joab trekked down the hill in no hurry to return to the cabin in the valley, bringing with him several large logs for the fire.

"Grandpa Church, I need to borrow my brothers a couple of days. Would that be all right with you?"

"Of course, son. I know what y' need to do. I say get busy and get this old house repaired. They's some stuff need'n to be fixed on the inside, too. May's well get that done while y' at it."

"Thanks, Grandpa! I knew you would see it that way."

"I'll furnish the wood, so y'll need to drive the buckboard on over to the mill and load it up. Get a-plenty now."

"Grandpa, you're amazing."

"Nah sir. *Grace* is amazing." He threw back his head and started singing 'Amazing Grace, how sweet the sound that saved a wretch like me' in old harp shaped note style. The whole Payne family joined in and sang it in parts like they used to do at meeting house. Tears ran down Grandpa's face. It was contagious.

Joab thought—this is an *amazing* day, a grand old time that I will never forget.

CHAPTER 23

WRAPPED IN WARMTH

I end not far from my going forth
By picking the faded blue
Of the last remaining aster flower
To carry again to you.

Robert Frost

Joab said sad good-byes to Rachel and Samuel, each promising to shed no tears. Besides, he would be back soon. They had every reason to live a more joyous and carefree life with every day counting for something good, something profitable. It didn't have to be in Union dollars. Those were few and far between. The attitude of the heart would bring an abundance of blessings. They could build on that.

"Mama, I'll be back, hopefully with Aggie as my wife, before Christmas. In time to decorate with Samuel. I'd like to have that attic room for a few weeks until . . . well, you know where I'll be going. We need to talk about that some more when the time comes."

"We will happily await the arrival of a new Payne, Joab. The room will be ready. I'll give thought to the Gettysburg journey, praying that God will lead you every step of the way if that's your calling. In the meantime, I'll make my new blue dress to wear at Christmas. And if Aggie wants to stay with us while you're away, that would be splendid."

"Thanks, Mama. I'll tell her what you said."

"And Joab—thank you again for all the hard work on the house. It looks so much better, and you and the boys did it so quickly."

"Frankly Mama, I couldn't have left here without getting that done. I know Jonathan and Isaac are busy, and I should have been here, but the way things have worked for me, it was not possible. Now the work's done and I will try to keep it up from now on. Maybe one day we can even paint the house. That is, if you want it painted."

"Right now, when I think about it, Joab, I want to keep it just like Thomas left it. He never planned to paint it, and I think it has weathered quite nicely. Do you?"

"Yes, Mama. It looks fine. We'll leave it just like Pa built it. I love you, Mama."

"I love *you* son."

Samuel stood by fighting tears, but he was a man. He hugged his brother and stepped back to put his arm around Rachel.

"Now, that's what I wanted to see," said Joab.

At four in the afternoon, Joab turned his horse north toward Oxford and rode in a steady pace. He would be there in two hours. His heart beat fast with thoughts of Aggie. He would go there first. Of course, he would. There would be no way he could wait another minute to see her. It was late in the day, Joab having planned it that way. He had spent most of the day with Rachel and Sam. And, he wanted to get to the Stephens' farm shortly after Aggie got home from The Thompson House.

His trip home had fulfilled all his longings to be there, that is, after he and his brothers had made all the repairs and the place no longer looked abandoned. He couldn't stand the thoughts of his mother having to cope with something she could not fix.

He breathed deep, filling his lungs with the fragrance of late fall. The dirt road was strewn with the crunchy brown leaves of the cottonwoods and the musty smell hung on the cold air that was by now far less humid. The last of the burnt orange and yellow leaves clung to the maple trees, and truck patches by the sides of the roads were still prolific with pumpkins and colorful gourds of all sizes and shapes. He loved fall, such a spectacular season in the deep South.

Aggie deserved a gift, but there was no place to make a purchase. He had intentionally spent his days at home, never once riding into

Sarepta. There was no need. On Thanksgiving Day, all his friends and family had come to Rachel's house. But he had commissioned the Jamison girls to make Aggie a quilt, a white one, trimmed with blue. He would give it to her after they married—if they married. He pulled Star to the side of the road and turned down a beaten path. Dismounting, he walked to the edge of the wood where he had seen blue wildflowers from the main road. He didn't know what they were, but they were beautiful. A gift for Aggie. The perfect gift, and they would be freshly picked. Blue flowers with a yellow center. Maybe they were Alpine Asters.

Joab was disconcerted. He had no idea what Aggie would say when he proposed marriage, especially since he wanted to marry her before Christmas—before he left Oxford for good. He aimed to take her with him. And after all was said and done, he would go back to work with Grandpa Church at the mill. He had visions of building his own house on the highest hill in Calhoun County. He knew where it was—on the outskirts of a little place called Reid. He would leave that thought and hope in the corners of his mind. Unlike Isaac when he built his house at Slate Springs, Joab would not be too full of pride to ask for help.

I love my brother, he thought, but what a rogue!

Joab veered toward Water Valley. He would be at the Stephens' house in just minutes. His heart beat wildly as he turned Star into the lot, dismounted and unsaddled her so she could feed on hay and drink from the trough.

Before he could make the short walk to the front gate, Aggie had sprung from the front porch steps and was jumping into his arms and he was kissing her face, her hair, holding her so tight she could scarcely breathe—with one hand, the other clutching the blue wildflowers. He released her and pushed her back then pulled her close again, kissing her lips. He felt her tears on his face, and in a speechless moment they stood in the cold November wind wrapped in the warmth of each other's arms. Joab was at peace. He had his answer.

When they could, they both spoke at once, laughed, and Joab said, "You first, Aggie."

"Now I don't know how to say how much I've missed you these days. Please, please don't ever leave me again. I don't think I could bear the thought of it." She took the flowers from Joab and tenderly held them in her hand.

"Aggie, do you really mean that—really?"

"Oh, yes, Joab. With all my heart I mean that. Please don't ever doubt it. I hope you had a splendid time with Rachel and your family, but I hope it is the last time—"

"What do you mean?"

"I hope it is the last time on this earth that you will spend time with your family—without me!"

"Well, I was going to wait until I mustered the nerve to be rejected, but I'm throwing all worry to the wind. Aggie, will you marry me, be my wife, love me for the rest of your life, and be a permanent part of the Payne family?"

"Joab, with no further thought or wonder about life and with no care what the future holds as long as we're together—yes! Yes, I will be your wife, take your Payne name as my name, love your family as my very own and . . ."

"Since we've just said our vows, now all we have to do is get over to Oxford and sign our papers."

Aggie laughed, her smile so warm that neither felt the cold wind that whipped about them.

"Aggie, I love you more than life."

"Joab, I love you twice as much."

"But I have a lot of things to tell you—to ask you, before you confirm that pledge you just made to me, and I think that is fair. If you have any misgivings or concerns, we can wait to get married until I have taken care of a few things. Or . . . or we can once again throw worry to the wind. But wait until I tell you everything. Can we go to the swing where this all got started? There's just something magical about that wonderful old swing."

"I love the porch," said Aggie. "My heart beats fast when I think of it, now. I need to put my flowers in water and tell Mama you're here. She'll bring us some hot cider, but I won't tell her about us until you have discussed your plans with me. That way, I'll know how to . . . well, I'll know what we're going to do. Oh, Joab, I'm beside myself with joy! Sit here."

Joab laughed, kissed her again, and waited on the swing for her to return. He looked around the old porch, loving everything about it. The chipped paint, the stone steps and banisters, the ivy that attached itself to the chimney on the far end, never changing through winter, spring, summer, fall. It was a beautiful old place. He was amazed that Daniel had kept it in such good repair with the few dollars available since the war.

"I told Mama we're on the porch, but I brought us some cider. She will see you when we go in."

Joab sipped the deliciously hot liquid, savoring the taste of cinnamon and cloves and apple and vinegar. He wondered if life could be better. Aggie, content to be sitting close beside him, said, "Tell me everything, Joab."

"I'll tell you some things and ask you some things," he said. "First, Mama loved the material you picked. And I told her all about you, how I'm in love with you; I even told her I was going to marry you before Christmas and bring you home with me at that time. So my first question is this—do you think your mother and Daniel will allow us to be married right away?"

"They both love you, Joab. I will give them the honor of saying, 'yes' but I know they will."

"Splendid! Next question—will you be willing to go with me to Calhoun County to possibly spend the rest of your life in near poverty?"

She laughed, knowing, hoping Joab was teasing.

"Of course. We will be happily poor. I would rather have you, Joab, than a bag full of Yankee dollars."

"Next—this is the tricky part and it is more complex. Do you want to stay with Rachel and Samuel while I travel to Pennsylvania? It could take me as long as a month to do what I need to do."

"That, dear heart, will take some thought. I need to talk to Mama and Daniel."

"I understand," he said.

"I don't want to just up and leave without giving them an opportunity to tell me what they think. The money I make at The Thompson House goes directly into that jar in the kitchen. It helps Mama buy the things she needs. I must give her and Daniel time to adjust or make other arrangements. I hope that doesn't delay our plans, but I wanted you to know. And, Joab . . . I don't have a dowry. We've been so poor since the war, and there has not been time enough to recover."

"That makes us on level ground, then," he said. "So, how about you stay with me at Rachel's until it comes time for me to leave. I'll bring you back to your Mama's and I'll head north. If they want to, Miss Caroline and Daniel can ride to Sarepta and take Christmas Eve and Day with us. Mama has plenty of room. Daniel can stay in the bunk room with Samuel. Miss Caroline can stay . . . she can stay in . . . in the attic room, which I've already asked for when we get married. Mama said, of course. She said we can stay there as long as we want to. I'll have to tell you the story of that marvelous marriage room some other time.

"On Christmas Eve, you and I can sleep on quilts beside the hearth. The boys and I have done that for years in the winter time. In fact, the last night we ever saw Pa and Henry alive, all of us boys slept on the floor in front of the fireplace. They left for the war the next morning. It was in January of 1862. So cold, in so many ways."

He was emotional, not only from thinking about T.G. and Henry, but thinking about sleeping on quilts in front of the fire with Aggie in his arms.

"Joab . . . Joab! Can life really be this splendid for us? Let's make it that way forever. All of this sounds like a story right out of my fiction books that I love so dearly. We can tell Mama this together . . . all of it. You've planned everything so splendidly. Mama will be as blessed by all of this, as much as I am. Oh, Joab, I'm so glad Mama loves you. You know, she even calls me *Aggie* now because you do."

"Does she really?"

"Yes."

"That's a good sign."

"Is there more, Joab?"

"I think I have listed everything in my thoughts. But, yes, there may be more that I'm too excited to remember at this moment. Except this—do you love children, Aggie? Do you want to have my children?"

"More than anything besides loving you, Joab. I will have your babies and love them to death."

The two sat on the swing sipping cider, shivering in the cold. The wind whistled through the spindly trees and rattled the old oaks. Music.

Winter music, thought Joab. The accompaniment to one of the best days of his life. He wished for many more.

<hr />

Joab left Aggie in the early evening, happy that he would see her the next day. It was dark already, a December moon shedding sufficient light on the trail. He turned his collar up and pulled his hat down for warmth and rode toward Oxford, turning his thoughts to Miss Mattie. Joab had left shortly after they buried Hiram. He was torn between leaving her and other things that he must take care of. More of that bitter sweetness of life. He knew Miss Mattie would need some attention and he would give as much as was humanly possible. He thought of Hiram and how seemingly easy it had been for him to slip from earth to heaven. You could never have told Joab that Hiram Raines would completely lose heart for living. Sorrow tends to trick the soul, he thought. Just when you think you have it under control—

"Joab, I'm so glad you're back, dear. I've missed you dreadfully, With Hiram gone and you away for a few days—well, it has been somewhat of a—"

Joab wrapped his arms around his friend and hugged her. "My mother sends her condolences. She wants you to know she understands your loss and prays God's comfort for you in these days. She invited you to her home any time you would like to come, and for as long as you would like to stay. Mama means that, Miss Mattie. I hope you know that. She appreciates you for all you've done and been to me in these days."

"Coming from her, a woman whose losses are equivalent to mine—I graciously receive and appreciate those thoughts and prayers."

"Let me make you some hot tea, Miss Mattie, and I'll have a cup myself."

"That would be splendid, Joab. I'm sure you have a lot to tell me. I can tell by the smile fixed on your handsome face something good has happened."

"You sound like Rachel, Miss Mattie."

"That's a compliment of the higher sort."

"Yes'm."

"The way I look at it, some good news would suffice right nicely."

"I just came from Aggie's house where I asked her to marry me—I asked her to marry me, Miss Mattie!"

"Well, I'm not the least bit surprised. What did she say?"

"Yes! She said *yes*!"

CHAPTER 24

SACRIFICES

*Joab's eyes filled with tears when he
recalled the story that day standing in the ashes
of Mr. Fleming's clothing store on the square.*

The darkest days in the history of the South had unfolded during the Civil War years. The accounts were endless. Jonathan and Isaac had told Joab many such stories out of their own experiences, another reason he was stirred to find out for himself what happened to his father and Henry. There was a sinister war connection for the people in Northeast Mississippi and his stay in Oxford had been sated with tales he was sure his own brothers had not heard and had nothing to do with his own father and Henry. Joab never knew a thing about *The University Greys*. Now he was learning they suffered a hundred percent casualties, either killed or wounded and none of them ever returned to the University after the war. Some of those young students and professors had no doubt fought side by side with T. G., Albert Henry and Jonathan at the Battle of Gettysburg.

Another account chilled Joab to the bone. It was Isaiah Fleming's story, though Mr. Fleming never told Joab. He was far too splendid a man to even mention the humiliating facts. Joab was sure the Jewish community in America—in the South particularly for this is where it happened—would never forget the shadow that fell across their personal freedom and equality in their New World during the dark and dismal days of the war.

Mr. Fleming was a Jewish immigrant who came to America with his wife and two daughters and three sons just eleven years before the War Between the States began. By 1861, Mr. Fleming was too old to fight, but he gave three sons to fight for the Confederacy. He had told Joab about it that day they met. They were all three killed in battle, two with Beauregard at Shiloh, and one with Lee at Gettysburg. Joab's eyes filled with tears as he recalled the story that day standing in the rubble and ashes of Mr. Fleming's clothing store on the square. He hurt for this man from the top of his head to the sole of his feet. Isaiah Fleming, like so many other southern fathers, gave all—every son he sent to war. None came home.

But that was not all there was to Mr. Fleming's story. When he thought about it, Joab recalled some things his father had taught him when he was a child. When you do something or you know something you're ashamed of, the proper handling of the situation is confession and absolution. He taught him there was a course to follow as a child of God in being forgiven and forgiving, but he also taught Joab that a vital part of growth as a godly person was to forsake the unmentionable past and never speak of it again. Joab struggled with this when it came to the war, thinking surely his father had not meant to include the unmentionable atrocities to the South. Joab guessed remembrance of what Grant did to the Jewish people tarnished the memory of Mr. Fleming's sons who died for the Confederacy and that Mr. Fleming never wanted to mention it again.

But Hiram had told Joab that same day when he first met Mr. Fleming—he told him the whole story. Joab was grateful for that, otherwise he may never know the importance of overseeing the building of Mr. Fleming's clothing store.

In December of 1862, Gen. Ulysses S. Grant issued an order from his headquarters in Holly Springs, a little town between Oxford and Memphis, a town Grant no doubt had chosen for the beautiful homes that stood in regal fashion beneath the age-old majestic oaks. He had winter-quartered at *Airliewood,* one of the Holly Springs mansions, in late '62, planning the siege of Vicksburg. His order was simple, to the point, and appalling.

GENERAL ORDERS NO. 11
HDQ. 13TH A.C. DEPT OF THE TENN.
Holly Springs, December 17, 1862

The Jews, as a class violating every regulation of trade established by the Treasury Department and also department orders, are hereby expelled from the department within twenty-four hours from the receipt of this order.

Post commanders will see that all of this class of people be furnished passes and required to leave, and any one returning after such notification will be arrested and held in confinement until an opportunity occurs of sending them out as prisoners, unless furnished with permit from headquarters.

No passes will be given these people to visit headquarters for the purpose of making personal application for trade permits.

By order of Maj. Gen. U.S. Grant
JNO A. Rawlins,
Assistant Adjutant-General

Official Records of the War of the Rebellion, Series I, Vol. 17, Part II, p. 242.

Expelled! Grant was going to expel the South's Jewish Community, those he called *this class, these people?* A few days later on December 29, 1862, there came to Lincoln a plea from some Jewish citizens that were deported by Grant. They wrote him from Paducah, Kentucky concerning the expulsion from Grant's department within twenty-four hours. These particular Jews were good and loyal citizens of the United States and residents of Oxford engaged in legitimate businesses as merchants, insulted and outraged by Grant's inhumane order which was a violation of the Constitution and their rights as good citizens. It would mean they were outlaws. They respectfully asked President

Lincoln to give Grant's General Orders No. 11 immediate and *effectual attention and interposition.*

On January 4, Grant's order was rescinded by way of a message from General-in-Chief H. W. Halleck, War Department, Washington. Grant had no alternative but to revoke his previous mandate, but not before considerable damage had already been done. On January 13, 1863, *The Jewish Record* in New York published an article that gave revolting details of the outrageous treatment of Jewish citizens by military officers of the U.S.

Joab was appalled when he read the only reply to the questioning regarding their expulsion from the Department. . . . they were *Jews and they were neither a benefit to the Union or Confederacy.*

By now Joab was wishing the war was still on and that he would have his opportunity. Those feelings he had the day he visited Brice's Crossroads were returning, mounting.

Hiram told him that although Lincoln's command to have Grant's order rescinded came quickly, in just a few days a lot of damage was done that would never be corrected. Mr. Fleming had managed to keep his family in Oxford, narrowly escaping the reproach before Lincoln's rescinding of the order. By then he had already lost two sons to Shiloh and in just six months his third son fell at Gettysburg, then in 1864, his store was burnt to the ground by Grant's men.

Light afflictions, thought Joab. I have *light afflictions*. I must always remember that. Some have sacrificed supremely.

Joab had already spoken to the men on the square. Isaiah Fleming's store would be the first one to go up. They were in full agreement, but it would be a surprise for Isaiah. Joab would proudly be a part of that rebuilding in the month of December before his wedding day. He wished Grant could see it before and that he could see it after. Treatment of the Jews was testimony that Grant had a personal war with the South and that he should have been censured for *General Orders No. 11*. Joab and the men of Oxford would do everything in their power to make up for Grant's insensitive and heartless treatment of the Jews in his *department.*

Early Monday morning, December 5, the men of Oxford assembled as usual on the square. Joab and a few men who had steady work at the mill paid for and loaded wagons with wood sufficient for framing

Mr. Fleming's store, Joab purchased the nails, and the men drove their small wagon train to the plot where the footings were already dug. In time, they would be able to purchase the bricks that would give his store a fine, strong finish.

There would be rejoicing in Oxford tonight.

CHAPTER 25

ONE PERFECT DAY

*. . . my richest gains I count but loss
and pour contempt on all my pride.*

Isaacs Watts

Joab regretted one thing about getting married in Oxford. His family would not be able to come. That would be asking way too much of them. But he could hardly stand the thoughts of taking this most important step without them. He must think of some way to make up for it. He and Aggie had settled on Saturday, December 17. Preacher Phillips had agreed to perform the ceremony, but Joab had already requested that it be quick and to the point; he and Aggie were going to say their own vows. The same ones they pledged to each other the day he returned from Sarepta. He hoped he could remember what he said. Knowing Aggie, she would have no trouble remembering exactly what *she* said.

Caroline Stephens brought out the long white dress she had sewn for Aggie, who was seeing it for the first time.

"Mama, it takes my breath!"

"Try it on Aggie. You'll look lovely in it. It was the best I could do on short notice, but as far as I was concerned, you were going to have a white dress for this occasion. I used my own wedding dress for a pattern. Took it apart piece by piece and sewed another one—just much smaller. Child, you are so small. Sometimes I wonder if you're large enough to be married."

"I can't thank you enough, Mama. You did wonders with that piece of cloth. Was there enough for a little veil?"

"No, but—"

Caroline brought out the veil she had designed from a piece of thin, white lace she found in her sewing trunk. She took some hairpins from her bun and affixed the veil into her daughter's hair and stepped back.

"Just two more days, Aggie, and you will be married and leaving. I don't know if I can bear it."

Aggie sighed, but not because of her mama's statement. She was looking into the mirror on the dressing table. "Splendid, Mama. The veil and the dress both are grand." And in the same breath, she said, "You and Daniel will be coming to the Payne's home for Christmas, and then shortly after the first of the New Year, I'll come back here to be with you for a month, maybe three weeks, while Joab goes to Gettysburg. That won't be so bad, will it? Of course, Joab and I will be leaving soon after the ceremony so we can get to Sarepta before dark and before the temperature starts dropping as the sun goes down. And then you and Daniel will be leaving here on December 22 to come to Sarepta. We'll all be together for Christmas. Everything should work out just fine, don't you think?"

"You're absolutely right, Aggie. When I think about it, I do get a bit excited. It has been so long since I got out of Lafayette County. A change of scenery will do us all good. Yes, to be quite honest, I am glad of that. And, it will give me time to get used to . . . well, to get used to your being married and eventually gone for good."

"You know I'll always be as close as a good hard ride away. I have never been so excited and Mama, I'm so happy. I dearly love Joab. You know that."

"Yes, I have no doubt about that."

"I must go and gather my personal things for the trip. I don't want to wait until the last minute. And I want to go to the woods and look for more of those Alpine Asters like Joab brought me that day. Or maybe I should do that now before it gets dark. I hope there will be some sheltered against the cold under the ferns. A wedding needs a few flowers, but I do have my doubts that I will find any."

"Just be careful, wrap up real good and don't stay long, for I'll worry. Listen to me. You're about to be married and I'm still hovering over you. I guess that will never change."

"That's okay, Mama. I don't want it to change, and neither will Joab. He knows how close we are and I think he is as much a Mama's boy as I am still your little girl. It was the war that made us like that. Don't you think so, Mama?"

Sarah Agnes didn't look at her mother and she never expected an answer. It would be hard for Caroline to speak while choking back tears.

"I'll go for the flowers first, and yes I'll be careful, and I'll pack up my belongings when I get back, then I'll be all ready for the little ceremony in—in just two days! I can't take much with me, for we'll be riding our horses, and I have to roll everything and tie it down in my blanket, but I'll wait till the last minute to do that, or everything will be all wrinkled. Oh, Mama, I'm talking in circles. Am I saying the same things over and over?"

On December 16, the morning before the wedding, Joab rode up on the campus and settled on a place under the cypress and pine trees in full view of the Lyceum. The ground was dry and covered with needles, a lovely place for people to stand for the brief ceremony at high noon. Quite frankly, he could pledge nothing but his love; times were still hard, money scarce, and it may be years before things got better from a financial standpoint. This was not the day to worry. He had better things to do.

He rode to the square, took his hammer out and tucked it in the pocket of his overalls, tied his horse to the hitching post in front of The Thompson House, and walked to Mr. Fleming's lot. What he saw pleased him—the framing and walls going up one board at a time. Soon it would be finished, perhaps before he returned with Aggie in early January. Mr. and Mrs. Fleming would be at the wedding. He would speak with Isaiah then.

Joab thought about Hiram Raines.

> *God, how I miss him! Somehow let him know how much he meant to me the few months we were together on this earth. I am reminded, once again, that life is fragile. Hiram endured the war and the loss of his sons then died of a broken heart. Would it be selfish if I asked for long life and perfect love with Aggie?*

Joab must cling to the assurance that *perfect love casteth out all fear.*

Mattie Raines was up before sunrise as usual and Joab, having finished the chores, stepped to the back porch to clean up before going inside. It was cold, but there should be a little outside warmth by high noon. The sun had set red the night before, giving hope for a clear day. He put the chunks of wood in the kindling box beside the stove and, shivering, he hovered over one side while Mattie patted out the last of the biscuit dough and put the iron skillet into the oven.

"This is your day, Joab. You should not be chopping wood and milking cows before such an important occasion."

"Miss Mattie, you know this is my last day here, and it is still my pleasure after all these months to do those things for you. I could never in a million years thank you enough for giving me the honor of staying in your home. You've treated me . . . well, you've treated me like a son, and I will never forget it. I will worry about you when I'm gone, but I will be back. The only thing is, there will be two of us! Will that be okay?"

"Oh, my, Joab! That will be splendid! I hope that's a promise."

"It's a promise. I love this place. It has been the only other home I've known except with Rachel. I only wish you could meet her. I know we will be able to arrange that in the future."

"I will be looking forward to that, Joab. Were you able to post a letter to her and Samuel about the wedding? I know you said they couldn't come, but does she know it is today?"

"Oh, yes ma'am. She knows, and I'm sure she is dying to be here with us. I have to not think about that. It makes me less of a man. You know . . ."

"I know, son. Now, you come on and sit down to some good breakfast. You're going to need your energy. Then we will get that water hot on the stove for a good bath for you. You have to get all scrubbed on your wedding day."

They both laughed and enjoyed hot cups of coffee and a hearty breakfast. Joab was proud of how Mattie had recovered since Hiram's death, at least she showed good signs of it, but then she had coped better than Hiram after the boys were killed in the war. Joab thought she would be just fine, knowing Hiram and the boys were together at last. Preacher Phillips already had her working with the women who needed emotional help. Mattie's strength of character would be encouragement for the younger women who were caring for severely wounded men and for women whose husbands or sons had died in the war. Miss Mattie was perfect for that job.

Joab rode up on the campus about ten minutes before noon, the first to arrive, so he thought. He sat on his horse for a moment, breathing deep. The cold air refreshed him. He was handsome in his dark denim trousers and the only white shirt he owned. Mrs. Raines had starched and meticulously ironed it. The pleats lay in tight creases across the front and the blousy sleeves fluttered in the slightest December wind. His hair was clean and straight, barely touching his shoulders. His face was clean shaven. He wore no hat, not wishing to accentuate any cowlicks today. Drawing a deep breath, he exhaled and relaxed as best he could on such a glorious occasion, praying that amidst the unsteadiness of the times this would be one perfect day. When he looked up wagons full of people and riders on horseback were coming out of the woods on that end of The University grounds. The whole town had turned out.

The men on the square, he thought. They must have passed the word. Daniel drove the Stephens' buckboard to the side where he and Aggie and Miss Caroline were to wait. Joab tied Star to an oak tree and took his place beside Reverend Phillips. He had no best man. Miss Caroline delicately walked across the pine needles, making her way to the other side of Reverend Phillips, smiling at Joab. She looked lovely. He could see Daniel was holding to Aggie, waiting for the moment when he would bring her and, in place of their father, give her away to Joab.

In that sacred moment a splendid sound came from the edge of the wood. Joab, knowing as surely as the noonday sun cast its golden streams across the pine-strewn ground on The University of Mississippi—it was Jonathan, Isaac, Samuel and Robert E. Lee Payne, and they were playing their violins. *When I Survey the Wondrous Cross on which the Prince of Glory died, my richest gains I count but loss and pour contempt on all my pride.* As they played, Daniel escorted his sister to Joab and placed her hand into his.

She whispered to him, "You're mother is out there. She's here, Joab, watching us as we make our vows."

Joab swallowed hard and whispered back. "I thought to pray for a perfect day. Amazing that God shows his approval in such splendid ways."

"Yes," she said, and they both turned toward Reverend Phillips. Joab felt someone's presence next to him. It was Samuel—his best little man, dressed in his khaki trousers and blue cotton shirt.

"We drew straws," he said, "and I won."

Joab smiled and turned his handsome face toward his lovely bride, who was holding a large bouquet of Alpine Asters and wild fern, firmly tied with a wide blue ribbon, against her white gown. He didn't know she had picked them herself.

Reverend Phillips read a passage of Scripture that described precisely how love must be, and then he prayed for Joab and Aggie. When he said *amen*, he nodded. Joab turned to face Aggie, took her hands into his own and said, "Aggie Stephens, with all the love and life that is in me, I throw all worry to the wind and beg you to be my wife, to love me for the rest of *your* life, even as I promise to pour my love out upon you for the rest of *my* life, and I ask you to be a permanent part of the Payne family . . . until death alone shall part us."

Aggie paused a moment, took a deep breath, smiled, and spoke. "Joab . . . Joab Payne, with no further thought or wonder about life and with no care what the future holds as long as we are together—yes! Yes, I will be your wife, take your Payne name as my name, love you with a never-ending love and take your family as my very own . . . until death alone shall part us."

Her voice trailed and Samuel nudged Joab, handed him a ring, and said, "Here, Mama wants you to have it."

Joab took the gold band and slipped it on Aggie's finger, while tears rolled down both their faces.

Preacher Phillips prayed over the young couple again and then said, "In the name of the Father, Son, and Holy Ghost, I pronounce that you are husband and wife. You may kiss your bride, Joab."

He kissed her long and hard, turning her toward the crowd as they cheered and shouted from every corner of the woods that surrounded them. Aggie went one way, and Joab pressed his way through the crowd to find his mother. He hugged Rachel, swung her around, and said, "This is a grand surprise, Mama."

"Well, son, when I received Aggie's letter begging for our presence at the wedding, I took counsel with your family and friends in Sarepta and as many as could come are out there in that crowd of people. I can tell you this much, all those who came to our home on Thanksgiving are here, including Grandpa Church. And look yonder, Dandy and Tibby, grinning from ear to ear."

"I never dreamed this would happen. I must introduce you to Aggie and her family and Miss Mattie and—"

"You're too late, son. Aggie has already introduced us to everyone. We all met at The Thompson House—behind your back I might add. Aggie arranged for us to be here early. And I think I'm supposed to tell you there's a reception compliments of the tea room. What a lovely, lovely place, Joab. And—such splendid people."

"If heaven is better than this, and I'm sure it is—I'm glad I will not miss it, Mama."

"Me, too, Joab. Me, too."

<hr />

Aggie had no way of knowing whether the Payne family and friends from Sarepta would be able to get to the wedding, but she had wanted it to be a surprise for Joab. It had, indeed. No longer needing to take her horse, she put her belongings on the back of Jonathan's buckboard as did Joab, and the two of them mounted Star, waved final goodbyes to Miss Caroline and Daniel and rode out of Oxford toward Sarepta on the late and cold December afternoon.

"Are you warm enough, Aggie?"

"So very warm next to you, Joab. This is where I will stay the rest of my life. I love you, dear heart."

"I love you more," said Joab, tightening his arms around the love of his life. "How did I ever come to deserve you?"

"And Joab, I love your family, of which I am now a part, of course. I am Sarah Agnes Stephens Payne. Please tell Rachel I will only wear the ring until you can purchase one for me. I cannot imagine that she would care enough to allow me the privilege of wearing her own wedding band."

They rode in silence for a few minutes and Joab spoke, "What did you do about The Thompson House, Aggie?"

"I told them I would be back after Christmas if they would have me, that I would work until you returned from Gettysburg. They were fine with that."

"The reception was splendid. Miranda outdid herself on the pralines and pastries."

"She said it was for her best white man, Joab! And she was so happy to be at our wedding. Did you get to see her before she returned to the tea room?"

"Oh, yes! I gave her a big hug. And Miss Mattie cried when I left. I knew she would. Not that I didn't want to myself. I had to keep thinking about you so I wouldn't. I have a hard time fighting tears these days anyway. I have noticed that is true with almost all of our people."

"Isn't it sad when good things end even though, for us, life just gets better? Some more of the bittersweet. Speaking of bittersweet, did you see Mr. Fleming, Joab?"

"He shook my hand and hugged me, kissing me on first one cheek, then another in the Jewish manner, I suppose, until we both cried and laughed at the same time."

"He's so proud of that store going up. Joab, you've been a son to so many men who lost theirs."

"In a way, that's what I set out to do, but then I lost Hiram, who was like a father to me."

"You didn't lose him, Joab. We haven't lost people when we know where they are."

"Well said, Angel. Well said."

Christmas came quickly that year of 1870 and having all the family together again did wonders to put another year between the Paynes and Christmas of 1861, the last one before all the heartache began. Times were getting better for them and now they had Aggie who was another blessing, an angel not only for Joab, but for all of the family. Joab allowed Aggie and Rachel were so much alike there was no way they wouldn't get along just fine. Miss Caroline and Daniel quickly became family, something Joab knew would happen. He also knew they would all visit Sarepta often while he was gone.

On January 2, 1871, Joab reluctantly and sadly took Aggie back to her childhood home near Water Valley, Mississippi, holding her close to him, warming her as best he could in the cold and driving snow.

"Joab, I'm glad you're going. I just wish it was not in the winter time. You will get cold without me, I fear."

"I will indeed, Aggie, but, quite truthfully, I planned on going in the winter time for a reason. Pa and the boys spent those winters in the cold and blowing snow. So did your pa. That will be part of my journey of remembrance—for all of them. Pray for me."

"Every moment of every day, Joab."

Part Two

CHAPTER 26

JOURNEY

*Not for fame or reward, not for place or for rank,
Not lured by ambition, or goaded by necessity,
But in simple obedience to duty as they understood it,
These men suffered all, sacrificed all, dared all, and died.*

Confederate Memorial
Dr. Randolph Harrison McKim

The Confederate Battle Flag intrigued Joab. It's significance tugged constantly at his heartstrings. Jonathan told his family how Thomas refused to abandon the flag at all hazards. It flew with him as he tramped on foot every step of the way from Sarepta to Gettysburg, and he died clutching it against his heart. It was the symbol of the South, of suffering and in the days following the close of the war, a badge of courage through persecution by those who didn't understand the South or its flag. Joab loathed the thought that it was so desecrated, used for a point of contention. Rachel made the flag that Thomas found in his knapsack when he got to Grenada the night he and the boys mustered in. Jonathan buried his father and Henry with that old battle-tattered emblem draped across their bleeding bodies on July 1, 1863, and two days later, he fought with Gen. Heth's Division at Pickett's Charge.

Joab wondered these seven years since the Battle of Gettysburg just what happened to that flag, and he wished he knew where his father and Henry's bodies lay buried on the battleground. Or if the Union had exhumed them and taken them to someplace like Richmond or another burial ground in the South. He had no way of knowing, but not knowing only stirred his passion to find out or to lay it to rest.

His visit to Oxford and Brice's Crossroads and Shiloh were supposed to have sufficed. They could have sufficed, but they would never satisfy. The men and boys who died on those bloody hills were not his blood kin. He had to go to Gettysburg. He knew that now. Concerned about what Rachel would do or say, he was pleasantly surprised when she went along with the first idea he dropped on her and the more they discussed it, the more she agreed he should go. She was fully aware of when it happened—his thought to travel to Gettysburg. He had, figuratively speaking, inhaled the stench of blood and sweat from the other battlefields, especially Shiloh where his lungs had, no doubt, filled with the black powder of ten thousand guns and cannons.

Jonathan drew the map that would lead his brother from Sarepta, Mississippi, to Gettysburg, Pennsylvania, as the freight cars traveled, for the most part. He and Isaac had gone through all of Rachel's letters from T.G., Jonathan, and Albert Henry to decide the route that Joab should take and then followed the newly repaired railways in as straight a line as possible hoping Joab could hitch rides on the freight or cattle cars from Memphis to Washington and then on into Gettysburg if possible.

For several hours the boys read all the letters, searching each for bits of information, weeping at the thoughts of what the men had endured, remembering that Rachel had faithfully kept the home fires burning during those sad years. Isaac shook and cried as he read Albert Henry's letter to Rachel from Goldsboro, North Carolina on January 17, 1863, just six months before Henry was killed.

> *Ma, maybe Ike (Isaac) has not gone to that company (Wheeler's Cavalry) and if he has not gone please don't let him go, no how in the world if you can help it. Tell him that I know he can't stand it and besides this, it would be more honor to him to stay at home and take care of his mother than to go to the army. There is no honor attached to them that die in the army. They are forgotten among those that were well. Ma, may the war end*

soon and in our favor and may we meet again at my sweet old home to live a life of peace and if we are not permitted to meet on earth let us meet in heaven. I live in full confidence that your prayers are continually going up for us. May you and the children have an easy time and not be interrupted by the enemy is my prayer. Tell Ike to be a good boy, tell Joab and Sam that me and Pa and Jon will come to see them by and by. I must close since there is a sermon going to be preached at three o'clock and it is nearly that time now. The preacher has got up. Goodbye, Ma. I hope not forever. Your son, Albert Henry.

Isaac had been fourteen years old when Henry wrote the letter. He didn't join Wheeler's Cavalry, but he did run away from home later that year when he was fifteen, trying to find his pa and the boys, but gave up and returned home. His father wrote for Rachel to send Isaac to him in early 1863. He arrived on the battlefield with full instructions from his father, but then T.G. sent him home just two weeks before the Gettysburg battle, mysteriously believing that something awful was about to happen and that he needed to get Isaac out of there. He wrote to Rachel, ". . . evidently something is about, but I can't tell what. Some think . . . Gen. Lee will make a forward move and will probably go into Maryland but . . . it is impossible for us to know until we receive orders."

Joab should have no trouble hitching a ride on most late evening cattle trains that had dropped their cargo and were riding empty. It would take him longer to get to his destination. He didn't want to travel hobo. In fact, it would be impossible because of Star; he needed to hitch as many rides as possible. Money was still scarce. Joab had sent most of what he earned at the sawmill home to Rachel, reserving a few dollars for his Gettysburg journey. The way he figured, it would take about three days to roll into the town where his pa and Henry fell, where Jonathan fought as did a hundred and thirty-five of *The University Greys*, and where his Uncle Marcellus Church was captured and sent to Point Lookout Federal Prison in Maryland, where he later died. Joab had no idea how he would get information. He also knew, while he could go several days without food, he would have to eat at some point in time.

The morning Joab left, all of Rachel's boys were at the old home place. They each shook his hand, hugged him, and wished him well on his journey. Joab had one more wish—that his brothers were going with him.

In 1863, Lee hoped fighting a battle on northern soil would put political pressure on Lincoln and the Radical Republicans to bring an end to the hideous war, or that it would lead to a military alliance with England and France on behalf of the South. A gray shadow hung over Lee and his army. Stonewall Jackson was dead. James Longstreet, *Lee's Old War Horse*, had his misgivings about what was taking place. And Jeb Stuart was missing—on a raiding mission of enemy supply trains. Stuart had lost communication with Lee. At the same time, Lincoln had lost confidence in Joe Hooker, and he replaced him with George Gordon Meade, placing him in charge of the Union's largest army. On the morning of July 1, Henry Heth's Division with A. P. Hill's Corps sent seventy-five hundred men down the Chambersburg Pike toward Gettysburg. Amongst the fighting men were Joab's father, T.G., and his brothers, Jonathan and Albert Henry, and his uncle, Marcellus Church. Heth's men clashed with John Buford at the store in Gettysburg. What had been, in that moment, all about shoes for the barefoot Confederate soldiers turned into all-out war before it was over. That was the day Joab wished to call back time. The day his father and brother were killed.

Joab had no way of knowing how emotional and heartrending this trip would be. He would have gone anyway, but he had no idea. He was deeply in love with Sarah Agnes Stephens and had left her with his own heart breaking to say nothing of hers. It wasn't exactly fair to Aggie, but he was constrained to go, and it was something she had consented to before they were married. Leaving his bride was as poignant as going to war, riding into a place that had been enemy territory during one of the fiercest battles of the American Civil War.

Joab rode Star north to Memphis, passing through Holly Springs, Mississippi. He was too young to know all the details of war, but his mother and Isaac knew that Grant was winter quartered in Holly Springs in November and December of 1862. That was too close for comfort—close to their home in Sarepta and not far at all from Oxford. It was a bustling community, situated just south of Memphis on a rail line, a good place for Grant to bring in and stockpile supplies for the war.

There was a large Jewish settlement in this lovely little town, mostly immigrants from Alsace, merchants who had passed through Holly Springs from New York and other urban towns peddling their merchandise, and when the railroad came through, it became a good trade route and a suitable place for them to settle. The U.S. Treasury Department had already mandated that southern merchants—those in the Deep South—must sell their cotton at twenty-five cents a pound. They even made the merchants and farmers take an oath to follow the government cotton monopoly. Many of the Union officers accused the Jewish traders of smuggling. That was all Grant needed to promptly issue his General Orders Number 11, expelling all the Jews, not only in Holly Springs, but in all the military district he controlled, even those Jews who were not involved in cotton trade. He said they were "a curse to the Union Army." That's when Lincoln stopped him.

There was not much sign of the war years in Holly Springs, though the Union troops had seized it in late 1862. Lanky limbs of bare oak trees and massive magnolias that tried to touch the sky lined the main street that would lead Joab through town and on toward Memphis, but not before he veered off the main road. He wanted to see *Airliewood*, where Grant had stayed while his army was there. He turned Star slowly up Salem Street until he came to the mansion that was situated on fifteen acres. It was stunning, but not nearly as beautiful as *Walter Place*, the home Grant chose for his wife and son to stay while he sat at the borrowed desk at *Airliewood* planning the siege of Vicksburg. Confederate General Van Dorn thundered through town and raided Grant's stockpile of ammunition then stormed to *Walter Place* to take Julia Grant and her baggage. Mary Govan, whose house had been seized by the Union for use as a military hospital, was staying at *Walter Place*, the owners being gone for the duration of the war. When the Confederates came, she told them Mrs. Grant was gone and that a southern gentleman surely would not invade a lady's bedroom to make a search. They left. Grant ordered that Holly Springs be spared the torches of war because of Mrs. Govan's actions that day.

Joab stopped often for Star to rest and drink, arriving late in the day, which was his plan, hoping to catch an empty cattle car to Chattanooga on the Alabama and Chattanooga Railway. He briefly told his story to the conductor at the tracks in Memphis. He was happy to accommodate Joab on one of the less than comfortable cattle cars. Joab didn't care. He never expected anything else. His car was strewn with hay and he had watered Star before they boarded. He took down the saddle, his pillow for the journey.

The train rumbled through Corinth in less than two hours out of Memphis. Corinth had been hard hit by the war, having come under siege by Union Gen. Henry Halleck in April and May of 1862. Halleck was the commander who had a great deal of contempt for Grant himself. It was this same Henry Halleck who, at Lincoln's command, had written the order rescinding Grant's General Orders No. 11 for the expulsion of the Jews. Later that year, General Rosecrans managed to push the Confederates back and take the little town of Corinth. They were after the Alabama and Chattanooga Railway. And they got it. Joab found it hard to believe he was riding across the battleground on the very spot from which Rosecrans had fought, directly on the Battery Madison. He stood to see as much as possible. He had come through Corinth on his way to Shiloh, had even crossed the railroad track, but he knew more now than then. This little town has been through a lot, he thought. Within minutes, the train had rolled through Corinth and there was nothing left to see.

He slept on the hay, his woolen blanket wrapped about his body from head to boot. It was a bumpy, jolting ride, and he woke each time the train stopped during the night, but he dared not move for fear of freezing. He saw that Star had bedded down for the night, right next to him. He could feel her warmth. Just after dawn, he sat up. They were nearing Chattanooga. He had never seen the mountains before. The train stopped in the shadow of Monteagle on the Cumberland Plateau, a treacherous stretch, even more hazardous in the snow and ice. For half an hour it sat on the track, the men doing their work to make sure it was safe to move on, then the train once again chugged toward its destination.

When they reached Chattanooga, Joab's teeth were chattering. It was cold, and he knew it would be getting even colder. He had to get off and change trains here, maybe even wait indefinitely for the next one. He could layer on his wool scarf and Jonathan's long coat when the train stopped.

A thin layer of snow dusted the tops of the mountains and the ridge that divided the city. Missionary Ridge. Following the Union's disastrous defeat at the Battle of Chickamauga by the Confederate Army of Tennessee under the command of Gen. Braxton Bragg, the Union routed Lookout Mountain, Missionary Ridge, Chattanooga Valley, Orchard Knob and Rossville Gap. One by one by one. When Joab visualized this, he felt sick.

With the trees bare, he could see from Lookout to Signal Mountain on Walden's Ridge at the southern end of the Cumberland Plateau. He wished to see it in the summertime. Better yet, in the fall when the leaves changed their color. It was past daybreak, the sun not yet brilliant, but in the light of the flickering lamps at the whistle stop, the snow cast a white glow across that corner of the world. Now it was coming down fast, accumulating on the mountains and piling up in Chattanooga Valley. Joab shivered. He would be glad when they stopped, would love to go inside the train station and warm by a fire. The engines, stoked by coal, sputtered and jerked and slowly the train came to a stop just past an old boarded-up depot. Strange, he thought. It was abandoned. There was, however, a shack of a depot with smoke curling out the chimney.

He had managed to keep the coal dust off his clothes for the most part by wrapping his blanket around himself. Brilliant, he thought. He tied Star to the hitching post and walked inside, hoping to be as successful here as he had been in Memphis. Southerners were the same all over the South. At least he hoped so, but since the war you could not be sure. He only knew his country, Calhoun and Lafayette Counties, and the most wonderful people on the face of the earth.

"Yes sir!" The man greeted Joab pleasantly.

"Good morning, sir."

"I see ya rode our cattle car. Come from Memphis?"

"Yes sir."

"Where ya goin'?"

"Gettysburg, Pennsylvania," said Joab.

"You don't mean it," the railroad yardman said.

"Yes sir. I'm trying to get there by cattle car or empty freight if possible."

"Whyn't ya just hobo it?"

"Oh, I've got my horse with me. I'll probably have to ride her from Washington City to Gettysburg."

"Mind me askin' your reason for goin'?"

"No sir. You see, my pa and brother died at the Battle of Gettysburg and I need to see for myself."

"You a Yankee?"

"Oh, no sir, I'm the son of Confederate Captain Thomas Goode Payne of Calhoun County, Mississippi. My brother, Albert Henry was a private. They both died on July 1, 1863, and my brother Jonathan was wounded at Pickett's Charge on the third. My brother, Isaac, fought till the war ended, made it home, and I was too young to fight."

"Well, son, what y' a-doing is commendable. Now, we got freight cars due in here about noon. If y' want to hitch, just take y' pick of an empty one. Be sure y' take one with sides and a door. It's awfully cold out there. Just clean up behind your horse once you arrive and everything should be just fine. Y'll take it through Bristol, Salem, and Lynchburg, Virginia, change there and take the Orange, Alexandria and Manassas Railway through Culpeper and Manassas Junction to Washington. On second thought, you might want to take an open-air car on the Orange. They's lots to see."

"You don't mean it!" said Joab.

"Yes sir! I thought y'd like that. Y'll be seeing where the fight at Culpeper took place, then First and Second Battles of Manassas. Y' train'll be goin' pretty fast, so y'll have to look fast. When y' get off the train in Washington, get on y' horse and ride downtown."

"Yes sir, I plan to do that. Thank you for your hospitality and for the ride. You've been mighty kind."

"Proud to hep y' son."

"Sir, I have one more question."

"What's that?"

"The building out there that looks like a depot, the one with bars on the windows—it's all boarded up and not in use. Looks like a good depot except for the bars. Why wouldn't you be using that instead of this shack?"

"Well . . . it has to have some work done to it. It was used . . . um, it's where the Yanks took our Confederate soldiers prisoners of war. It was our good railroad depot. We don't rightly know how to treat it. They's blood on the walls, and you know, son, that was the blood of our fightin' men. The Union armies pretty much devastated this part of the country . . . Grant and Sherman and Rosecrans. Why, they was s' many battles fought right here. They finally just called it the Chattanooga Campaign. They won all those battles except Chickamauga. It was bloody bad around here for a long, long time. Don't know if we will ever get back to normal. It affected us all. Son, y' know exactly what I'm a-talkin' about, don't y'?"

"Yes sir. Just losing my pa and my brother and my uncle was hard. It was very hard. But you people lost family and friends *and* all this beautiful countryside was ripped up. Thank you for sharing your experience with me. It's all a part of my journey to Gettysburg. Good-bye sir, and thank you again for the ride."

The year 1870 was bittersweet for Joab. He was satisfied with the decisions he had made, especially the one that had taken him to Oxford and The Thompson House and Aggie Stephens. But it was before he met Aggie that Joab made up his mind he would see the battlefields of the Civil War. He had been made aware since the day he first spoke with Aggie just how far the war had reached. She lost her father to Shiloh Battle and then there was Will Cavanaugh's untimely death, giving up the desire to live after the war took so much from him. Hiram Raines had come into Joab's life the same day as Aggie. He had lost two boys, one to Shiloh; one to Chancellorsville. And Joab had lost a dear friend in Hiram, who died of a broken heart. Mr. Fleming's sons—all three of them—had fallen in battle.

Gettysburg would be Joab's last attempt at bringing this war under subjection as far as he was concerned. If he could find one little bit of peace from this journey, it would not only suffice, it would satisfy.

He had indeed chosen an open car for the leg of his journey that would take him to Lynchburg. He remembered his father writing to Rachel about the beauty of Virginia's countryside. He had also written that The Mississippi 42nd was joined in November of 1862 by the Mississippi 11th. Joab had just recently found that *The University Greys* were attached to the Mississippi 11th. Both were a part of Gen. Joseph Davis' Brigade. That brought the war even closer to Joab because of his new relationships in Oxford.

The Paynes had skirmished with Davis' Brigade in "regular picket fighting for twenty-three days" up near Suffolk, Virginia. Jonathan wrote home about it, saying "I have never seen so many men broken down in my life—thousands lying along the roadside. Far better to be home but never mind that . . . I am willing to do all I can to save our country . . . My country needs me and I will stay here."

The train whistle pierced the midnight hour with its lonesome call. Joab was lonesome himself, missing Aggie, wishing to see her face. When this was all over, he was going to cling to her eternally, never again leaving her side. He wondered what she was doing, if she were keeping herself busy thinking about their future together, a future they would have to build; they had nothing. He didn't mind. No one in the South had much of anything since the war. They would all be building together, just like on the Oxford square.

The train rolled into Culpeper in the late night hours and stopped to load up with coal. Culpeper was the birthplace of Ambrose P. Hill, his father's corps commander. Since he would not be able to see anything in the darkness, he decided to lie as still as possible, hoping to get an hour of uninterrupted sleep while the train was stopped. They should arrive at Manassas Junction early in the morning, which would be the fourth day of miserable jostling on the cattle cars. Joab would be glad to step off onto non-moving ground and to search for someplace to clean up and get some coffee and a biscuit. He was beyond hunger. He wondered how many days his father and Jonathan and Henry had gone without food when they fought for the South. He quaked when he thought that except for a few rides on the cars, they had marched on foot from Kentucky to Pennsylvania.

He stood in awe as the train slowly pulled into the Virginia town. Snow lay two feet deep on the hillsides where men from both sides fell in the largest and bloodiest battle to that point in the war. Confederate generals made their country proud in First Manassas. Joseph Johnston, P.G.T. Beauregard, Thomas Jackson, Wade Hampton, Jeb Stuart, Kirby Smith, Jubal Early, Arnold Elzey. Gen. Jackson got his nickname, *Stonewall*, at First Manassas. These fierce warriors routed the Union troops, sending the shattered army running all the way back to Washington. Joab had to laugh when he thought it may have been the Rebel Yell that caused the Union soldiers so much angst. It was disturbing the first time they heard it. At Second Manassas, it was to do all over again with Lee's Army of Northern Virginia under the command of Maj. Gens. Stonewall Jackson and James Longstreet, again bringing victory to the South. The Greys had been there, having fought at First and Second Manassas before they joined up with A. P. Hill's Corps and the Army of Northern Virginia. Joab thought, if our men could only have lasted, but there were not enough of them to fight for four years.

It was too cold and the snow too deep to tramp around Manassas, but Joab had four hours to wait for the next train. He walked back down the railroad track to Bull Run River, a tributary stream of the Potomac that originated in the Bull Run Mountains in the next county over and flowed south to the Occoquan River where the battle was fought. Not once but twice. Johnston and Jackson had ridden down from the Bull Run Mountains to Manassas to protect the Orange and Alexandria Railroad. Joab was standing on those tracks. He could see the ruins of Stone Bridge over Bull Run. Manassas was near to Washington, and Bull Run River flowed into the Potomac.

He walked back to the train station built of logs where two fires blazed, one in the potbelly stove and one in the fireplace. It was warm and it felt good. He hovered over the fire a few minutes then walked around inside in search of someone who might know the whereabouts of some coffee.

By late afternoon, the freight cars rolled in, their flatbeds loaded with everything from lumber to steel. Joab was obliged to help unload them for which he received a few Union dollars. They needed his help, and he could sure use the money. But that was not all; they would be herding livestock into the cattle cars. Joab hoped there would be a car left for him. It was late when the last of the cows and hogs were loaded. Two cars were left; Joab selected one and commenced to cleaning it out with a shovel. He pitched several rakes of hay into the car and decided it would have to suffice. The train would pull out of Manassas Junction by eight that evening. He returned to the hitch at the station to get

Star, but first stepped inside to speak to the cargo conductor, the man who had temporarily hired him to help unload and load.

"Much obliged for the ride, sir."

"Much obliged for helping us out."

"Yes sir," said Joab.

"Say, you had anything to eat today?"

"No sir. Can't say that I have."

"Come with me," the man said, and he led Joab to the back room where he shared a slice of beef, some bread, and a good cup of coffee.

Joab was more than happy.

CHAPTER 27

HIS OWN NATIVE LAND

*Breathes there a man with soul so dead,
Who never to himself hath said,
This is my own, my native land.*

Walter Scott

By the time Joab reached the train station in Washington, D.C., he was as tired as he'd ever been. He had slept little, had eaten even less, and riding in slatted cattle cars for hundreds of miles in below freezing temperatures, he had near frozen to death. And what was more troubling, he had it to do over again back to Memphis. There was one thing for sure, he must use a few of those dollars he earned at Manassas Junction for food. Where, he had no idea.

He cleaned the car and shuffled some hay about, jumped Star to the ground and rode to the station. A light snow covered the dirt packed roads of the Nation's Capitol, and the trees were bare except for the myriad evergreens. It was early morning and the lamplights were still flickering. He crossed the bridge over the Potomac River and searched the horizon for the dome of the Capitol. Breathtaking. And there was no scaffolding to the top. Joab guessed they had completed the work that was suspended during the war. For that matter, *everything* had been suspended during the war. He rode toward the building that was much farther away than he thought. He wanted to see what it looked like on the inside. He could not imagine. He remembered how beautiful he thought the Lyceum to be, and it was. But this beggared all description. The closer he got, the more enormous the building.

He rode Star as far as he dared and tied her to a hitching post, secured his rifle with the blanket, and hoped his horse would be there when he returned. He wasn't too worried. Star would resist anyone she didn't know. It was the chance of a lifetime, and he may never pass this way again. He took the steps to the top, more steps than he had seen or likely would ever see on a single building. Joab entered the grand Rotunda and stood with his eyes passing over a thousand moments of beauty. He must take it all in. He removed his hat and stepped toward the center of the Rotunda and lifted his head. In 1865, at the end of the Civil War, a man by the name of Constantino Brumidi painted what he titled *The Apotheosis of Washington* in the eye of the Rotunda. It was a glorious rendering, in fresco technique, of George Washington rising to heaven in glory, flanked by figures of women named Liberty and Victory-Fame and surrounded by six different groups, each having significance. A rainbow was at Washington's feet and thirteen maidens symbolized the original States. The idea of the masterpiece was to glorify George Washington to the rank of a god, but perhaps more importantly it was the glorification of Washington as an ideal.

Joab's mother taught him much about George Washington, who was a southerner, a Virginian, a slave owner, who loved his people and his country. A wealthy man, but a generous one. Robert E. Lee had married Mary Anna Randolph Custis, who was Martha Washington's great granddaughter. Rachel had also taught her sons Washington's ideology by having them memorize the eulogy Henry "Light-Horse Harry" Lee offered at Washington's funeral.

> *First in war—first in peace—and first in the hearts of his countrymen . . . His last scene comported with the whole tenor of his life—although in extreme pain, not a sigh, not a groan escaped him; and with undisturbed serenity he closed his well-spent life. Such was the man America has lost—such was the man for whom our nation mourns.*

"Light Horse Harry" was Gen. Lee's father, a connection that was significant to Joab, for Robert E. Lee was his own father's General-in-Chief.

Joab silently walked the great rotunda and the first floor of the Senate wing through the vaulted ornate Brumidi Corridors taking in the magnificent murals that depicted every scene imaginable. Most of the walls and ceilings were completed. Some were still being painted. Brumidi designed the murals and all the major elements included on the walls and ceilings. Many artists were helping with the not-yet-finished artwork.

Joab's footfalls echoed through the National Statuary Hall, the meeting place of the House of Representatives until 1857. He marveled at the whispering gallery, which he would like to have tried for himself. He would take John Quincy Adams' word for it. It was an amazing building. He paced the hall where the founding fathers once sat to frame the Constitution, form the Bill of rights, and create the laws of the country.

Not wanting to leave, Joab mounted Star and, gaining confidence that this was his Country, his Nation, he reluctantly rode toward the White House. He was not dressed properly to enter. He knew that, but he could circle the residence of President Ulysses S. Grant. His insides churned with thoughts of the past. He had nothing but contempt for Grant and Sherman. The war was over. Grant was *his* president. "Forgetting those things which are behind . . ." Why was healing practically impossible?

Joab needed food. He dared to stop and inquire of a well-dressed gentleman about a place to get coffee in the heart of the city.

"The Old Ebbitt Grill," he said.

"Am I dressed properly?"

"Doesn't matter, son. Before the war, it might have mattered, but things have changed. You go. It's a grand place to get a lot of breakfast. It's a saloon, mind you. President Grant goes there from time to time; likes the bar, of course."

Joab hitched his horse to the rail with many others, washed his hands and face at the pump, and walked inside. He knew he was not properly dressed and likely did not smell fragrant. He ordered coffee and breakfast of eggs and ham and pastries. Ravenously hungry, he fought desperately to keep from shoveling the delectable food into his mouth, leaned back and with coffee cup in hand, breathed deeply before continuing. It was just about the best food he had ever tasted, though he would never tell Miranda.

He looked around quite like he did his first day at The Thompson House in Oxford and relished the beauty of the place. The freshly oiled hardwood floors and dark wood framing around the glass dividers and the crown molding at the ceilings were all polished so much that he could see his face in them. The glass windows were lavishly embellished and the pieces that divided the seating arrangement were etched with inscriptions and writings, one suggesting that the British sat drinking at this pub while Washington burned.

Interesting, my great-grandfather fought the Revolutionary War so that our country—The United States of America—could be free from the strong arm of tyranny. He drank an extra cup of coffee, toasting his Grandfather Jonathan Payne who fought and survived that Revolutionary War while the British sat right here mocking the very existence of America. He was equally as sure that Grant had sat here with Lincoln drinking whiskey, discussing war strategy as the North aggressively sought to crush the South just a few years ago. The similarities were astounding, though he was consciously seeking to put everything into perspective.

Joab was fine, seeing these places, knowing some of the nuances of the wars for independence first hand were all a part of the healing. He would be a better man for it, and he knew in due time, it would all make sense to him. He would tell his children and his children's children—everything. He was too young to fight, but he was just right to see where it all took place.

Satisfied with food and refreshed for the last miles of his journey, Joab rode back to the railroad depot of the Baltimore and Ohio. He stepped to the ticket counter and inquired about a hitch to Hanover Junction.

"We can get your horse on the car with some other livestock, no charge, but you'll have to ride a passenger car. Do you have the fair?"

"I have very little," said Joab. "I was counting on a hitch in a cattle car, and I can wait if there's one coming through empty."

"We run mostly passenger cars between Washington and Hanover, but we do maintain one car for horses and one for rigs, but they're going to be crowded. I wouldn't want you to ride like that. Where are you going, son?"

"To Gettysburg," said Joab.

"So you'll ride to Hanover then ride your horse to Gettysburg?"

"Yes sir. I have to see for myself where my pa and my brother fell in the battle."

"Where are you coming from?"

"Mississippi. I've been traveling four days on cattle cars."

"Wait right here, son. I'll be back with you in a few minutes."

Joab paced the floor at the depot, waiting as patiently as he possibly could. This would be the last miles of his journey, but it was too far to ride Star all the way. "Lord, make a way," he prayed quietly, waiting for the man to return. After all the grueling hours of riding on cold and open cars with very little food, he felt much like Jonathan and Henry and their father had felt after trudging endless days through sleet and snow and mud up to their knees. They were infantrymen. They had no horses. At least he had Star. He had come a long way. He must not even think to complain now. The ticket agent returned.

"Son, I would like to accommodate you for a ride to Gettysburg, but we are to capacity today and tomorrow. However, if you would like to do so, you may ride with the rigs. The train leaves shortly, so get your horse loaded up and you'll be in the car right next to the livestock. Just take a seat on any of the carriages. That shouldn't be too bad."

"You're very kind sir. How much do I owe you?"

"Nothing. Nothing at all. You'll not be taking up a seat as such. Just hop on and enjoy your ride. It's going to be freezing cold, so layer up as best you can. There may even be a blanket on one of those rigs. Now, you will have to change trains at Baltimore Camden Station, but everything should be exactly the same—to capacity—so get off, get your horse and follow the crowd to Bolton Station. Just tell the ticket master you hitched from Washington and with my permission. My name's Edward. You'll be fine."

Joab was elated. He had made the entire journey hitching. He wanted to do the Rebel Yell, but he refrained.

"Thank you. Thank you, sir! I'm very much obliged."

"Glad to help you out, son."

Joab had resigned himself to the probability he would have to walk from Washington to Gettysburg. This was extraordinary news for which he was thankful. He had no idea what was facing him on his journey back home. For the most part, there had been no chink in his plan, and he was none-the-worse for the long, tiring journey.

On November 18, 1863, Abraham Lincoln took this exact same ride. His party boarded the cars on the Baltimore and Ohio Railroad in a special reserved train with only four cars, gaily decorated for the occasion. The train left at ten minutes past noon and arrived at Camden Station in Baltimore at twenty past one that afternoon. A team of horses pulled the train through the streets of the city to Bolton Station, which was the depot of the Northern Central Railway. The switchmen added a baggage car especially for preparing lunch for the president, and the train left the station at two o'clock that afternoon. They rumbled north toward Hanover Junction in Pennsylvania, which was a mere forty-six miles north of Baltimore, reaching Hanover about five in the evening, switching trains, and arriving in Gettysburg at half past six that evening. Coffins bearing the bodies of southern soldiers were still stacked on the open platform at the red brick train station. Between the two armies, more than 51,000 men lay dead and the citizens of Gettysburg were left with the hideous burden of properly burying the bodies. Lincoln's speech was ten sentences long and he delivered it in a few short minutes. Weary from the trip, following his speech, he stayed until early evening then boarded the same railroad cars and returned the way he came, back to Washington.

CHAPTER 28

SOME RICH MAN'S CARRIAGE

Did the man have no humanity about himself?
No wonder he was hated
even by his own countrymen.

Joab wondered if he were hitching on the same train that bore Abraham Lincoln from Washington to Baltimore to Hanover Junction to Gettysburg—in his finery as the most powerful man in the world.

Riding comfortably in some rich man's carriage, Joab borrowed the warm blanket that lay neatly folded under the seat, thinking about home, wishing for Aggie, missing her so badly he could hardly stand it. He pulled the fresh, clean blanket to his face and relished the warmth. It was a fine blanket. Five days seemed like a long time when he doubled it. Ten days just traveling or maybe even more if he had to wait for rides going home. But he would not stay long in Gettysburg. He knew what he wanted to do. He just didn't know what to expect. He was not in the South. In fact, he was in a country that, from all indications and according to Senator Sumner of Massachusetts, didn't accept southerners.

He was feeling grimy and dirty by now, wishing for a stream in which to bathe; however, it would be extremely cold, and he didn't know if he could stand it. But he couldn't go much longer without a bath. He thought about his father. How had he stood it, day after endless day of marching, scavenging for food, sleeping on the ground, feet blistered and burning. Joab would not complain. This had been his idea, his choice. Soon it would be over and he would have a lifetime of memories. Each year that separated him from his father and Henry got a little harder to bear. Because he was getting older, he guessed. He hated that the memories of their faces were beginning to fade. He never wanted to forget them, never wanted to fail to honor them for their sacrifice. They had not asked for this war.

Joab wondered if his father and brothers had to listen to campfire tales about Senator Charles Sumner of Massachusetts who hated the South and its people. He was one of the leading Radical Republicans that had argued the plantations owned by southern white men should be taken from them and divided among the slaves. And it was largely Sumner who used his political influence to prevent European help for the Confederacy during the war. He called southerners *cruel and barbarous and savage* and said they were the *detested example.* When the president was assassinated, in his eulogy Sumner called Lincoln's address a "monumental act," and that ". . . the world noted at once what he said, and will never cease to remember it. The battle itself was less important than the speech."

When Joab read that in one of the papers from Rachel's quilt box, he quaked. What an awful thing to say, even about both sides! The man was without a conscience, thought Joab. "The battle itself was less important than the speech . . . ?" Great God, my father and brother died in that battle! Did the man have no humanity about himself? No wonder he was hated even by his own countrymen.

Joab needed to calm his thoughts, stop dredging up old thorny memories. He was about to arrive in Hanover Junction where he would truly begin the last leg of his epic journey. It had been ambitious on his part. He had never been far from Calhoun County until he went to Oxford and Shiloh. Now he was hundreds of miles away from his birthplace, lonely and alone. He shivered at the thoughts of arriving at the battleground that rivaled all others. What would he see?

He closed his eyes, hoping for sleep.

It was midnight when Joab's train thundered into Hanover Junction. Lanterns flickered in every window of the three-story, flat-roofed train station. There were several tracks that crossed each other and one turned sharply and led in another direction. Across the tracks was a three story red brick hotel with attic windows and balconies on the middle two floors that faced the station. A large sign on the side of the building facing the train station simply read, *Junction.* It was the Junction Hotel. He was going to ride Star the last few miles to Gettysburg, but he could not do it tonight. It was dark, cold, and snowing. Joab was going to the hotel. He hoped it cost only a few dollars, which he would gladly give up for a good night's sleep and a hot bath.

Cars loaded down with wounded soldiers rolled through this junction during the war years. And in November of 1865, a nine-car train bearing the body of assassinated President Abraham Lincoln slowly passed through Hanover Junction on its way to Illinois. The windows of the cars were all draped in mourning for the fallen president. The train did not stop in Hanover Junction that night, but slowed to about twenty miles an hour when it passed through, the crowd of people no doubt remembering when he had come that way before to dedicate the Battleground.

Joab neatly folded the borrowed blanket, left his cold but comfortable seat on the carriage, and hopped off the car. He got his horse and rode across the myriad tracks to the hitching posts at the hotel. He stepped inside to the warmth of a large brick fireplace piled high with burning wood that spit and sparked. The barmaid winked at him as he passed and he looked straight ahead pretending not to have noticed. He was in no way interested. He thought about Aggie. She was beautiful, sweet, kind and gentle. He missed her so much he could hardly stand it. He continued on to the clerk's desk where he inquired.

"I'd like to stay the rest of the night, but only if I can get a hot bath, a shave, and a bite to eat. I have money, but very little."

"Yes, well, all right, let's see how we can accommodate you. Do you have a horse?"

"Yes ma'am," said Joab politely.

"You're from the South, I take it," she said, obviously taking notice of his marked southern accent.

"Yes ma'am. From Mississippi."

She looked him over as if the interrogation were about to begin, but instead she said, politely, "How about one of our attic rooms. They're the least expensive, but they have a nice, clean bed and a wash bowl where you can shave. We'll have to bring in a bathing tub and hot water."

"That sounds fine. And, ma'am?"

"Yes?"

"I will bathe myself."

"I understand," she said. "That will be $1.00. Includes the bath and a light breakfast, and we'll take your horse to the barn. Once you've had your bath, just come on down and we'll find you something to eat."

"Much obliged," he said. "I just need to get my saddlebag. And, ma'am, could someone wake me around seven o'clock, please? I've been traveling for five days and I'm plenty tired. Afraid I'll go to sleep and not wake up."

"You bet," she said. "Here's your key. Just go to the third floor, take the attic stairs on up, and the number's on the door. Hitchcock will be right up with your water."

By now, Joab was so tired, he could scarcely put one foot in front of the other. He dragged himself up the stairs and fell across the bed waiting for the tap on the door and—Hitchcock.

Morning broke, and there came another tap on his door. It was seven o'clock.

"Thank you," he said and rolled over.

An hour later, the morning sun beamed off the snow that lay deep on the rolling meadows across the way and woke Joab for the second time. He jumped up and walked about the low-ceilinged room to get his bearings. The bath had done wonders, he had washed his hair, and obviously Hitchcock had returned to take the water. Joab had been dead to the world and had not heard the knock. Neither had he gone down for food last night. Now he was really hungry and in need of coffee. He pulled back the thin curtains and watched the sun cast long golden streaks across the wood floor. For a moment he thought about home and the attic room. He wanted to be there. In fact, he longed for home and his new wife. Soon, he thought.

Joab shaved and dressed in clean clothes from his bag for the first time in over five days. He rolled up his clothes, grimy from the cattle cars, and pushed them into the other side of his saddlebag, knowing he might have to put them back on for the trip home. But today he was wearing his khaki trousers and long-sleeved blue shirt. He looked splendid.

Down the narrow attic stairs and three flights to the first floor, Joab found the dining room and ordered coffee. Last evening's barmaid,

Amanda, who was now the waitress, brought coffee and croissants and jam. A basketful of croissants. Joab was elated, thinking, this is all I need, and she said a *light* breakfast. He ate until he could eat no more, thanked Amanda, and climbed the stairs to the attic room. He gathered his belongings, layered himself for the ride and descended the stairs for the last time. He thanked the desk clerk copiously and headed for the barn to get Star. It was cold but clear and sunny, perfect for riding thirty miles. He had seen few days like this since he left Sarepta almost a week ago. He had a clean body, a clear mind, and a heart that was uncertain—uncertain of how it would react to what it was about to experience. He knew the battleground was now a military park, a tourist exhibition. He also knew it was on northern soil—dedicated to Union soldiers.

He sauntered alongside the railroad tracks toward Gettysburg, his heart pounding.

CHAPTER 29

THE WIND AT HIS BACK

So it ends, this lesser battle of the first day,
Starkly disputed and piecemeal won and lost
By corps-commanders who carried no magic plans
Stowed in their sleeves, but fought and held as they could.
It is past. The board is staked for the greater game
Which is to follow . . .

Stephen Vincent Benét

The wind blew hard against Joab's face, but that would change when he rounded the bend. It would be at his back. He was happy to be riding his horse through the beautiful Pennsylvania countryside, the rolling hills covered with untouched snow, reminding him of his native hill country of Mississippi on a cold wintry day, though the snow would not be so deep.

Through the peach orchards now, the trees bare of leaves and sketched with snow like an artist's rendering, Joab still riding the road that ran alongside Hanover Branch tracks, the same route that Lincoln took on November 18, 1863, when he dedicated the battlefield. Everything reminded him of Lincoln and his tragic end. So much water had passed under the bridge since the war ended in 1865. Lincoln's assassination, Johnson's partial term, Reconstruction, though it had stalled and struggled and failed, and then Grant's election just a year ago. This was Radical Republican country, something completely foreign and foreboding to southern Democrats.

About ten miles toward Gettysburg, with twenty more to go, Joab stopped at a stream for water. Trembling at the thought of arriving at his final destination, he rode up on the hill and around to the north and west side of town to Chambersburg Pike, the route Gen. Heth's Division took that Wednesday morning, July 1. He remembered Jonathan's poignant description of the battleground; and for a moment Joab smelled peaches and corn silks and tassels and felt the heat of an unforgettable midday inferno. As cold as it was, he stopped and removed Jonathan's long coat and strapped it behind his saddle with his blanket. The thought of the beginning of that day and how it might have been caused sweat to form on his brow and his pulse to beat wildly against his frame.

He was looking for the store. There was only one out that way. Joab stopped, adrenalin forcing hot water to his mouth, his heart still pounding. He got off his horse, hitched her to the rail, gathered his wits, and walked inside. The old gentleman behind the fabric counter stepped out to greet him.

Joab swallowed hard and addressed the elderly man with all due respect. "Sir, my name's Payne."

"What can I do for you, son?"

Joab, getting quickly to the point, said, "Were you the proprietor or owner in 1863?"

"As a matter of fact, I was. I own this store and have for many years," he said.

"The first day of that battle, did Confederate Gen. Heth's men come here looking for shoes? I know this may be a sensitive subject, but this is my first stop in Gettysburg after five days of hitching rides on cattle cars all the way from Memphis. My father was a soldier in Gen. Heth's Division of Lee's Army of Northern Virginia."

The old man lifted his eyebrows, gave a sly grin, then realized he should not have done that. It was insensitive.

"Did you lose your father in the fight?"

Joab nodded. "My father, Captain T.G. Payne, and my brother, Albert Henry. I lost them both, and my Uncle Marcellus Church was wounded and captured and imprisoned at Point Lookout. He died a short time later. My brother, Jonathan, was severely wounded at Pickett's Charge on July 3. It was a terrible day for a lot of us in

Mississippi when we got the word. My mother—well, my mother was overcome with grief."

Joab watched the man's countenance fall, but he continued. "Sir, I know none of that was your fault, and I'm not here to place blame. I'm here to see where they died, for you see, we never found out what became of their bodies. My brother buried them on the field—together—but we heard the southern men and boys' remains were dug up and removed but that some of them might still be buried in Gettysburg in unmarked graves. If that's the case, we will never know."

"Son, I'm so sorry for your loss. It was bad—terrible, in fact, for both sides, and I hate knowing it was right here at my store where Buford and Heth's men clashed. I'll never forget it."

"Yes sir," said Joab, beginning to shake. Standing in the presence of a man that could possibly have seen his father and Albert Henry that day was overwhelming. What was more troubling was that he had seen them barefoot and hungry, wasted. But surely he had seen how they met the contest and fought as if they had shoes on their feet and food in their stomachs.

The old man continued as if he had read Joab's thoughts. "I will tell you this, son. I've never seen anything like those southern boys. They were dirty, bearded, thin as rails, and what was worse, they were fighting barefoot. Some of them had pieces of shoe soles tied onto their feet with strips of coarse cloth. Yet they were proud and almost haughty, for when the fighting broke out, they commenced to yelling—all of them—like it was something they all learned from the same teacher."

"Yes sir, it's called the Rebel Yell, sir."

"Yes, well, I watched from the window, the way they handled a squirrel rifle was . . . it was mystical. When I had time to sit down with my wife and ponder what I had seen, I cried, wanted to round them all up, offer them a clean hot bath, a fine meal, wanted to outfit them with fresh new clothes, give them socks for those feet that were oozing sores and blood, and new boots. In fact, if I had it to do over, that's exactly what I would do. I always felt bad that war was one-sided and that Lincoln had a lot more men to call up. There was no way the South could endure. Though they had us whipped with fortitude."

By now Joab was sobbing. There was something about the conversation that was touching him. This man had shown sympathy, real feelings for the southern soldiers who were doing their job with what they had. They were giving the very *last* of themselves. That *last full measure of devotion*, Lincoln had called it, and although he was speaking of the Union soldiers, it had been more than true about the South.

"Sir, visiting with you has been well worth my trip to Gettysburg. You likely saw my pa, and if you did, it would have been two years after I saw him when he left Calhoun County in late 1861. All we have is memories and letters to my mother, and this is important to me. The beginning of this Gettysburg chapter. I'm much obliged, sir. I'll be going now. Thank you for the talk. Oh, just one more thing. Could you show me a pair of boots, size ten, something that would be suitable for a soldier?"

"Sure." The man went to a shelf on the back wall of the store and searched for a pair of black boots, size ten. "Sorry, I don't have a ten, but here's a half size larger. Will that work?"

"Yes sir," said Joab. "I just want to see what they look like."

The man opened the box and Joab took one of the boots and held it in his hands. With tears in his eyes, he said to the man, "You didn't have Albert Henry's size that day, so he bought a pair for our brother, Jonathan, instead. Jonathan was not with them at the store. He was up on the hill with A. P. Hill's Corps waiting for them. Henry ran with my pa and the others to the railroad cut to take cover. When Jonathan found Henry's body, he had those boots tied together and around his neck. Jonathan knew what he had done and buried the boots with him out of respect for the most selfless person on the face of the earth. My brothers were splendid soldiers, sir."

By now the old man was crying, wiping tears. He cleared his throat and spoke. "I remember that. In fact, I'll never forget it. That boy paid for those boots with Confederate dollars and I . . . I overcharged him . . . thinking their money was worthless. I remember him tying the strings together and wrapping the boots around his neck. He barely made it before the clash and he was gone, caught up with the others."

Joab wiped his eyes and said, "I'm much obliged you told me that, sir."

"You know Gettysburg is a National Military Park now?"

"Yes sir. I know about the Gettysburg speech and Lincoln and the dedication. I took his same train route from Washington, stayed at Hanover Junction last night and rode my horse the thirty miles over."

"If I were you, I would go to the entrance. You can follow the progression of the war. It'll be hard on you, son, but you're strong. You can do it. I wish you well, friend."

"Much obliged," said Joab. "That's what I'll do. I know Pa was killed in the railroad cut."

"It's still there," the man said.

"And the peach orchard?" said Joab.

"Yes. You can't miss it."

"My brother died there."

"Son, you go now and gather your memories. You'll never be sorry."

Joab tipped his hat, left the store, and turned Star out onto the Chambersburg Pike until he found the entrance to the battlefield.

He rode slowly across the rolling hills, Star leaving the first prints in the snow on this beautiful cold morning.

CHAPTER 30

HEROISM UNEQUALED

We may not fire a soldier's salute over your dust,
but the pulses of our hearts beat like muffled drums,
and every deep-drawn sigh breathes a low
and passionate requiem.

Dr. John L. Girardeau

From June 24 to June 30, Lee was ". . . engaged in crossing his army over the Potomac into Maryland and Pennsylvania, his progress . . . effected with trifling opposition."

Lee and Jackson had succeeded big in Chancellorsville and Union Gen. Hooker was cast down, his once boastful spirit dampened so that he declined battle in Virginia. Lee now had the advantages and Hooker relinquished his post. There had been other Union generals who tried to conquer Lee. Hooker joined them on the proverbial Union shelf, and the command of the Federal Army was given to Gen. George G. Meade.

Lee was taking his army to the North, and the thought of Confederate troops tramping across their countryside did not bode well with its people. They were outraged at the sounds of the Rebels as they made their way across the Alleghenies and along the tributaries of the Potomac. Lee's movement into Union country awakened urgency in Lincoln to call up a hundred thousand more troops. Northern states answered the cry for help and came to the rescue. Washington City was in danger. So was Philadelphia. The North was afraid of Lee. Afraid of the devastation to their people and country. But what they didn't realize was that Lee was "superior to a warfare waged against noncombatants, and any depredation upon private property was expressly forbidden." He never permitted his soldiers to be known as murderers and intruders. He made sure no harm came to non-military citizens and he did not allow destruction of their subsistence, unlike what Grant and Sherman had allowed to the South. When Lee's men needed food, he paid for it in Confederate dollars or they went hungry.

The clash with Buford's army on the Chambersburg Pike by A. P. Hill's corps resulted in the repulse of the Union. It looked good for the South in that splendid moment. But it was on that day, July 1, 1863, that Joab's young life changed forever, to say nothing of Lee's hopes and aspirations for the South and an opportunity to win this war and move on with life in the Confederate States of America. It was not to be.

As the merchant suggested, Joab left the entrance and rode Star in a gallop around the perimeter of the battleground west and north until he was back on the Chambersburg Pike where the battle first started. Where Heth's men clashed with Buford and where A. P. Hill's Corps pushed the Union army of General Reynolds back to Cemetery Hill. Reynolds was defeated and fell mortally wounded.

This was not going to be easy for Joab. He rode hard from Chambersburg Pike to the railroad cut and slowed Star to a walk. He was sick, but he turned her into the entrance of the trough, the railroad bed, though there were no tracks laid. He could see how Gen. Joseph Davis thought it was a breastwork and led his men into it for cover. It was more like a wide canyon and there was no way they could escape the barrage of fire from Reynolds army. For the first time since his father and brothers joined the Confederate Army, Jonathan was not with his father and Albert Henry. He had told Joab the whole story. From a distance Jonathan saw his father running and he couldn't get to him in time. His father stumbled and fell. Jonathan cried out and he and Andrew McAllister ran as close to the ground as they could to get to the men in the railroad cut; they were receiving a heavy volley of fire, and the men in the cut were falling and dying. When he got to the edge, Jonathan jumped in and his father was already down, bleeding. He pulled him up into his arms and begged him not to die. Pleaded with him. He was barely hanging on to the brittle thread of life when he spoke Rachel's name and pulled the Confederate Battle Flag to his lips and died. In Jonathan's arms.

By now, Joab was on the ground, crawling on his hands and knees in the snow, crying, sobbing. It was right here. His father fell right here in the railroad cut with many of the men from his company. Joab tried to relive the moment, the pain and agony of war, his father dying in Jonathan's arms. It was beyond comprehension. He sat on the ground for an hour trying to come to grips with the truth of war. His father, whom he had always thought invincible, had fallen in battle and Joab was sitting in the railroad cut where it happened. T.G. served honorably for the South, though he was older than the age limit required. He had fought with his sons. He would not let them go without him, and he had bravely died for *The Cause*. Seven years had passed, but it might as well have been today, this moment, as far as Joab was concerned.

He stood to his feet and stretched out his arms and begged, "Jesus, help me!"

He mounted Star, sobbing, and rode out of the railroad cut south toward the peach orchard. He had no way of knowing where Henry died, but he had to be close. Jonathan and Duncan Jamison had gone looking for him and found him under a peach tree, clutching his squirrel rifle. Joab dismounted and walked through the snow touching the naked trees along the turn row, each one outlined in white. It was an emotional experience; Joab's heart was touched for the pain that Henry endured before he passed from this life. He, too, had fought bravely that day and some Union soldier, obviously out of ammunition, had run him through with a bayonet. Jonathan talked about how thin and small Henry looked curled around the base of that peach tree, his life's blood poured out upon the ground beside him.

A.P. Hill had won the battle for the South that day, but Joab had lost. Lost his father and his brother, and his Uncle Marcellus had been captured and taken to prison where he later died.

The wind blew against Joab, cooling his face that was hot with tears. He had one more place to visit.

The second day of battle had been vicious, turning hard against the Confederates. There was silence the morning of July 2; the fighting had not started until late in the afternoon. The Confederates lost some grand officers. Gen. William Barksdale, the old Fire-eater, a Mississippian by choice, was one of them. Our enemies hated him, thought Joab. They called him "haughty Rebel" and mocked him for asking for a cup of cold water as he lay dying. He shuddered when he thought about it. But he smiled when he thought of what Lee called him—"my Mississippian." Jonathan fought alongside him on that day. Barksdale's men took him to the Jacob Hummelbaugh Farm. Joab could see it from where he sat on his horse. A beautiful white farmhouse on Taneytown Road, it was the field hospital for both sides, amputated arms and legs piled to the windowsill on the back side of the house those three days and, truth be known, months following that battle. Barksdale died there before dawn on July 3. They buried him on the grounds, but his wife came and got his body and took it home to Jackson, Mississippi for proper burial.

On July 3, the enemy was entrenched on the heights of Cemetery Hill, and what took place at the bottom of the hill was already written in the annals of history. Jonathan was there, fighting with Heth's Division on the left of Pickett and this is how it went.

> . . . there was now to occur a scene of moral sublimity and heroism unequalled in the war. The storming part was moved up, Pickett's division in advance, supported on the right by Wilcox's brigade, and on the left by Heth's division, commanded by Pettigrew. With steady, measured tread the division of Pickett advanced upon the foe. Never did troops enter a fight in such splendid order. Their banners floated defiantly on the breeze as they passed across the plain. The flags which had waved amid the wild tempest of battle at Gaines' Mill, Frazer's Farm and Manassas, never rose more proudly. Kemper, with his gallant men, leads the right; Garnett brings up the left; and the veteran Armistead, with his brave troops, moves forward in support. The distance is more than half a mile. As they advance, the enemy fire with great rapidity; shell and solid shot give place to grape and canister; the very earth quivers beneath the heavy roar; wide gaps are made in this regiment and that brigade. The line moves onward, cannons roaring, grape and canister plunging and plowing through the ranks, bullets whizzing as thick as hailstones in winter, and men falling as leaves in the blasts of autumn.

Joab rode to Emmitsburg Road where the Rebels met a severe fire storm from the enemy that first day and got pushed to Seminary Ridge where they entrenched and recharged. He rode back around to Round Top and turned north again, following Little Round Top past Devil's Den back through the Peach Orchard and across the Wheatfield to Chambersburg Pike. The railroad cut was north of Chambersburg. The clean-up and removal of Confederate soldiers' bodies had long since been accomplished and if any were left on the battleground it was unknown to the powers that be.

He rode along the fence on Chambersburg Pike where the snow had started to melt. Puddles of water stood, likely from the marshy place and he dared not get too close for fear of bogging down. He rode for a mile in either direction on one side of the fence and returned to where he started. He then rode the same distance on the other side of the fence, west of Gettysburg, for that is where they were, to the north and the west along Chambersburg Pike—his father and Henry.

Joab was emotional. He couldn't stop crying. He was seeing every inch of the battlefield trying to visualize how it might have been without snow, in the hottest month of the year, stifling, bloody, thundering loud with canister and grapeshot for distance and close-up fighting. Three days of it. For some reason he was finding it hard to leave. He knew what he was searching for, but he also had a feeling he would never find it. Not in the snow. Not in any weather, especially not seven years after the battle. He was sure excavators and scavengers had searched the battlefield for any articles that might have been useful in identifying the dead.

He was about to call it quits when he spotted something red, a corner barely visible but distinctly red against the white of the snow about two feet from the fence. He dismounted and slowly walked toward it, reluctant, hopeful, but afraid. He reached for the corner and gently pulled. It didn't move. With both hands he pushed the snow back, uncovering a large piece of sturdy cloth partially buried in the ground. He dug into the soft mud and carefully lifted it out, and immediately he knew. He took it to one of the water puddles, washed it as best he could, and laid it out on the pure white snow, then turned it over to the back side and read the words embroidered by the hands of his mother, Rachel—"Captain T.G. Payne, MS 42nd, Co F." Hot tears rolled down his cold cheeks. Rachel had sewn the Confederate Battle Flag for her men and put it in T.G.'s haversack unbeknownst to him until he and the boys found it the first night in Grenada after they mustered in.

Joab didn't know if it was just a hunch he had about where the flag might be from what Jonathan had told him, or if Divine Providence had led him to the spot. Jonathan had buried them in a shallow grave on the wheat field, but Joab knew searching the field would have been futile especially in the snow. It had occurred to him that, if their bodies were dug up and taken to the South for reburial, the flag might be someplace out there and that a likely place would be against the fence. The grave diggers would not have wanted a Confederate flag. They would have tossed it.

He was sufficiently satisfied that their bodies had been taken or the flag would have still been buried. It was not buried. It was stuck in the mud against the fence where the ground was too marshy for burying the men.

Without a thought of anybody that might be within a mile of him, Joab let out the loudest Rebel Yell he could muster. He laughed and he cried. And he shouted "hallelujah" to the top of his lungs.

CHAPTER 31

DEFINING MOMENT

*If Joab were ever to relinquish and abandon
hate and contempt in the light of eternity,
this would be the defining moment.*

Joab sat close to the hearth of a blazing fire in Hanover Junction all night, thinking, remembering as much as he possibly could. He had lots to tell Rachel and his brothers and his wife, and he didn't want to forget a thing. He buried his head in his hands and sobbed. This time he shed tears of hope, happiness. He had come. He had seen. He had felt. And now he was going home and he had the bullet-riddled Confederate Battle Flag with him. It had been almost twelve days and he didn't know how long it would take to get back. At least five days. He had one more stop to make that might delay him by a day. He had given it a lot of thought, and his conscience was telling him to do it. He wanted to trust his conscience, but he was not sure he could, so he prayed for God to give him leave to do it—only if *He* willed. Joab would know at the proper time.

It would be easier going back. The switchmen, conductors and yardmen would remember him, and they would know—they would know he was going home. The only way for him to return was like he had come.

It was near daylight when the first train pulled out of Hanover Junction. Exhausted, he sat, once again, on the leather seats of some rich man's carriage and slept like a baby for the ride into Baltimore Camden Station where he changed trains to Washington.

At half past one in the afternoon, Joab rode Star toward The Old Ebbitt Grill, but he didn't stop until he was on Pennsylvania Avenue. He had no appointment. He would soon know if he had come at an opportune time. Still dressed properly in his riding pants and blue shirt, he was none the worse for his day on the battlefield. The barmaid, Amanda, had arranged for him to shave before he left Junction Hotel. He was grateful.

He hitched Star, leaving his rifle firmly in place, hidden by his blanket, and made his way to the security entrance where Grant's men searched him from head to toe. Grant was out and out military, and he had brought an entourage with him, never forgetting that Lincoln had been assassinated. Joab entered the White House and was ushered to the receptionist. He stated his reason for being there and was told to take a seat. An hour passed and Joab, anxious to get to the train station, stood to leave when the door swung open and he was ushered into the president's office. President Grant stood and greeted him. The guard stayed.

Joab had hated Grant. He thought of him as crude and rude, the man who had been primary to destroying the South. But now, with all due respect and honor—if he thought Shiloh and Gettysburg had been the healing place for him, he knew without a doubt the moment he laid eyes on Grant, the war was over for him. Finally. No amount of mourning and hatred would ever bring his father and brother back. They had willingly given. It was time for Joab to accept the healing and to do that, he would have to forgive—forgive the man who was symbolic of everything evil and hurtful about the War of Northern Aggression. With all that he had accomplished on the long, long journey, this would be the coup de grâce.

He took a step toward the President of the United States of America and extended his hand. He gripped Joab's, firmly shook it and said, "Son, you're quite the man for coming here like this, and I greatly admire you for it. May I say to you, I mourn your loss as I mourn my own. Our country has suffered unmentionable destruction. It has left me sorrowful, with despondency that covers me like a shroud, something I live with every day. You've spoken about your family. May I say to you my wife, Julia, is my beloved, and I adore our four children. Without them, I would be lonely, left with my sickening thoughts of war."

Joab was stunned that Grant expressed contempt for the war and an intense love for his family. That could be the binding tie; Joab felt the same way. Grant appeared to be a very modest man, shy and reserved. In the past he was a farmer and had worked in his father's leather store before the war. Suddenly Grant was no longer a rude and crude cigar-chewing tyrant. He was a real person with passions not unlike Joab's. For the first time since Joab was mature enough to know the role this man played in the Civil War, he felt compassion for the commanding officer who, under military orders, was responsible for the killing of thousands of Confederate soldiers and the destruction of the South. If Joab were ever to relinquish and abandon hate and contempt in the light of eternity, this would be the defining moment. Lincoln was dead. Grant was standing before him, a man of like passion, a human being who loved a wife and four children.

Joab could continue hating Lincoln for giving the orders and Grant for carrying them out, or he could seek peace from God, not because of Grant or Lincoln, but in spite of them and the havoc they inflicted on the people of the South. Joab reached into the depths of himself and said, "Sir, I came here hoping to have this precise conversation. It is the last page of one chapter in my life that can now be closed with a much more splendid conclusion than I could ever have imagined, and I'd like to thank you very much for these moments of your time. Good day, sir." Joab shook his hand, nodded respectfully, and turned.

The President called his name, speaking a little louder as Joab walked away. "Joab?"

"Yes, Mr. President."

"Thank *you*!"

Joab grinned through tears that rolled down his cheeks, thinking that he saw a few on Gen. Grant's face.

The Gettysburg chapter was part of a saga that would be read over and over again, figuratively speaking, and the memories of the sacrifices of his father and Henry and Jonathan and Isaac and Uncle Marcellus and all their Calhoun friends of the Mississippi 42nd would never be forgotten. He would see to that. He had left the hatred in the railroad cut, the peach orchard, the wheat field, on Cemetery Ridge, in the marshy place where he found the flag, and in the office of the Commander-in-Chief of the United States of America.

The trip before him would be long and lonesome and tiring, taking Joab five days after he left Washington, D.C. He could hardly wait to get home to his beloved Aggie and the rest of his family.

*

Aggie, having selflessly consented to the long trip, waited as patiently as she possibly could. They had been apart for two weeks at a time, before they were married, but three weeks had come and gone without a word from him. He had posted no letter. In fact, he had not planned to write her while he was away. She knew that. In the back of her mind there was the fear something dreadful had happened to him. The fact that he would be going through Washington City into Union country terrified her, though he would not be trespassing. Mississippi had been restored to the Union.

It was late when Joab arrived in Memphis. He slept overnight in the train station. His once smoothly shaven face was now covered with six days of beard. He was dirty, his clothes dusty and grimy with coal from hundreds of miles on the slatted cattle cars. He was sure he smelled like a barnyard but maybe Aggie would not mind. He trotted his horse the last few miles toward Water Valley and turned her into the familiar lot at the Stephens' farm.

He thought of his meeting with Grant. He had described his lovely wife, Julia, shyly telling Joab how he loved her and their children and how he loathed being away from her while he was in battle during the war. Joab's hatred for Grant had slipped into oblivion at the thought of his humanity and his passionate love for his wife and children. Joab found comfort in that, though he needed no one to tell him how to love. God himself had taught him how to do that the first day he laid eyes on Aggie. He had missed her, had longed for her arms about him, her sweet lips touching his, sleeping close by the hearth or on the feather bed in the attic.

It was late in the day, and she had been standing with her face pressed against the window when Joab rode up. Before he could remove the saddle from Star, she was running to the barn, crying out, "Joab—Oh, my darling Joab!"

She jumped into his arms and kissed his dirty unshaven face a thousand times, clinging to him like honeysuckle clings to the plum trees on a hot summer day. Joab swung her around, kissing her in return—a thousand kisses on her lovely face and neck, his passions rising with each touch of her lips to his. He was in glory—three weeks of crossing the hills of Mississippi into the Cumberland Mountains of Tennessee, the Shenandoah of Virginia, and the rolling hills of the Susquehanna, his emotions rising and falling like the winter waters on the tributaries of the Potomac River—Joab was now where he wanted to be.

Before he could say he needed a bath, Aggie and Miss Caroline were already at work. He allowed they, too, thought he needed one. They heated buckets of water on the wood stove and filled the bathing tub. It was early, but darkness had fallen when Miss Caroline excused herself and went to bed. Daniel finished his chores and followed her up the stairs after he stoked a high burning fire in the kitchen fireplace and moved the tub close. Joab poured in the hot then pumped cold water to finish filling the tub, shed his filthy clothes, and stepped into the warm water. It felt good. Aggie took the round of soap and gently washed his face and hair.

"I'll shave tomorrow," he said.

The fire crackled and flickered, spitting sparks onto the hearth, the lamp on the mantle the only other light.

Aggie whispered, "We're going to sleep by the hearth in the big room, Joab. Daniel laid us a fire, and I've got our blankets and quilts and goose-down pillows ready. Will that be okay with you?"

"It will be splendid, Aggie."

He stepped out, Aggie draping him with the best towel she could find. He dried himself and pulled on some of Daniel's night clothing Aggie had brought down. She would gladly scrub Joab's clothes tomorrow.

She ran her fingers through his long, straight hair, tousling it then brushed it with her own brush until it fell dry to his shoulders. He put his arms around her, snuffed out the lamp and they walked arm in arm draped in a flannel blanket to the hearth in the big room. Joab had not intended it, but he fell sound asleep, never moving until the crowing of the rooster and the first light of day.

He would not talk about his trip until he could tell his story to the entire family.

Rachel was uneasy about Joab. She would not rest until her son was home. Soon he and Aggie would be in Sarepta for good and that would be one less worry for her. Like the rest of the family, she had no idea when he would be home and what he would have to tell them. Joab had posted a letter to Isaac and Jennie to meet him at Rachel's on January 20, but Rachel had no way of knowing that. Having stayed with Rachel while Joab was gone, Jonathan and Cassie and Lee would already be there.

Joab, Aggie, Miss Caroline, and Daniel hitched the mules to the Stephens' buckboard and climbed on, this time with all of Aggie's belongings. Joab was leaving Star behind. They would all return to Oxford in ten days and Samuel would be with them.

Joab's plans were somewhat altered with the trip to Gettysburg, but he must keep his promise to Rachel. Samuel would stay with Mattie Raines, doing all the chores that Joab once did early of a morning. He would take Samuel to the square to work with him and the other men on rebuilding Isaiah Fleming's store until early afternoon, when they would go to the mill and pull a saw until dark. He wanted his brother to know these people and to love them as much as he did. He also wanted Samuel to see real Reconstruction at work.

They would not be long in Oxford, just a few weeks. Of course, he and Aggie would stay with Miss Caroline and Daniel. Joab would never leave her again. Besides, she would never again agree to it. She's almost childlike, Joab thought. So small, so cheerful, a little pleasant clinging vine, the way he wanted it. The war had done that to both of them. There was always a sense that someone would leave, someone would die. Times were still unstable. They all clung to one another and they probably always would. That was not a bad thing.

Joab knew he could not always live at home. When all of this was over, he would stay in Calhoun County and lay claim to that highest hill where he would build a house for Aggie and their children.

It was dark and cold when the little Water Valley party topped the ridge to the Payne home in Sarepta. Lanterns flickered in every window and smoke rolled and boiled from the chimney.

"I can hardly wait to hover over a good fire, Joab," said Aggie.

"I know you're cold, Angel. Rachel will have something hot for us to drink. And I bet there will be a buttermilk cake made with figs and nuts and jam."

"Oh, that sounds splendid," she said. "I love you, dear heart."

"I love you more."

"Not possible," she said.

They both laughed and Aggie moved closer to her husband. He pulled the blanket to her chin, put both arms around her, and drew a deep breath when they got closer to the house. The buckboards were there. Isaac and Jonathan. His heart was in his throat when he thought about the flag that was neatly folded in his saddlebag. He had washed it in the horse trough and dried and smoothed it by the fire at Hanover Station the night he left. Amanda had taken the smoothing iron to it, Joab having told her the story that night. She folded and steamed it down under a damp cloth and Joab neatly placed it in his saddlebag, wondering what Rachel would do when she saw it.

"Aggie, I have kept a secret for this special occasion. I did it on purpose. It concerns my family of which you and Miss Caroline and Daniel are now a part. I just want you to know I may get emotional." He swallowed hard.

Aggie tightened her hold on his hand and said, "Joab, you are most handsome with tears in your eyes. And I've known since you returned from Gettysburg that you have something to tell."

"You've been patient."

"I knew you were waiting to tell us all at one time. I'm sure it will be worth the wait."

"Are you every man's dream of a perfect wife?"

"No, but since I can't be perfect, I'm just trying to be the woman you deserve."

Joab shook his head in disbelief.

Daniel pulled the mules to a stop in front of the house. Joab jumped down and helped Miss Caroline and Aggie with the bags.

"Leave them on the porch and wait for us so we can all go in together."

He hopped back on, and he and Daniel took the mules and wagon to the barn.

Laughter rang through the old Payne cabin, everyone greeting and hugging, like holiday all over again. Rachel announced coffee and cake in the kitchen where it would be warm and cozy. Everyone gathered around the table that her beloved Thomas built over twenty years before, the center filled with candles for just enough lighting.

"Joab," said Rachel, "please tell us your story. We're all eager to hear everything. Aggie, you sit on the corner for inspiration, and Joab could you just stand beside her so we can all see your face?"

Jonathan and Isaac and Samuel stood, offering the chairs to Miss Caroline, Cassie, Jennie, and Daniel. The Payne kitchen table was, once again, filled to capacity.

Joab began to relive his journey from the very beginning, leaving out nothing. When he got to Manassas, Jonathan broke down, recalling the night he and his father and Albert Henry sat around the campfires of Grenada while a young southern recruit told the story as he had heard it—a battle the South so gloriously won—the Battle of Manassas. It sparked memories of T.G. sitting on a camp stool draped in the flag Rachel had sewn, smiling at the young soldier's embellishment of the battle, an image Jonathan would never forget.

Captivated by Joab's epic account, the family listened intently—the night in Hanover Junction—the story of Lincoln and his stop there before riding into Gettysburg to dedicate the military park where the Payne men had fallen.

There were no dry eyes in the room when Joab told of the last miles of his ride onto Chambersburg Pike. Cassie stood and put her arms around Jonathan, who was by now shaking. The store where Albert Henry had bought the boots for him—Joab went there? He talked to the man that sold Henry the boots? And the man remembered. Jonathan was spellbound, as if he were frozen in time.

"I rode from the store on Chambersburg Pike to the entrance of the railroad cut. Jonathan, it's still there—where Pa and Henry were trapped."

Tears began to fall off Joab's face, but he never stopped telling the story. "God Almighty gave me grace to relive Jonathan's account of what happened that day. I spent an hour in the railroad cut wishing I could have been holding Pa when he drew his last breath. Jonathan, you were honored to do so."

Rachel cried aloud and lifted both hands, "Oh, Jesus! Jesus!" Tears streamed down her loving cheeks. Joab knew this was hard on her, but in the long run, it would be precious memories with which she would live out her days.

Samuel put his arms around his mother, Joab's mantle having fallen on him. What a comfort and how blessed Rachel was to have all her boys in the house—all those who were left.

"I rode up through the peach orchard and touched bare and lanky limbs of those on the outer edge and along the turn row."

Cassie, who was by now shaking, cried aloud, "Oh, Henry! Our beloved Henry!"

Joab continued. "Jonathan, no doubt you could have touched the very tree—I wish you had been with me, for you could have taken me to the spot where you found him and where you buried Pa and Henry. But so many of our men's bodies had already been dug up and taken to other southern cemeteries and buried, maybe in trenches like Shiloh. I concluded that didn't matter. God Almighty will get them at the Resurrection.

"I rode along the fence near the marshy place out close to Chambersburg Pike, up one side and back down the other real slow, when I saw just a small corner of something red against the snow. I stooped down to get it and it was stuck in the mud. Not buried, but stuck just under the soil. It wouldn't release, so I dug in the mud and gently lifted it out. I washed it in a puddle of melted snow in the marshy place and commenced to yelling—the Rebel Yell. Wait here, and I'll show you what I found. Don't go away, now."

Joab went to the bunk room and returned with the battle flag unfurled. Rachel gasped—they all gasped—and he handed it to her.

She read the words she had embroidered—"Captain T.G. Payne, Mississippi 42nd, Co F."

She said softly, "Joab, you found it." She held it to her lips and hugged it to her heart.

"Yes, Mama. I found it. It's yours now. Papa would be proud and happy you have it."

He looked around the room that was shrouded in memory and pain and said, "But I have good news in all of this sadness, and I believe Pa expects this of us all, especially from his vantage point. I experienced something on the journey that I hope we can all embrace. It was a healing for me. I remember when that came for Isaac a few years ago, and to Jonathan on his way home from Gettysburg when Andrew McAllister told him the story of the death of Stonewall Jackson. I had to do my own letting go of the hatred and bitterness of that war. At times I thought I had laid hold on forgiveness and then I would think of Lincoln and Grant and Sherman and it would hit me all over again. For Lincoln, I left it at Hanover Junction in Pennsylvania, on the tracks where the train bearing his dead body rumbled through on its way to burial in Springfield, Illinois.

"As for Grant, you will never in a million years guess my level of audacity. I went to the White House, waited outside the president's office for an hour. I was about to leave when his door opened, and a military guard escorted me in."

Joab told the story.

"I was compelled to forgive the man. Whether or not he felt he needed to be forgiven was not the point. I needed to forgive. He called my name and thanked me for coming to see him. I was taken by his response and the sadness on his face and in his voice. He has his own political corruption problems, and I was told on the street he drinks a lot. He may not live a long life. Who knows how that will turn out? But I cleared my own conscience concerning him and the Union without relinquishing one whit of love and respect for the Confederacy.

"I have reached my journey's end. And I did it for all of us."

"The war's over, dear ones." He took Aggie's hand and pulled her close. "Life begins this night, Angel."

"Oh, yes, dear heart. This very night."

A lot of happy people hovered over Joab that night in Sarepta, Mississippi. Around the same table where T.G. and his boys laid their plans to go to war for their country in 1861. Aggie clung to Joab as she would the rest of her life, and Rachel clutched the flag stained by the blood of her beloved, representing a body broken, a life given for the love of the Old South. Not as though it was all she had left of T.G. She had Jonathan and Isaac and Joab and Samuel and Lee.

Call them what you will—Rebels, Confederates, Southerners. Remarkable men lived and loved, died bravely, and left an amazing legacy for *The Cause*. And what may have been equally remarkable was how those who were alive and remained picked up the pieces and rebuilt the South, literally from the ground up with their own blood, sweat, and tears.

Afterword

Never forget that *Joab* is a work of fiction. It is based on history to the best of my research and knowledge. There are nuances, of course, one of them being the store on Chambersburg Pike. The idea that there was a large shipment of shoes in Gettysburg and that Heth's Division went there to try and get shoes is declared by some writers to be mythical, but some writers maintain they were looking for shoes. History reveals that many Confederate soldiers were fighting barefoot, and elements of both armies collided west and north of Gettysburg on July 1, 1863. My fictional story about the shoes is just that, and it stays, my supposition being as good as the others.

I have stayed with the logistics, events, and dates to the best of my research ability. I know from the Clark war letters, copies of which I have in my possession as a family member, originals copyrighted and archived at The University of Mississippi, the boys wrote home that times were hard, days were long and they became weary of marching. They were infantrymen who only stopped during the war years to winter quarter. I've tried to imagine how difficult it was to march from Sarepta, Mississippi, to the Potomac River on foot, seldom taking the railroad cars. They complained little, and by the time they got to Gettysburg, my best-calculated guess is that they were totally exhausted, hungry, and barefoot.

My description of countryside comes from having visited the battlefields about which I write. Brice's Crossroads, Shiloh, Corinth, Holly Springs, Vicksburg, Natchez, Chattanooga, Missionary Ridge, Orchard Knob, Lookout Mountain, Chickamauga, Oxford, Gettysburg, Appomattox. I lived in Chattanooga in the shadow of Lookout Mountain and Missionary Ridge, when my husband was in college, at the corner of Orchard Knob and Union Avenue, walking distance to the Military Cemetery and a short ride to Chickamauga Battleground. I grew up in the Delta of Mississippi, just forty miles from Vicksburg. My brother was born there and has lived there for many years. My father loved the battleground and he never went to Vicksburg without stopping to pay his respects to fallen Confederate soldiers of that battle.

As always, I owe a debt of gratitude to my cousin, Charlie Wayne Clark, who has assisted me with information in all three books of the trilogy. His essays on the Clarks were used as a backdrop for the Introduction to *Confederates Killed in Action at Gettysburg* by Gregory A. Coco, Thomas Publications, Gettysburg, Pennsylvania, copyright 2002, in which Charlie shares the story, in part, of our forebears, T. G. Clark and his sons, Jonathan and Albert Henry who died at Gettysburg. Charlie has donated DNA in hopes of identifying any dust of the remains of our fallen heroes whose bodies were never found after the battle, and he has spent a large portion of his life putting their story together, preserving our heritage, and keeping their memory alive for the Clark family.

Charlie has a wealth of details as it relates to The Mississippi 42nd Company F, organized in Calhoun County, Mississippi, under the leadership of T. G. Clark, who was its Captain until he and the majority of his men were killed at Gettysburg. Mr. Coco called the battle "the apex of the great calamity." The struggle of our people during the war years could not be more real to me because the Clarks are my family.

Thomas (T.G.), Jonathan, and Albert Henry first mustered in at Sarepta in January of 1862, for sixty days, as a "local defense measure only." Clark Company F of the Mississippi 42nd came to be in April of that year. By June of 1863, T.G. wrote to his wife, Margery Rodgers Clark (Rachel in my stories) telling her that "something is about, but I can't tell what. Some think . . . Gen. Lee will make a forward move and will probably go into Maryland but . . . it is impossible for us to know until we receive orders."

The move was more real than T.G. could have imagined—north into Pennsylvania. Union country. The 42nd Mississippi was now a part of Gen. Joseph Davis' Brigade with Gen. Henry Heth's Division, placed as history tells us, in the heat of the battle on July 1, 1863, where the railroad cut came into play.

Information concerning Grant's treatment of the Jews in Holly Springs and other southern locations of his Department were gleaned from an Article in *The Jewish Records*, New York, January 13, 1863, and from military records citing Orders No. 11, which was quickly rescinded by President Lincoln, but not before damage was already done and Jewish lives were affected. Isaiah Fleming's character is fictional, typical of how it might have been for Jewish merchants in Oxford and Holly Springs during the war.

Once again, I am indebted to my late friend, Bill Stenhouse, his family, and Barbara Massey of Greenville, South Carolina, for the book, *Life Work and Sermons of John L. Girardeau,* The State Company, copyright 1916, Columbia, South Carolina, excerpts of which I gleaned concerning Girardeau's love for his native South Carolina, his conversion to Jesus Christ, and other relevant nuances of his life.

I availed myself to prolific online Civil War data, some of the writers contradicting others, but all of it informative and poignant and delivered to the best of the contributors' knowledge.

Thanks to my son-in-law, Bob Danner, for the gift of *Collector's Library of the Civil War* to my husband, who shared those books with me. In *Richmond During the War* by Sally B. Putnam—first printed in 1867, New York, G. W. Carleton & Company, Publishers—there is a poignant chapter that covers personal moments when Lee made the decision to move into Union territory after the glorious victory at Chancellorsville, taking the war to the North. It was then that Lincoln called up an additional one hundred thousand troops, which the South could never match. It was the beginning of the end, but not before the South had exhausted mind, heart, body and soul to win the War for Southern Independence. The portion in *Joab* describing Pickett's Charge is from Sally Putnam's rendering. Jonathan—Jonathan Clark, that is, my great granduncle, fought at Pickett's Charge and died there. My readers of *The Mississippi Boys* know that I brought Jonathan Payne home from the war. I could not bear to have them all die as it actually happened. When you think about it, Joab and Samuel and Isaac Clark had to give up their father and two of their brothers to the war.

All Scriptures are taken from the *King James Bible.*

My Thanks . . .

To my publishing associates, and there are many working seamlessly, some behind the scenes, some out front. In my humble opinion, you are the publisher's greatest asset. Deborah Cantrell, you worked on my behalf, and I'm most appreciative. Mars Alma, thank you for always moving the front process along superbly and for giving me that comfortable feeling from the start. Jill Serinas, you are amazing, a total joy to work with. You liaison with a great design team, always bringing me a beautiful cover and a finished book that makes me proud. Jerry Barker, you come later and provide exceptional service with those book orders. All of you perform your special service in remarkable ways. Thank you from my heart.

To Joab Clark's closest living descendants who willingly shared memories of their great-grandfather and told me about the highest place in Calhoun County—the hill upon which Joab lived out his days with his beloved wife, Mary Frances (Sarah Agnes in my story).

To my nephew, Dewey Davidson, my Mississippi Agent! He has worked diligently with me for events and book signings all over the State of Mississippi. His genius for marketing and messaging is superb. Thanks, Dewey, for pressing me on and for connecting me with the New Albany Historical Society. Who knows, maybe we'll open a manuscript with another Mississippi setting, dating back to "The Burning of New Albany." Fly the Flag!

To my brother, Mike Bennett, Vietnam combat veteran, purple heart, Union County, Mississippi, Veterans Service Officer, and member of the Sons of Confederate Veterans, and his wife, Gloria, a Mississippi historian, retired librarian, and member of United Daughters of the Confederacy, who have labored tirelessly to gather information about our Clark family and the war years, trekking from one hill country cemetery to the next to put names with information, and searching courthouse records and ancient newspapers for articles and obituaries of family members who have gone before us and who left a legacy that we pass down to our children and grandchildren. Thanks, Mike and Gloria, for building and preserving the family genealogy and for supporting my books.

To visit Oxford, Mississippi, is to understand my love for this grand old city of the South. Thanks to Emmie Lou Mooney Greene for filling me with great information about Oxford and introducing me to some notable people. She made it possible for a great book signing at *Cedar Oaks Guild* with women who work endlessly to preserve the legacy of the South and its antebellum treasures, and she extended that signing to her famous city restaurant called *Phillips Grocery*, which is on the street named for one of Oxford's most prestigious Confederate patriots and statesmen, L.Q.C. Lamar. She also introduced me to Jack Mayfield.

Thank you, Jack Lamar Mayfield, historian, author, and columnist for *The Oxford Eagle*, for your endless stream of information and wealth of knowledge, much of which helped me greatly in writing JOAB, especially as it concerns the history of Oxford, home of L.Q.C. Lamar, Ole Miss, and The Thompson House! Thanks for reviewing JOAB for "all things Oxford," for introducing me to the world of William Faulkner in very tangible ways, and for a meaningful tour of the University of Mississippi where memories of the Civil War years live on.

To Glenda Hall Griffith of Yalobusha County for opening doors with the historical society and for introducing me to the lovely restored hill town of Water Valley.

To Jimmy Giles of Clarksdale, that "Mississippi Man" who hosts my Delta signings in the beautiful and historic Old Greyhound Bus Station, which is now the tourism building, and for all my Clarksdale High School friends (class of '58 and others) who support my books and who are life friends. I love you, CHS'ers!

To my granddaughter, Holly, who hosts my Memphis signings in her lovely home in Cordova, and my granddaughter, Nichol, who rallies all our people. I love all of my grandchildren and great-grandchildren.

To Panera Bread in Trinity, Florida, for hosting my local signings. And to all my "Café Eclectic Friends"—so many, who buy my books and support me in a place where North meets South. A special thanks to photographer, Dale Caperell, who always comes to my rescue with posters and prints and photographs and other marketing material.

And to Havana Dreamers Café in the lovely bungalow community of Longleaf in Trinity, Florida. Looking forward to signing JOAB with Scott at Havana!

To my "Forever Friends," all of us originating in Memphis and now scattered all over the USA. Thanks to all of you for supporting my books and especially Karen Corbitt who "keeps us together."

To my beloved military friends, serving and retired, too numerous to list. God bless you for serving our country in the good times and the bad. You wear the badge of courage and make us proud.

To all the Clark family who are members of United Daughters of the Confederacy and Sons of Confederate Veterans. So proud of all of you! Charlotte Crocker Brown, Betty Crocker Abdo, Sally Hellums Woolley, Burlon "Sonny" Crocker, Larry Hellums, John Benton Long, Michael Clark Bennett, Dewey Davidson, Charlie Wayne Clark, Renee Clark Wright, Creekmore Brunner Wright, III (Trey), Briley Alexander Wright, and Teresa Clark Dunn.

To my son, Peter, for sharing his wealth of writing knowledge, and to his bride-to-be, the lovely Vonne Rhylenne Guzman, who cheers for me from the Philippines. Hurry to America, dear heart. To my beautiful daughter, Tracy Danner, who gives me encouragement and takes amazing author photographs. To my beautiful daughter, Angie Grossman, who is there for me at every signing and gives me incredible support. To my beautiful and brilliant daughter, Phyl Lippy. I love all four of you endlessly.

To my husband, who loves me as Joab loved Aggie. You are my biggest fan and I am yours, and I love you beyond all *intellectual capacity*.

To my Savior, the Lord Jesus Christ, who loves me even more and who blessed me with a *goodly heritage. The lines are fallen unto me in pleasant places* . . . (Psalm 16:6).

Extending thanks is never ending, and I am always fearful of forgetting someone. So let me say here—I know I have forgotten someone. Please forgive. With that said, I rebel against bidding my "Payne" family farewell and hope to say hello to another stand-alone before I go hence. I think there is room for one more writing of a good book. Thanks, Jack Lamar Mayfield, for your encouragement. I look forward to working with you, perhaps on *Redemption* that will star Samuel Payne.

My best regards and thanks to all of you, my faithful readers.

Jane Bennett Gaddy
Christmas Day, 2012

CPSIA information can be obtained at www.ICGtesting.com
Printed in the USA
LVOW131059260213

321748LV00001B/100/P